DRE

NYSSA WINTERS

DREADFUL

For any information please contact
authornyssawinters@gmail.com

First Edition

Cover by: Shepard Originals

Edited by: Celtic Edits

Paperback ISBN: 978-989-33-4216-9

For Dani.
My bestest friend. My partner in crime. My little sister.

DREADFUL

Playlist

Love You Like Me – William Singe

Heavy in your arms - Florence and the Machine

Breve - Diogo Piçarra

Lovely - Billie Eilish

Expectations – Lauren Jauregui

Vengeance - Zack Hemsey

Love is a bitch - Two Feet

Who (feat. BTS) - Lauv

I feel like I'm drowning - Two Feet

You should see me in a crown - Billie Eilish

Radars - Alina Libkind

Do It For Me - Rosenfeld

Blue & grey - BTS

Falling - Harry Styles

Heaven - Taemin

DREADFUL

Author's Note

This book contains strong language and several topics that may be sensitive to some readers. The content includes, but is not limited to: death of a child (off-page), cheating, homophobia, and harassment.

Please read responsibly.

DREADFUL

Nine Years Ago

People do not tell you how painful or fucked up life is. When I was a teen, I used to think my parents had my entire life paved for me. I used to think that, no matter how well I did, I would never live up to their expectations. It was one reason I ran away from home. From them. You cannot grow wings in a place where you feel weighed down. You cannot chase after what you want when you are in someone else's bubble.

Life is a funny thing. It's also complicated, emotional, and overall messy. There are lucky people in this world. Those who never had their life turned upside down and struggled to figure out their next move. I was never fortunate in the same way. Not even when I was a child.

Father, or my mother's husband as I prefer to refer to him since the first time he laid his hands on me, was one of those men to whom women don't matter. They taught me, from a young age, that I had to cater to my future husband's needs. How men were more important and would bring more meaning to the world than I ever would. He even had me serving drinks to his associates during business meetings. The old bastard did not care if

I was not comfortable in a room full of middle-aged men. I was not there to be at ease. I was there as a maid. Some of those people were often inappropriate in how they talked to me. They expected me to suck it up. At fourteen, I knew very well how I didn't want a man to look at me. Not since he was going to look in a way I deemed inappropriate, as my father's colleagues did.

So I ran away to the other side of the country. I wanted peace. I wanted to live. I wasn't expecting to meet someone who would interest me enough. Let alone for the person to be a man. The same man who now I keep stealing glances at.

It is day six of him riding the bus with me and I still haven't told him my name. Not because I don't want to, but because I don't understand why he keeps coming along.

"So let me get this straight," I say, shifting in my seat and turning my back to the bus window. "You have a car?"

"Yes."

"But you've been riding the bus this whole time, despite it?" He nods. "Why?"

"I took the bus the other day because my car was at the mechanics. It's been ready for three days, but I keep coming here because I don't think you should ride the bus alone," he admits and I raise a brow. "Call it a precaution."

"Why do you have a car if you live in the city?"

"I am expected to have one. It also helps in my

line of work."

His accent thickens around certain words. I wonder how my name will sound coming out of his lips. I try to not admit it, but it is sexy as hell. "You don't sound American."

He smiles. "I was born in France. My family suggested I study abroad. The plan was for me to go back, but I think I'll stay. I like the city." He looks at me as he speaks. His brown hair falls in front of his eyes and his mouth turns up as if smiling is second nature. Green eyes borrow mine for a second before he continues. "How about you?"

"Sort of the same thing." I tilt my head, not wanting to get into details about my past. If I keep the conversation about him, then we don't have to talk about me. "I have a feeling you are on the stubborn side. It's been what? Five days?"

"Six. I told you, I will take this bus for as long as you take it. You would make my life easier if you told me your name, though."

My cheeks burn and I am pretty sure they are pink because he bites his bottom lip, gazing at me as if it's the first time he sees someone blushing.

"So what will happen when I stop taking the bus?" I ask him as the said vehicle comes to a halt.

"Well," the stranger says, sitting by my side, leaning closer, and again, his perfume invades me. It takes me only a second to realize why I like it so much. It's peppermint. "When it happens, I hope to have taken you on enough dates, so you allow me to drive you home. Then none of us has to take the bus again."

I snort before I can stop myself. The man raises a brow, studying me. I could think of his insistence as stalking, but he hasn't made a move yet. I am pretty sure if I tell him I am not interested, he will let me be. For six nights this stranger has entered the bus with me and then watches me leave. We don't deepen our conversation. He doesn't ask where I live. He talks to me and makes sure I get off the bus safely. Today he even bought me a cupcake which I bit into after he proved it was harmless for me to eat by taking a bite of it himself.

A girl can never be too careful.

"You seem confident I will say yes if you ask me out."

"I am."

I turn to face him, folding my arms over my chest and he widens his eyes at me before the smile that had me blushing moments ago appears again. For the second time in less than five minutes, I have no clue why it happens.

"But I don't even know your name. You should understand I don't hang out with people I don't know."

The stranger leans forward. His breath blows against the soft skin of my lips, and he glances down for a second. His eyes then lift to mine, and he whispers something in French before speaking in

English.

"We should take care of that. I'm Dorian."

I look at his hand and decide to hell with it. My former life made me rethink every interaction between men and women. I had to be a good girl. I had to make sure our family's name was out of the mud. It all went down the drain when my father caught me kissing the girl he believed was my best friend. The old man called me multiple things. The sweetest term he used was slut. Sometimes I still get scared he is right, and other times I decide it doesn't matter what he thinks.

So I relent. I give in and decide since I moved here, I will begin a new life. The one I want for myself.

My hand wraps around Dorian's as I speak. "Ariella."

1
Dorian

She's cheating on me.

I lean back on the chair, clutching my hands into fists and attempting not to let the fury taking over my body burn against my skin.

"Can you send them today?" I ask, or rather demand, to the guy on the line using the deepness of my voice to make sure he understands this is not a request. I need those photos. I need to know if the woman I love has given up on us.

The man on the other end of his phone doesn't reply. Not right away, and I move the chair to face the window. Summer is fading away, disappearing from the background. The wind swirls, taking the golden leaves across the backyard and carving the perfect color pallet. One where it almost seems the sun is kissing the branches as they all turn into different shades of auburn.

My horses, the pride and joy of my work, move around, taking in the last minutes of light before heading inside for the night. Soaking in nature's beauty, I almost forget the issue at hand.

Almost.

If it was anything else, I could brush it aside, but knowing Ariella is cheating… fuck. No matter how bad this marriage has become, it hurts like hell. I knew we were going through hardship, but this?

"Yeah," the man answers after what feels like a handful of minutes. "I can send them today."

The call ends and I place the phone on the desk behind me. My eyes close as I let the air conditioner cool down my troubling thoughts.

Ariella is having an affair.

One of my biggest fears is coming true. I am losing her.

My wife has changed over the last year. She did not leave the house for months. Now she works late, has nights out with colleagues, and almost never acknowledges me when I'm in the house. I cannot blame her for the last one since I sometimes avoid her as well.

We have been struggling, not able to heal, and during our last fight, I was an asshole to her, saying things I shouldn't. It was months ago when we still talked after fighting. Not like we used to, but we talked. At some point, I thought she was about to ask for a divorce. Ariella showed no sign she was leaving me and I settled back into our routine. The one where we ignore the obvious problem in our relationship and also don't mention how different our lives have become.

A knock on the door brings me back to the present. "Yes?"

I don't want to deal with work now, but my attention is required. The girl walks into my office wearing a piece of clothing some would deem inappropriate for work.

Still, I try not to stare at how her hips sway as she approaches my desk, leaving a file in the corner. With a shy smile, which I know is fake, the girl places her hair behind her ear, leaning forward. For a brief second, I get a glimpse of her cleavage and even the delicate line between her breasts. I look away as soon as I realize it, knowing it was her plan all along to get my attention.

"The new client file, as you requested, Mr. Vaillant," she purrs, batting her lashes. "Do you need anything else?"

"No, Ms. Young. That will be all."

The small sigh she gives has the corner of my mouth twitching down while Zoe leaves my office. I am always amazed at how some people react to others. A quick glance, a smirk, a glimpse of skin, and they are hooked. I have seen my friends seduce women by breathing around them. To Zoe, however, it seems to talk to her, and giving her enough attention makes her think something else is going on. She seems to drift sometimes and stares at my lips, thinking I don't notice. I was considering letting her go, but the truth is she is good at her job and with everything I went through in a year, I haven't found the time to find someone as adequate.

With one last glance at me, trying to hide the evidence of her annoyance, Zoe closes the door behind her. I spend the last few minutes of my day examining the file she left before deciding it's no use. My brain doesn't seem to focus on work until I get those photos of Ariella and the other guy. I take my keys and head to my car to meet Josh and Eli at the pub.

The drive is short, and I blast music in the car loud enough to silence my thoughts. I don't care about the bad lighting of their favorite place, since the food is great and the conversation between the people muffles everything around us. It makes me forget how fucked up my life has been for the past fourteen months. I slide onto the seat at their table and stare at Eli, who chews on a chicken wing. His tie is missing, and his shirt wrinkles in certain areas. Eli drives out of the city at least once a week to meet us. Or so he says since both Josh and I know he comes for the food and beer. With a small dip of my chin, both my friends lift their beers, acknowledging my presence.

But then the oldest raises a brow. "You seem upset. Did something happen at the office?" Eli bites into the meat, sparing me a few seconds of attention. He pulled his light hair back, revealing his face. The same face the woman from the table next to ours cannot seem to take her eyes away from. "Another fight with Ariella?"

"In order to fight with my wife, she had to speak to me." Josh takes a bottle from the bucket at the table and pries the cap off. He slides it towards me and I take a long sip. "She doesn't even look my way when I am at the house, so what do you think?"

"What about therapy?" Josh asks, his hair clinging to the side of his face. He picks up another chicken wing and makes me wonder how many he has already eaten, and even how he can get in those tight jeans he wears. Sometimes I envy his metabolism. But I am aware of how much he works back at the stables, burning all the food he inhales.

"Therapy?"

"Yeah. Weren't you two going?"

"I am, and so is she. Separated now, after the fight we had two months ago. But I don't think it works when one of us is cheating."

Eli chokes on his food, coughing and hitting his chest while Josh laughs before deciding to help the oldest of us three. These two can go through something life-threatening, but if one does something stupid, the other will laugh. It's how we handle each other. They are the older and the younger, always making jokes. I am the middle child, passing unnoticed.

We did not grow up in the same house, nor are we blood related. But they are the closest I have to a family. They have been ever since college when I found myself in a foreign country all by myself.

"Ariella is cheating?" Eli asks, and I dip my chin with my eyes trained on the beer label as I peel it off. "Are you sure?"

"No," I reply, and Josh rolls his eyes at my answer.

He is always the practical one. I am aware the guy will tell me I can't do this. I can't make assumptions or decisions when I am being controlled by my emotions. How my wife and I went through something others wouldn't know how to handle. I have seen the numbers. Most couples split after something as difficult as what happened to us. I still love Ariella. We are still married despite all the shit thrown at us. And something in me needs to know where my wife is spending her time. Especially if it is with her lying beneath someone else.

"But she is never home early anymore. She has been spending time with friends, and there's this guy I heard her talking to on the phone a few times."

"What guy?" Eli asks.

"Louis."

Even saying his name makes my fucking eyes twitch. I saw him once at an art event Ariella had to attend about three years ago. I did not have any suspicions back then, which is why I think whatever is going on between them is recent. About two months ago, Ariella got busier with work. My visits to her office stopped around the same time. It's hard to walk those corridors knowing that fourteen months ago, whenever

I went to visit, our lives were so much different.

"Maybe he's just a colleague," Josh suggests, watching me. "I don't think Ariella would cheat on you. She loves you, Dorian-"

"No, Josh," he doesn't get it, he never will, and as I am about to speak, as I am about to say the words that drag my heart across the floor, my lip twitches with the pain. "She *loved* me."

One beer after the other, I try to explain to them the reasons for my suspicions, although I don't think I am successful at doing it. Why do I stay awake at night wondering how to fix what's broken? Because it's how we are. Broken like a porcelain piece. There is a faint memory of my childhood, when my mom tried to fix one of the expensive porcelain vases she had after I crashed into it. She glued all the pieces together. It took her days to do it and she was proud when she finished. But I could still see the cracks where it broke apart. I could still see the repairs and I knew it would never be the same.

My marriage reminds me of my mom's vase.

Ariella and I need fixing, but I know even if we put all of our broken pieces back together, the cracks are there. The thought of someone other than me touching my wife, touching the woman I have been with for the last nine years, has me drinking another beer. Is this the third or the fourth? I can't remember. All I know is that I drink while my friends talk among themselves. I drink so I don't let my thoughts crowd my mind.

My phone vibrates across the wooden table and all of us look at the notification.

Ari: I'm staying at work to finish something. Don't wait for me.

Another excuse for arriving home late. Great.

"So…" Josh says, staring at me. "How are you going to know for sure if she is cheating or not?"

"I hired a detective," I reply, placing the half-empty bottle on the table, the foam running on its sides. Both of my friends raise their brows. "He has been following her for a couple of days now. I had a call with him about some photos earlier."

Josh sighs. "You are being paranoid. Even with all you have been dealing with, if the relationship isn't as it was, I am sure Ariella would never cheat."

The light on my phone appears as I pick it up to read the notification. An email, the one I have been waiting, pops onto the screen. I type the password only for my blood to freeze in my veins. The phone slips from my hand and falls on the table with a loud thud.

The sound has both my friends staring at me as I lean forward and cover my face with my hands, trying to make sense of the images.

Images of my wife and Louis.

I can't breathe. My chest aches and the room

spins as I try to focus on both my friends. The hope for thinking Josh was right vanishes. Replaced once more by the idea that the woman I am married to has not been faithful. I dare a glance at the phone and pain strikes again with the images of her hugging and dancing with her colleague.

My head spins, my breathing becomes uneven, and the words seem to fight to come out of my mouth. "What is it?" Eli asks, putting his drink down and trying to realize what's happening.

My hand works fast, turning the device on the table for my friend to see, and I catch as his eyes double their size before he taps Josh's arm. The younger one glances at the phone, then at me, and maybe the words get stuck in their throats as well because none of them speak.

"She is cheating," I mumble, dragging the words out and folding to the front.

The woman I love, the woman I wear the ring on my finger for, is cheating on me. There's a loud sound filling my ears, but I soon realize it's my heartbeat.

"Maybe they were just having a nice time," Josh says again and I narrow my eyes at him.

"How much more do you need to understand it, Josh?" I ask through gritted teeth. "This should be enough for any other man. Ariella hasn't been coming home at normal hours. I know she isn't home now."

"Dorian," Eli calls, noticing the way the words all come together as I speak while I stand up.

It doesn't seem like I can stay in the same place. So, glancing at him, I try to move, failing to do so in the full pub. To try, at least, a vague attempt at peace. To prevent my heart from bursting out of my chest and running away scared of being hurt again.

My nails disappear while my teeth pull the small remains of them. Her laughter. The mornings spent in bed talking and loving each other. We were inseparable. Not only as husband and wife. Ariella was my best friend. She was the person I knew would never turn her back on me. It seems as if all the smiles, laughter, tears, pain, all we endured, all we've been through, means nothing. *I* mean nothing.

"Let's think this through," Josh says, putting one hand on the table. He is trying to be reasonable, which will not work on me tonight. Between the three of us, I am the one who has emotional reactions and I know right now I can't see whatever full picture he wants me to see. "Ariella can just be hugging him because she is having fun. You said months ago she has been fighting depression!"

"Yes, but-"

"Listen to me," Josh continues, holding out his hand. "I don't think she is cheating, but I am not the one married to her. You are, and maybe you need to confront her about this before assuming anything. You two have been through hell, Dorian. She wouldn't do this to you. You know her."

I hate when he has a point, but I also cannot stay here. My mind needs to focus on something other than how my heart crushes inside my chest. I drink the rest of my beer, avoiding concentrating on how the room seems to spin, or how the floor makes me stumble. I pick up my wallet and phone from the table before Eli stops me.

"You will not drive home after drinking. I'll call you a cab."

And he does, walking with me to the door, and waving his hand in the air as the car pulls to the curb in the humid street. Eli pats my shoulder, whispering words of courage that don't stick in my brain because right now nothing he says is able to stick with me.

Nothing but the way Ariella smiles in those photos.

Could this be emotional cheating? Or is it a physical thing? Does she like him? Is she in love with him? The idea has me fighting to keep my alcohol in my stomach. She wouldn't be in love with him... would she? Then again, I never thought she would be capable of sleeping with someone else, and it's not like we have been intimate. I don't know if she even wants us to. Ariella has been the only woman I have touched for a decade. But if she is cheating... well, it would make sense why we now have therapy separately.

"Josh is right," Eli says, closing my door and speaking through the window. He searches for something in my eyes as it seems I can't focus on him, not on the way my mind isn't letting me be still. "I'll drop by your office this week to speak with you. Zoe is usually around during lunch, right?" My chin dips as I take a deep breath. "How drunk are you?"

"Not drunk enough."

He smirks. "Don't freak out yet. Try to stay calm. The photos mean nothing."

In fourteen months, I haven't seen my wife smile, or even be happy. Yet, as another man held her in his arms, the beautiful curve of her lips appeared. My breathing gets shallow thinking about it, because ever since I have known Ariella, I am one of the biggest reasons for her grin.

As she is mine.

"Where to, sir?" The driver asks me as I blend against the smelly seat of his car, watching my friend walk inside the pub again.

I can go home and face her as soon as she arrives, but I don't think I should do it in this state. Because I am not ready for the impending fight, I give the driver my office address.

2
Dorian

I pay the man for his crappy driving, noticing the displeased sneer he gives me for not handing a tip. It's his fault. He passed a red light and almost got us killed. By the time I turn around, something or someone bumps into me.

"Mr. Vaillant," she groans, rubbing the spot she hit in my chest. "What are you doing here?"

Zoe stares at me, blinking her eyes like a puppy waiting for an answer. But my current balance doesn't allow me to give her one. I drank too much; my eyes are foggy and my discernment is clouded. Not a good combo, as it doesn't seem I am thinking things through. But how can I when every time I close my eyes, those damn pictures haunt me? Even if she isn't involved with him, as Josh told me, Ariella is still living a separate life from the one I am a part of.

"I left my keys here. I'm just stopping by to pick them up."

My feet betray me and reveal my lie as I wobble across the sidewalk and Zoe helps me regain balance. She pushes her lips together while I adjust my shirt and make my way to the door. Even the horses complain about the commotion I am causing.

"Why are you still here?" I ask the girl, who doesn't seem to let go of my arm. "I thought I sent you home when I left."

"You did," she mumbles, not meeting my curious gaze, instead gripping me tighter when my balance threatens to fail me. "But I had a report to file and paperwork to finish."

It may be true, but I still hope she will leave as soon as I turn the lights on. When my fingers find the switch and Zoe doesn't move away, disappointment fills my chest. Zoe follows me around the room while I take my jacket off and open my office door. She walks behind me, not taking her eyes away from my every move. I let my coat fall on the chair in front of my desk and pray to God to take my secretary away from here so I can crawl on the small sofa in the back and rest. I need to sober up before going home. "I am fine now, Miss Young. You may leave."

Yet the girl doesn't move, adjusting her skirt as she walks behind me before I go to my chair. Her eyes narrow and a small, barely visible wrinkle appears on her forehead as she stares at me, attempting to appear sober or less drunk.

"I think it is best if I stay, sir."

A grunt dreads to escape me. "Might as well wait then," I tell her and pull the last drawer open, signaling for her to sit in the chair where my jacket now rests. She does, carrying a smile on the corner of her thin lips. From the drawer, I take two mugs and then move to grab two cold brew coffees from the mini-fridge.

"You're going to drink coffee at this hour?" She asks, amused.

"Yes."

For some stupid reason, my short answer makes her chuckle. I pass her the coffee, aware when she touches my hand while grabbing it. The softness of her fingertips brush against mine, but I don't react. It's not the first time a woman has tried to touch me, even in the most innocent way.

Zoe sits in front of me, her gaze pleading for me to look at her, but I don't. My attention is on the liquid inside the mug and the tormenting thoughts I keep having. Ari at home waiting for me. Ari smiling when I asked her if she would be my wife. The day she gave me the happiest news she could ever give me. The day I saw her in the hospital bed. Our life together could split in moments like those, and despite everything, I would still go back to her.

"Is there a reason for you to be here?" Zoe asks, forcing me out of my mind. For a minute, I forgot she was here.

I'm not thinking straight. I know as much. Yet I want someone from the outside to give me their opinion. Someone who doesn't know my wife and me, or everything we have been through. Zoe began working here about a couple of weeks before it all happened. She never figured it out. She was not one of the people who could know what was wrong in my private life. Ari and I only shared our heartache with our closest friends, and even then, it was heartbreaking to watch their faces crumble.

I want to know if I am overthinking, seeing things where they don't exist, and finding reasons for Ariella's distance.

"Why do people cheat?" I blur out, avoiding the weight of the ring on my finger or how it shines against the light, sending a sharp strike through my heart.

Zoe's eyes settle on mine, drinking in the image of me leaning back in the chair, a craving swirling in them as she draws a sip from her coffee. She then glances at the window.

"I'm not sure how to reply, Mr. Vaillant," she states before placing her mug on top of the wooden desk. "I think it varies. Some people cheat because they are not happy with their partners. Others for need of something more. Curiosity, or just foolishness."

"You think people cheat because they are upset?"

Closing my eyes, I don't allow the burden of the words to hit me. I have been in denial for months. First, it was the phone calls. Ariella would walk out of the room to take them as I stayed at the table. Then it was the texts, the lunches, the staying late at work. My wife turned from numb to cold around me.

I know where it went wrong. Yet I cannot fix that, to amend the tragedy that befell us and broke us apart. Maybe we should have fought harder, but grief blinds us.

"Or because they want to," Zoe says, enunciating the words. "People who cheat think about themselves. As most narcissists do."

I raise a brow at the girl and try to focus on anything but the way my stomach swirls with anticipation. She notices how my eyes wait, inviting her to continue, and enjoying the attention I give. Zoe sits straight, her breasts fighting the restraints of her thin blouse, and I glance away from her cleavage. I am not cheating on Ariella. Especially with Zoe. But I cannot deny it feels so satisfying to have someone listening and understanding.

"There are a lot of reasons to cheat, but if the person does it often, if *she* doesn't feel guilty about it, then it's about pleasure. About seeking, in others, an answer to their needs."

"You seem to know a lot about the topic," I joke, raising the mug to my lips.

"I talk from experience."

Zoe crosses one leg over the other, leaning back on her chair. Her skirt rides up her legs and I spot the inside of her thighs. It's been months since I have touched a woman, months since I have felt the comfort of someone's delicate lips kissing me.

Ariella and I haven't been intimate. Not since last year. Fourteen months, to be more precise.

With alcohol running in my blood, a woman tempting me would not be the best of ideas. But in all this time, I have never felt the need to reach out and touch someone else. And as Zoe shifts in her chair, uncrossing and crossing her legs once more, I feel nothing.

"You cheated?" I ask her, maintaining my eyes on hers and avoiding the way her body seems to move as I speak. "Why?"

"I did, and I don't regret it. My relationship was dead when it happened and being with someone who could please me, made me aware of it. I missed the sex and then I didn't. I was unhappy and then I wasn't."

Unhappy. When I hear the word, I fight the urge to look into a truth I'd rather not face. Because I have been unhappy. I haven't smiled, laughed, or done any other thing expected in a relationship. I don't feel loved.

"So, you don't think fighting for someone is worth it?" I ask again, and this time Zoe stands.

She takes a deep breath, and the buttons on her shirt fight to stay together before she walks towards the window. "Not really. If it's broken, leave it. If it's cheating on you, then it's not worth it. If it's not pleasing you, why bother?"

"You are straightforward tonight, Ms. Young."

She seems to find amusement in my remarks, which was never my intention. Zoe stares at me. I can see her by the corner of my eye biting on her lower lip and I become aware of the dangerous situation happening here. This is a girl who has shown signs of being interested in me.

She is also my employee, and I am married. All reasons for me to avoid her. Which I do on a normal day. And tonight, it is no different. I place the now empty mug on the table, trying to lift myself from the chair, only to fall back once again when Zoe stops me.

Her hands fall on top of mine, scorching against my already warm skin, her eyes holding me hostage as she demands my attention for the brief span of seconds. "Tell me, Sir, are you unhappy?"

"No," I lie.

Zoe pushes her lips together, considering if she should continue with the questioning. It doesn't take her long to lean a few inches forward and try to speak while seeming serious again. Her breasts brush against my arm and lift the hairs on the back of my head. Her nipples perk underneath the fabric as if awakening with the subtle touch.

"And pleased?"

I brush her hand aside. "Ms. Young," I warn her. "That's private."

She doesn't move. Still leaning, the girl takes a small breath, glancing at my lips inches away from hers. Her scent invades me, the fragrance of an orange field, fruity and inviting, a craving for something sweet after the sour months of my life.

"You're right. But it's my job to answer your needs." Her breath tickles against mine as the girl stares me in the eyes before continuing. Her hand tugs my shirt out of my pants.

I grasp her wrist to stop her. "Ms. Young-"

"If what you told me is true," she whispers again, her fingertip brushing against the buttons on my chest. "And if your wife is cheating on you, then why bother containing what you know we both want? I have seen the way you look at me. I know you want this as much as I do."

She leans forward and I place my hands on her shoulders. I cannot do this. No matter what I think Ariella is doing, I cannot damage our marriage in the same way. Zoe frowns as I stand up and put her at arm's distance. She still tries to unbutton her shirt and I grind my teeth, looking away.

"Ms. Young, for both your sake and mine," I say, glaring at the ceiling. "I advise you to leave my office this instant."

"Mr. Vaillant, I thought you-"

"You thought wrong," I say before she can finish the sentence. "Tonight was a mistake. I apologize for my behavior or if it led you to believe anything would happen between us. It was not proper conduct for me and I am sorry. But there is no way the professional relationship we have will develop into something else."

I'm drunk, but I'm not *that* drunk. I step away and towards the door, opening it. It's clear when the idea that nothing is going to happen sinks in for Zoe. Her shoulders slump and she takes a long breath before buttoning up her shirt again and readjusting her skirt. Zoe is beautiful, but I am not seeking the mistake of a night.

Not right now, and not while I am still married to Ariella.

The idea, although tempting, is wrong. Zoe is a beautiful girl, but I cannot and will not get involved with her. She turns and walks towards the door as I stand by it, waiting. When Zoe reaches me, she stops, her hand touching my chest and gliding up and down. I frown at her and am about to stop her, but she raises her brow.

"We both know this is going to happen one day, Mr. Vaillant. You don't love your wife anymore. No matter how much you fight it, the chemistry between us is clear." I grab her wrist, but she leans forward and brushes her mouth against my jaw.

"Zoe…leave," I demand, stepping away.

Her hands fall to her side and she sighs but steps outside the office. I shut the door as fast as possible and rest my head against it. I stopped it. But shame still lurks around my heart and mind. Because for a brief second, my discipline faltered.

For a moment, I almost gave in to temptation.

3
Dorian

I open the front door as the night grows long. The house where Ariella and I planned to begin our lives as a family. We didn't want to live in the city. Not if we were planning to have kids. My wife's only request was for the place to be spacious enough in the hope either she or I could work from home when we had children. It was a must for both of us to be as present as we could.

It took me a while to come home, to drive, and get rid of the alcohol in my system. To face my wife after almost cheating on her. The idea crossed my mind. Zoe was right there. She wanted it to happen. But I don't think I could ever forgive myself if I hurt Ariella. I could not forgive myself if that was how my marriage ended.

Consciences are a weird thing. Some people ignore theirs. I can't seem to shake off mine.

I put the keys on the narrow table by the door. The place is dead silent, as it has been for almost fourteen months. The cackle of the keys hitting the plate Ariella chose so long ago as the key holder spreads through the house. She chose most of the furniture and details. Elegant and with no clutter. I try to listen for something, but there is no sign of my wife. I walk around the empty rooms and notice the door at the end of the hallway is closed. It's always closed. I can't help but question myself if she is in our bedroom or inside this one. Crying again.

I try not to give it much thought. I try not to think back to the hurtful memory of my wife crawling in the sheets and hugging herself to sleep. This was before she closed the room's door, and also herself to me.

My naked feet step into the dark kitchen, and I fill a cup with water. The coldness of it calms me as I grasp my thoughts and work out how I will talk to Ariella tomorrow. I need to tell her, to let her know I am aware of Louis, and maybe even tell her about what almost happened tonight. We can still mend this.

The empty kitchen, once full of laughter, now only shows how sad our lives are. How broken and fragile our marriage is. When I turn, my eyes fall on an envelope on top of the table. The light brown color of it makes it stand out against the white wood, yet it's the name of the well-known lawyer's office at the top corner that grabs my curiosity by the belt. Before I can stop myself, I reach for it.

"You're home," Ariella says as she walks into the kitchen and reaches for a cup, filling it with water.

"I didn't hear you arrive, and you didn't tell me you were going out. I was wondering if I should call Josh to check on you."

Ariella walks around me, knowing I am reading the document she left here. She waits, sipping from her cup. "You want to divorce me?" I ask, my voice only above a whisper, still staring at the papers.

"I think it's the best, Dorian. You… I think we should."

Her voice carries the usual strain when we speak. As if she is tired of me, of us, of how our life is holding itself together. She looks serene, but as I dare glance in her direction, her fingers tap against the drink in her hand.

"Ariella…" I mumble, letting my fingertips press the bridge of my nose. "You're asking me to sign the divorce papers when we never even talked about it? We never spoke about divorce."

I turn to face her, only to find no traces of emotions in her brown eyes. They stare at me as calm as the sea before a storm. They don't resemble the fiery woman who would have me scream her name in every way known to man. Her dark blonde hair falls to the side of her face, struggling to stay in place. But it's her beautiful full lips pressing together that draw my attention.

"We did Dorian," Ariella sighs. "During the last session we had together, we talked about it."

"No. I asked if diving into work and staying out

till late was a way of distancing yourself from me, and you were the one who said if you wanted to do it, you would ask for a divorce. You never gave me a hint about it. You never-"

My voice fails and my hands fall by my side, closing in and crumbling the papers, as I swallow my ache. I should not lose my calm. It's one thing our therapist told us to work on. Ariella and I need to talk, and it will be best if we can do so without raising our voices. Or, without one of us speaking about whatever it is we know will hurt the other.

It's human nature, and I need to fight it. Hurt people hurt others.

"Say it, Dorian," she demands, raising her chin at me, her eyes sparkling with tears she doesn't set free. "Say what you are thinking."

Fire sparks in her eyes as I realize the fury, the hunger I love since we met, still lies somewhere inside of her. Just not for me to see. "You never talk to me, Ariella. You bury yourself in work and doing God knows what with whom."

"What do you mean?"

My wife takes a step forward, crossing her arms over her chest and daring me to continue. When I don't, Ariella glares, taking a deep breath but not breaking eye contact with me. She never does, she always stares me in the eyes. Memories of how those fights ended invade me, and I force back the lump in my throat.

I miss it. I miss touching her and talking to her. Our life as a couple is what I miss the most. My hand reaches for hers, but the woman I love pulls away and it's then that I lose it. I miss her, and it's only making me angrier to know she doesn't care about it at all. She doesn't want me in the same way anymore.

"I mean, maybe the vows we swore years ago mean little to you."

Ariella scoffs, sliding her fingers through the loose curls of her bun and they fall around her shoulders. Her long hair rumpled from the bed she was laying in. I stare at her in a mist of adoration, sorrow, guilt, and anger, not knowing which one needs to come out first.

She turns around and then the words slip out of me. "It's why you want a divorce, isn't it? I know what you've been doing and I don't think-"

"I don't know what you mean, Dorian, but I cannot let this go on. You are clearly hurting and this marriage is holding on by its fingernails. We have been struggling for too long. It doesn't need to be this hard. It's time."

Ariella walks out of the kitchen and leaves me alone in the darkness. With the paper in my hands, I realize how easily she can make me lose my temper. She knows I will do what she wants.

"I am not signing, Ari," I call after her and she freezes.

I know I have stopped calling her by her nickname, yet my heart speeds when she doesn't move. Her shoulders slump, and I assume she doesn't want to fight. But that's not her. My wife always fights back, and she makes sure she wins. Ariella glances over her shoulder, a tear threatening to fall from her eye, but she doesn't let me see her cry.

Not anymore.

"You will. You are tired of this, and so am I."

I grunt, rising from the sofa, unfit for someone who is over six feet tall to sleep. The night was long, and I didn't rest. Neither did Ariella. She will never admit it, but I heard her footsteps. I listened when she entered the other bedroom and closed the door behind her. And then when she got up as the first rays of sun came into the window, cleaning her sweet eyes from all traces of tears.

She hasn't cried in front of me for months. Maybe over a year now.

At first, I thought she was carrying on, gathering courage so we could keep our lives on track. Yet she distanced herself from me, and not even therapy helped us reach each other. The therapy she suggested. Somehow, I feel it has drifted us apart. My wife, the beautiful soul I fell in love with, is now a ghost. A shell of the woman she once was.

I hear the coffee machine, so I stand up and head to the kitchen while trying to make the strings of my hair less rebellious. There is nothing better in the morning than the smell of crushed coffee beans filling the air.

I step inside the kitchen, hesitating when I notice Ariella already there. She has one of her favorite skirts on. The navy-blue fabric hugging her hips and fighting to stay put, the jacket covering the back of the chair, while she sips on her white mug with the words she loves so much.

The ones she doesn't listen to anymore.

"*Bonjour,*" I mumble to no one.

"Good morning."

Ariella murmurs the words under a breath as I place my mug on the counter. It's a relief she is speaking to me. I glance at her figure by the table while pouring my coffee. She hunches over her notebook, scribbling down one of her ideas. A small wrinkle appears between her eyebrows.

When did she become so cold with me? It wasn't right after the accident. Something broke then, but the cold slipped in later. It was months after when we stopped looking at each other, when we stopped speaking, when we stopped living.

Ariella keeps the three-letter word out of her sight. I think the pain from yesterday is making her the most vulnerable since she didn't take that mug from the kitchen cabinet for two months. Today, however, she needs the memories connected to it.

Maybe I should deny what she said last night. Correct her. I am hurt, but I love her. Somehow, in the heat of the moment, I didn't deny her accusation.

"What time is your appointment today?" I ask.

"In a couple of hours," she replies, not taking her eyes away from the drawing. "Thea asked me to remind you that yours is after lunch."

I snort at the note from our therapist before trying to figure out what to say. Even with all the struggles of our past, I don't want this marriage to end. If anyone knows anything about Ariella, it is Thea. She is one of the few people in this world who can help me understand what is going on inside my wife's head.

"I'll be there," I reply, putting my now empty mug in the sink. For the last year, every time we fight, I can't seem to stay quiet and the last word has to be mine. "Do you still want me to come to the gala tonight?"

I glance at her over my shoulder, my hands gripping the sink, but Ariella doesn't take her eyes away from the sketch. Her long finger slides over the pencil as she pulls her brows together, focusing. It's what she has done for months, working so she doesn't deal with life. Maybe the same reason she is fucking someone else.

"It's up to you, Dorian. My colleagues like you, my boss as well, and it would be good to have you there. But I'm not forcing you to come to the event. I know you can get bored."

"I'm asking because if you want me to sign the divorce papers, what's the point of going, anyway?"

Ariella stops, her hand hovering over the sketch, and she closes her eyes. She mumbles something, but not loud enough for me to hear. My wife takes a deep breath before staring at the table and speaking. "You do whatever you want. You always do it anyway. What's the point in trying to make up for me just because it's my job?"

"What does that mean?"

"It means," Ariella shifts in the seat, staring at me instead. Her gaze pierces mine like fire melting snow. "You accuse me of cheating when you still have that perky secretary of yours around. You know who I am talking about. The one who undresses you with her eyes? The one you hired a little over a year ago?"

Nausea hits me. It's not the first time we fought about my secretary, however, this time Ariella is on to me because I keep Zoe around even though it's not the best idea. The last time she brought the subject up, I told her I would fire Zoe if she wanted me to. But then our conversations became dry, our therapy sessions together ended, and Ari never spoke about Zoe again. I shift my weight to my other leg, grabbing the counter to gain some composure but failing when my wife waits for me to speak.

"Are you ready to talk about you and Louis?"

Ariella scoffs. She picks up her bag and jacket, throws the latter over her arm, and I notice the way her eyes come alive once she grabs the mug. She lets her fingers caress the engraved letters on it, sliding against the black before she blinks the memories away.

We always fought. It's common for a couple to fight. However, our fights would not last. Not like this. We would never go to bed angry because one would admit to being wrong, or the tension would build to the point we ended up having sex. After sex, it seemed we could always work everything out.

I fell in love with the fire in Ariella. A fire she kept hidden from most people. One I haven't seen for so long, but it’s showing signs today. Seeing her standing up for herself, even if against me, has me recalling all those times we ended up making love right on top of the kitchen table.

They say anger is not the opposite of love. Indifference is. I can now agree.

“I already told you all I had to say, and I will not stay here listening to you blaming me for how our lives turned out again.”

“What?” I ask, my voice becoming louder. “When did I blame you for it, Ari?”

My wife stands against the kitchen’s backdoor before saying the one thing I can't ever comprehend.

“You blame me for the accident, Dorian,” her voice breaks before she has the chance to realize it.

"You will always blame me for that day."

My hand is quick as I take the steps needed to grab her wrist and turn her to me. Tears dance in her eyes and beg me not to say anything. Yet this time, she doesn't step away from my touch.

Her words get caught up as I try to read her gaze when her eyes trap mine. When her breathing hits my lips and her perfume invades my lungs, I am thrown back to those nights when we would dedicate ourselves to showing the other how we felt. Worshiping her body with my lips, hands…

"I have to leave," she mumbles under a shaky breath, easing away from my grip and taking away the flowery scent with her. "Try to be on time at home tonight. The car is picking us up at seven."

"Ariella," I yell after her as she walks out of the house, leaving me and my fading anger alone in the kitchen.

The memory of the hardest day of my life invades me as if it's still happening. I lift my gaze to the intact mug on the table, along with my wife's notepad. Curious, I open it. She smeared the sheets of her drawings with her tears. Proof my wife still has a heart and still hurts. Then, being extra careful, I pick up the mug, staring at the three-letter word. It is one of the few things we keep in the house. In the months after the accident, we gave most of the stuff to people in need but kept a few pieces of clothing and some stuffed toys. The mug, however, seems to be Ari's most treasured item. It will always leave a scar on us. One we can never heal from, as his laughter keeps me awake every time I remember how he looked when we last saw each other.

The word *mom* stands out against the white mug as I lay it inside the sink.

4
Ariella

"Well, that's how it is," I say, with a mocking grin.

"That's your opinion?"

Dorian pretends to think this through. A smirk charms his lips as he looks at me before staring ahead again. The dark street helps to hide the blush on my cheeks. However, I catch Dorian eyeing them as if he can see the pink spreading on my skin when I pull my hair behind my ear.

I am never this blunt, especially with men. But there is something about him. I feel compelled to say whatever is on my mind to him. Maybe it's because I know he is interested in me. He made it clear before. If not with words, then with his actions.

I never had a man wanting to do things for me, or wanting to hang out. The bar is low, but I still have standards and so far Dorian's patience is proving to be a big one.

"Yes," I reply and watch, amazed as he absorbs every word I speak. "Sex is as important in a relationship as talking. I understand not everyone feels this way. But for me it is."

Dorian smiles and I think he does this without even realizing it. Men misunderstand how quiet I am because of my shyness. I don't let people in. Being on a date with Dorian was already something out of my comfort zone. He pikes up my curiosity. The smile he gives me. How his green eyes see the world.

The date was amazing. Three hours had passed with us sitting at the table talking before we realized. It was the best date I have been to since I came to New York. All the other people, especially the men, were too eager to get to know the part of me I don't share. And when I explained I wanted to take things slow, the men didn't understand. The women did. But so far, both times I developed a relationship with a woman, it didn't last for longer than a few months.

However, since the first night, there was something about Dorian. He never tried to do anything I would consider too much. He doesn't ask questions I am uncomfortable with. But the best thing is he cares. Or I think he does. I have little experience to compare him with, but no one else I dated before took the bus six nights to make sure I was safe. I am pretty sure he was off from work last Saturday but still showed up at the bus stop. The second I saw him, my heart stumbled on itself.

"Can't say I disagree," he replies, and I am pulled out of my thoughts.

I stop, twirling my body to face him as we come to a halt in front of my place. The bricks are fading in color, looking paler, mixing with what was once a bright building. It still holds some magic. A mix of old and contemporary buildings on a street that has seen better days. The rents in the city aren't cheap, and I am not the *biggest fan of being around people I don't know. I had to compromise. It's not like the money I saved before running away would last me forever if I lived elsewhere.*

Dorian frowns, looking at the building behind me. From what I understood, he lives outside the city. Something about a family property. I don't think he wants to get into detail, so I didn't push for answers.

"You live here?"

"Yes. This is home, for now at least," I reply, glancing over my shoulder. "If I get the job at the fashion studio, I may leave and search for another place. But it's not a terrible building. I mean, my landlord is kind of shady. But my neighbors are honest, hardworking people. The Indian couple across the hall even gifts me with meals from time to time."

I turn to face him, but his eyes are already waiting for mine. Whenever I talk about the future, it seems to make Dorian happy. And I cannot understand why seeing him smile makes the butterflies in my stomach go crazy.

"Sounds like a plan," he says, and I fight it, but the corners of my mouth turn up in amusement.

"I'm someone who enjoys having things planned."

If this isn't one of my biggest truths, then I don't know what is. I don't like being surprised or caught with my guard down. When things happen my way, it's easier. Less messy. I have been called a control freak before.

"Thank you for tonight," I say, and his eyes borrow mine for a second as Dorian leans toward me. Enough for him to be closer, but not enough for us to kiss. I find myself disappointed about it. It's the first time in months

I've wanted to kiss someone. "It was fun."

His hand brushes mine, and the contact sends tingles down my spine. The good kind. The ones who make me realize where this can lead. The ones I missed. "Can I pick you up for work tomorrow?" He asks and my brow raises. "I won't try anything if that's what you are worried about."

"I'm not worried about you trying."

He comes closer. His expensive perfume invades me, and the hints of peppermint warm my entire body. Dorian glances at my lips when I trap my lower one with my teeth. Sparks light up his green gaze, and I swear if he does nothing, I may combust.

"Then what are you worrying about?" He murmurs, and I know he is making sure. I know he realizes I have kept my walls up for too long. Waiting for consent only makes him more attractive.

I'm screwed. So screwed.

"You try nothing at all."

Dorian's lips brush against mine, lingering around the kiss we both want to happen. The soft skin sends a jolt of electricity through my body, and his hand rests against the small curve on my back, pulling me to him.

*"*Tu vas me ruiner*," he murmurs against my mouth, and I make a mental note to search for the translation. I am pretty sure he said something along the lines of ruining him.*

I tiptoe, reaching for him, and he closes his lips to mine. My hands crawl on the side of his arms until they stop on the nape of his hair, not wanting him to go anywhere. I don't think he would, to be honest. He doesn't deepen the kiss, and although I barely know this man, something in me tells me he is harmless. That I am protected when I am with him.

When Dorian pulls away, and we both open our eyes to each other, it seems he is fighting a battle with himself. Dorian talks. A lot. A lot more than I do. He has to fill the silence whenever we are together. Even when I didn't know his name, he still made small talk. Right now, he seems to have all these words trapped inside him, wanting to come out. But he doesn't let them. He doesn't say what's on his mind for whatever reason.

"You're thinking," I say, and he smirks.

"I do that a lot."

"About?"

Dorian glances at my lips. "How badly I want to know you better. I am thinking so many things, my mind is all over the place. I am thinking I have to do this right and move at your pace, not to scare you away."

His lips touch my forehead. Oh God, he is going to wreck me. I know it. My mom always told me that some people enter our lives, and we know they should never leave. The way Dorian looks down at me makes me realize how true that is.

His lips trace mine as he whispers into my mouth. "I'll pick you up at 8 a.m. From now on, I am taking you to work and I'll bring you back home." I open my mouth to argue, but he stops me. "You can try to talk me out of this, but I am not changing my mind. It's my car or the bus. If we are going on another date, I am not letting you walk these streets alone, Ari. Not anymore. You have me."

I have him.

I never had someone in my corner before, and then came this man. This tall man holding the entire universe in his eyes and dreams I cannot understand. I have tried to fight my attraction to him since the day we met. But each time he looks at me, with all the patience in the world and wanting nothing more than to listen to the sound of my voice, I feel my resolution falling further. I wasn't expecting Dorian, or to like him so much.

I also wasn't expecting tragedy to strike us like it did.

"It sounds lovely," my therapist interrupts my speech as I finish retelling about the first date my husband took me on. "He even walked you home."

"I gave him the divorce papers yesterday."

By how she frowns, one would think I said the moon is falling from the sky and killing us all in the next few minutes. Thea furrows her brow, shifting in her seat while taking notes on the small leather notepad. Buying time into figuring out how to continue with the session as I remain here, without saying much. Something she hates. She is professional enough to keep her opinions to herself, but it is obvious I am filling the time by not speaking. If I don't speak, she doesn't write in her damn notebook. In the last few sessions Thea has asked me to talk about memories, especially the happy ones. It's almost impossible to think about the happy memories when one terrible memory has tainted them all.

"Ariella, you can't give your husband the divorce papers without talking to him first."

"Why not?"

She bites the inside of her cheek, staring at me. Thea has been with us for the last year. At this point, she is the only person I talk to or at least open the slightest crack in my heart to speak my mind. We don't have a friendship, but the way she relates to me is what made me come back to her sessions. Thea doesn't talk to me as if I am going to break apart and burst into tears. I want to, but I have kept myself together, especially around others. It's the reason I'm still here, not giving up on comprehending my thoughts and emotions. Or trying to.

"You never mentioned it before, and Dorian doesn't cope well when he is facing a hard situation."

Sort of true. She has a point, but it's not like my husband and I even talk. I'm aware of my role in this failed marriage, but I don't think he is. I don't think he knows anything about me anymore.

"What is your suggestion?" I ask, crossing my arms over my chest.

Thea's eyes linger as I recline against her Safire couch. Pretending. Always pretending I am well enough. People don't know how to approach me otherwise. No one knew what to tell me after I lost my son.

When someone has been through the pain my husband and I have suffered, people give support. However, they expect us to hold our heads high and carry on with our lives. It's what *he* would have wanted, a family friend of Dorian's told us once. I almost told the woman to fuck off, but Dorian walked us away before I could. My son was a toddler. He did not know what he wanted besides his favorite toys and cartoons. How does she know what he wanted? How am I supposed to carry on with my life if I don't have him in it anymore?

So I pretend. I pretend I am well and I am coping when the truth is so much uglier.

"Try to keep Dorian on your good side," Thea advises. "Be with him at tonight's gala. Stay close to him. Avoid the colleague he thinks you're having an affair with."

"Thea…"

Therapy is helpful. After leaving my old life behind, therapy with Thea has shown me I should have done this years ago. But having Dorian go to the same therapist as me isn't easy. I confide in Thea. I trust her with my darkest thoughts. Dark enough to scare anyone else in my life. This woman used to walk me around the block or through the park from across her office during our first sessions. It was her way to make me open up to her when I didn't want anyone in my life anymore. When I didn't want to live. I still don't, but at least now I have something to look forward to.

It was she who made me speak when all I wanted to do was scream when the thoughts of the love I held inside of me weren't enough to survive. Thoughts I can't go back to. Her first rule was to treat each other on a first name basis, to make me more at ease. But she explained time and time again that we were not friends. We couldn't be. The moment we became friends, she would have to stop being my therapist.

Sometimes I wish it was that way. Sometimes it is so lonely to face the world, I wish she was by my side.

"Try Ariella. If he doesn't sign the papers after you ask him nicely, we can discuss what to do next."

She places the pen and notebook down and I know the session is almost over. Her long light hair cascades to the front, falling and covering her shoulders as she takes her glasses and massages her nose to get out of her doctor's mindset.

"Are you having an affair with Louis?" She asks, and I scowl.

"No. Why would I have an affair with him?"

Why do they think Louis and I are together? Dorian hasn't liked him since before everything happened, but over the last few months, I have noticed how he gets tense whenever Louis' name comes up in conversation. His fixation on my colleague, to the point Thea is trying to know as well, is getting out of control.

"Dorian seems to think you are."

"Dorian makes a lot of assumptions."

"But you are seeing someone," she states, and I don't meet her eyes. I am aware of what I will do or say. Because it's not as simple as they think.

Thea is the only person who can break me since it all happened. She sees through the facade I have. If I open my mouth, if I dare to speak, she will dig deeper.

"I have to go," I blurt out, standing up and grabbing my coat. "Same time next week?"

"No. A week is too long between sessions. I will text you to check if you're available in a few days."

Thea calls for me as I close the door, but I pretend I did not listen. I can't answer her question. Not yet. I am not jeopardizing my plans.

"Finally," Louis shouts with a mouthful, waving his fork in my direction. "Where the hell were you?"

"Therapy. You know, the thing people resort to in order to make amends with themselves?"

"I thought you were doing couple's therapy." He takes a fork full of pasta and shoves it into his mouth.

"Please chew your food. You will choke."

"Ariella," he raises a brow. "Food needs to be eaten and savored. I can't do it if I don't stuff my face."

I chuckle as I pick up the menu to choose my lunch. "Well, you could have waited for me."

"I did. I waited about ten minutes."

With a signal to the server, I call the young man's

attention who hurries to the table. It's the same restaurant we usually eat at. The one Louis loves and where everyone already knows him.

"Next time I choose where we are going to eat," I say, thinking of one of my favorite places I haven't visited in a while.

I order my food and as soon as we are alone again, Louis charges back with questions. "How did therapy go?"

As the girl with a high ponytail passes us twice in a row, batting her eyelashes at him, I reply, "You know you can eat slower? My food hasn't even arrived yet." He doesn't even acknowledge the girl who seems to give up. Louis has a happy marriage, and I envy it every time I am reminded of it.

Not because I want the man. Far from it. I envy his relationship because it reminds me of how mine used to be. The shared glances, the soft touches… It reminds me of how Dorian and I used to be around each other.

"Yes, but this way I can eat twice. Don't avoid my question and answer me."

I stall him for a few seconds, drinking my water. With a smile on my lips, I decide I can't avoid my friend anymore and reply to his question before he forces me to speak.

"It went fine. My therapist doesn't see much progress on my part over the last couple of months."

"And from Dorian?"

"He tried," I explain and stare at my hands. Speaking about my husband trying to make things better makes my heart ache. The thought of him trying is painful. "I gave Dorian the divorce papers last night, but he says he won't sign them."

Louis almost spits the food out of his mouth. I feel time slow down as I realize I'm about to be scolded. "You filled out the divorce papers? Did you talk to your husband about it?"

"No," I sigh, thanking the server who places my carbonara pasta in front of me. "I didn't file for divorce. I had an attorney drafting the documents. It has to be done now. I know Dorian. It would never go in the way I need it to and if he sniffs around, it's about to get messy."

My fork spins in my hand as I ignore the man sharing a table with me, knowing well my friend is glaring from his seat. It's not normal for me to act on a whim. But then again, nothing has been normal.

"Did you two get into another fight?"

I roll my eyes. "We shared some words."

"At least you talked. How is he?"

I keep moving the food on the plate, unable to eat. Louis's question is the one I avoid answering myself. Especially since over the last months I have come to terms with the decision I made. I can't keep Dorian around. I can't drag him into the mess I am creating in order to get my answers. My husband blames me, and I understand him. I blame myself too for the car accident that took our son's life. But although I recognize my mistakes, and how guilty I am, it doesn't mean my husband is 100% right either. Because we are both hurt. The difference is I tried. For over a year, I tried to reach him. But the only thing we could not do was talk about it. The accident and how everything went after. Dorian doesn't seem to bring the subject up, and I have to confess it breaks me apart every time Thea forces me to dive into the memory.

The ache in me right now, knowing I am not loved anymore, seems too much to go on with the facade of marriage. He may still love me, but he is not *in love* with me.

And I don't want Dorian to hurt, which will happen if I keep him around. Nothing else in my life has a purpose but the plan. Nothing. Not even the love I still hold at the ends of my heart, the same love that hurts me every time it dares to surface.

"I don't know Louis. I haven't asked."

"Ariella, this game you're playing is dangerous. What if he finds out?"

"He doesn't know about it and I will not tell him until the right time comes," I say, patting my friend's hand, reassuring him he has nothing to worry about.

It would be funny on any other occasion for Dorian to consider Louis someone able to cheat. Louis is married, doesn't know how to lie, and doesn't even know how to inflict pain on another human being. No matter how annoying someone is. Despite his size, this man is like a big teddy bear. He is incapable of hurting someone. I once applied the same principle to me, and yet here I am now, sniffing for blood in the water.

"What time are you and Dana heading to the gala tonight?" I ask him.

Chewing, I stare at the man, who smiles at me at the mention of the woman he loves. "Around seven."

"I know you like to leave early," I reply, and a laugh leaves his chest.

To this day, I am pleased Louis is on my team. The only thing that made me return to work all those months ago was his friendship. Especially since everyone used to stare at me for the first couple of weeks. The people who knew about Raphael seemed to be eager to bring up the subject of his death every chance they got. It was the last thing I wanted to talk about. I only wanted to work. Focusing on it allowed me to forget my life. Louis has been the person who holds me in place when I cannot even stand. The one letting me drown in work and forget about my life.

Louis and his wife have been there for me when I need someone, when I want to clear my head and forget the pain. When I need to smile instead of cry.

Not my husband, and it's both of our faults. Dealing with the pain of our hearts being taken away from us, we drifted, and maybe he channeled his anger and his grief toward me.

As I did.

5
Ariella

Silence fills the car. Dorian sits close to his door on the other side of the seat. As I fix the strap of my shoes, the partition rises, separating us from the driver.

My husband's hand closes into fists on top of his leg as the other rests on his chin while he stares outside. Keeping his anger and opinion hidden from me, but fighting against it. Dorian wants to talk, but I think he doesn't know how to.

"Is Louis at this party?"

A sigh is my small reply because with all I thought he would ask, this is not the question I was expecting. The divorce papers, the accusation, last night's alcohol, and the smell of another woman on his clothes all are to blame as he glances at me.

I don't know what he did, but I suspect. Still, I can't blame him for it, since our love is numb. His love for me has died, which makes it harder for me to understand why he keeps saying he isn't signing the divorce papers.

Despite it all, despite the way we grew apart, I still want Dorian to be happy. And he isn't happy with me. How can he be when I am the one who caused him the biggest heartbreak of his life? Plus, if I play my cards right, all the work I put in for the last year will show profits. When it does, I think it's for the best if he isn't around. If Dorian knows the truth, I doubt he will understand.

He chose to let go of his anger and grieve in peace. I chose to hold on to mine and search for answers.

"Yes. He has to be. Fashion week is close, and he is my right hand. It's beneficial for me as it is for the company to have Louis talking to investors. You know this."

Dorian is trying to pick a fight. I don't think we can ever fix the distance between us. It wasn't on purpose, at least not for me. I closed myself so I could breathe again. But now my husband and I almost don't look at each other.

I don't want to keep doing this. I don't want to crawl into our bed at night with my back against him and cry as quietly as I can until I am so drained, I fall asleep. I have been doing it for over a year now. I don't want to be weak. I don't want to make others see I am weak. I don't want to feel the despair every night of not knowing how to fix things.

I don't want to hurt anymore.

And every time Dorian passes by me and doesn't

even spare a glance in my direction, that's precisely how I feel. It's how I've been feeling since last year. Since his eyes held so much pain in them, it was difficult to look at my husband. It seemed wrong to do so. From knowing our son did not survive. From knowing I did. I hurt, I shred, and I break all over again the same way my body did all those months ago. Every time he talks to me like this, I am taken back to that night at the hospital when I woke up and he was already in the room.

Love became numb, cold, and distant. So I found something to replace the void it left in me.

Revenge.

"I know a lot of things, Ariella. I am just waiting for you to admit them." Dorian continues. "Do you want a divorce so you can be with him without guilt?"

"Louis and I are not together, and I already asked you to sign the papers. What happens after is no one's concern."

"The vows we took mean nothing to you, do they?"

As he turns to face me, the anger in his eyes spreads and I grow aware of our surroundings. There's nowhere to run now and I cannot avoid him. When I began this, when I came up with the plan, no matter how hurt I was, it was never in my heart to break Dorian. To break us.

Yet it happened, and now I need to deal with everything. It is for a greater cause. All the nights I said I was working until late, all the meetings he thought I have been to. Everything I did, even the things I didn't want, I did for a purpose.

"You keep accusing me of cheating on you," I reply, tilting my head and facing him as well. "And yet, you are the one who arrived late last night with his shirt all messed up."

There it is, the soft gaze I love. As an intern, I fell head over heels with the tenderness in his eyes. Dorian always acts first, until someone makes him see where he is wrong, and then he stops. He apologizes and tries to make up for his words. Either with big gestures or small ones. He can melt me and bring me to the verge of tears when he swears his feelings. This time, however, I am not blaming him. If I am cheating – or some form of it - he has the right to do the same. I am not a hypocrite. However, knowing he may be with someone else brings a new kind of pain to my soul.

"Maybe you are right," he mumbles, staring out the window as the lights from the venue appear. "Maybe we should get a divorce."

It stings, but I shake the feeling away. I have to let him find someone who is worthy of him. I still love my husband, even if he isn't in love with me anymore. It's because I love him, I need Dorian to be happy.

Life is miserable as it is. Dragging him into this dreadful sadness lingering around us all the time, it's not fair.

"It's not like we can even be around each other, Dorian. It's for the best."

My husband glances at me, but then looks away. His shoulders slump and I can tell his resolve is wavering. "Can we at least talk this through? I need to know more before- "The car stops. The front door opens and Dorian sighs, knowing whatever he is about to say will have to wait.

"We are here. Please behave."

"I always do," he says, but it seems the words have lost the bite they had moments ago.

Flashes of cameras cover our eyes as we smile. Dorian walks around the car, avoiding even glancing in the photographer's direction. Coming to my side, he opens the door, extends his hand and places his arm so I can interlock mine through his.

Dorian doesn't do things for others to see. He never did. The fact that he is being courteous tonight has my stomach swirling. It's the most we have touched for months. Even while sharing a bed, I only slide under the sheets once I know he is already deep in sleep.

I want to ask him about it. Where does he think it all went wrong? When did the man faking a smile by my side stopped loving me and began hating who I had become? But I know the answer.

"You look beautiful," Dorian whispers, not even looking at me, and I raise my chin as the doors to the house open.

"You look sharp as well."

Which he does. The suit he wears is my creation. The black jacket with silver strings lets the black silk button-down shirt stand out. I don't hate or resent Dorian. I never will. Making clothes for him is proof of it. It takes time, and patience, although I know my husband would look handsome in anything.

As we walk into the main room, people turn to look. It's not only because of my position at the company but also because of my husband. They love him. To talk to him. To stare at him. To be the focus of his attention. Dorian's surname helps to draw people in as much as his looks do. His height and build, the angelic lips, and the voice able to make anyone swoon. His family is one of the wealthiest in Europe. Even if my husband drifted from the affairs his father attends to. The Vaillants' have a vast hotel chain. Dorian's love for animals made him follow his passion and now he acquires and sells horses. His family implied he will one day take over their business, but for now, he is living his life.

My dress skirt moves as I walk. The dark green fabric sways away from my hips and shows my legs as I approach the shareholder in front of us. My shoulders are in full display, the body part Dorian never forgot whenever we made love. Whenever he wanted to tease me, he would kiss, grasp and bite.

"Ariella," the old man says, beaming as we

approach him. Dorian takes his arm away, resting his hand on the curve of my back. I stay in front of him to greet the pervert who pays my paycheck at the end of the month. "What a stunning dress."

I see his eyes wandering over my cleavage. Men. Show them boobs and they forget we are talking. Dorian clears his throat. My boss acknowledges his presence and stops ogling at me. Something common in these events is that the elders seem to like to watch the women walking around and eating them with their eyes instead of speaking.

But I notice how the small grip of my husband's fingertips on me tightens, and my heart beats faster as I realize he is still possessive. Even if not willingly.

"Mr. White, always happy to see you."

The lies I have to tell to keep my job. They can't afford to fire me. My designs are some of the most requested in the city. The store is always busy, so custom-made outfits are quite common. One store for now, but the promise is to expand soon. I have worked with them since my internship, and I have witnessed and helped build up the brand.

We make small conversation. Even Dorian talks about the horse he is trying to buy. Everyone appears content in this overpriced rented manor, which welcomes about five hundred people tonight.

"Ariella," my friend's familiar voice makes me turn my head to catch Louis walking towards us with his wife. Dorian stiffens. His hand slides from my back to my waist and I am pulled to his side. "I thought I had seen you. Hi Dorian."

Dorian dips his chin, the grip on my waist tightens, and I regret not having told Louis this over lunch. It's embarrassing to even think about it and honestly Dorian should have let it go by now. But I should know better. Louis glances at my husband, trying to understand the silence. Dana looks between them before her gaze falls on me.

"Your dress is gorgeous, Ariella. As always."

"Thank you. I love yours as well. Did Louis design it?" She nods. "I'm surprised it looks that good."

"Hey," Louis says and I beam at him. "I spent hours on this."

Dorian makes a sound, and I take a deep breath. Not the right time for him to start. Louis is too deep in conversation to notice anything, and I walk away with Dorian by my side. "What?" He asks.

"Behave."

"I am behaving."

"You're poking around for something that does not exist, Dorian. He is a friend. Let it go."

"Okay. If it's not Louis, then who or what is it? Because something is up, Ariella. We both know it."

I roll my eyes at him, noticing someone staring at us. Hidden in the crowd, eyes deadly set on my figure and the way Dorian's hand stays on my body. I try to avoid it, not to look in that direction, knowing a fight may begin when no one is around.

It's not like I look forward to our moments alone. If we fight, it will make everything more difficult.

"I need to go to the bathroom," I tell Dorian as one investor approaches us.

"Ari-" he whispers as I pat his hand and slip away.

Dorian groans as I leave him without an answer, and before he can say anything else, I walk towards the end of the room. For a moment, I almost told him the truth. But the mess it would create... I glance over my shoulder and instead of going to the bathroom like I said I would, I approach the bar. Where the one person I cannot cut ties with is.

"Stop staring," I whisper.

My hands on top of the cold marble surface, I don't even dare to glance at Irene who stands, leaning against the bar. Her eyes are still clinging to my husband, who is now making small talk with someone from the accounting department. He always knows how to fit right in, and Irene doesn't. She sighs, turning around to face the window behind the bar as if gazing at the garden instead of everyone at the party.

Irene takes a long sip of her champagne before she allows herself to peek at me. "He is lucky, and he doesn't even know it."

A deep breath fills my lungs as I thank the bartender for the drink. I need alcohol tonight, and the icy champagne helps to ease my nerves. "Why are you here? You didn't mention you were coming. In fact, you seemed oblivious when I told you about the gala."

Irene grins. "Because I needed to see you tonight."

"Irene…"

The warning escapes me. I am unable to control it as she looks around before tilting her head towards the hallway. Her red hair reaches a little over her shoulder now. It was shorter when we first met. I follow her, knowing I have to or everything may end up down the drain. One man looks at Irene as she passes by. His eyes are drinking up the woman who walks ahead of me in a two-piece suit.

Under the white pants, her slender hips curve slightly. Irene takes the jacket off, showing how the delicate fabric of the bright red top she wears does nothing to hide her back. The man is about to stop her, but she ignores him. From the corner of my eye, I catch Dorian drinking and laughing. Irene and I step into the hallway, our figures hidden by the walls, and she opens one door as I approach her.

Soon as the door is closed, I am pressed against it, her lips on my neck. She bites my earlobe, sniffling my perfume as her hand roams to the gap in my dress in search of more skin. I press my lips together to stop myself from speaking something I shouldn't.

"I have been staring at you since you walked in," she breathes out in a whisper, and I force a whimper out of me when her fingertip brushes my hip. "I haven't seen you for over a week, Ariella."

When her mouth opens on mine, when my hand grasps the silk of her top and I know she is putting her walls down, I twirl Irene around and press her against the door. I need to put some distance between us. Her eyes crinkle a little as I lean forward, and open the silver buttons of her ruby blouse as slow as I can, revealing the red silk bralette covering her breasts. I arch my brow at her, who snickers in reply, biting down on her lip.

"I know how much you love red," she whispers, brushing her finger against my collarbone before twirling it in a loose curl.

Irene is right. The red color against her pale skin creates a sinful effect. As if she were innocent. Another lie she likes to spread.

"I wonder what that husband of yours would think if he knew about us."

"Leave my husband out of this, Irene."

She shrugs. "I don't have plans to bring him *into* this. I am just wondering."

Always pushing my buttons. By now, I am not only used to it, as I am adept at shifting her attention away from Dorian.

My thumb caresses the hem of the bra where her skin appears. Her nipples perk under my touch while I lean forward and caress her lips with mine. I glide them further down on her jaw, kissing her skin until reaching the fabric.

She hisses when my bottom lip lifts the fabric before nipping it with my teeth. With my hands on her hips, I force Irene to stay still. My mouth takes her nipple, savoring the delicate skin as if it's the most delightful sweet I have ever tasted. It's not, but she doesn't need to know it. She also doesn't need to know how my mind has a battle with my heart every time I touch her. Irene is the type of woman I would date when I was single. However, I cannot let go and do what she wants me to do when I am still emotionally connected to my husband.

"Ariella," she purrs, wanting me to hurry as usual. This is the most I have touched her in two months. It is a desperate move and I am glad she doesn't realize it. My fingers travel the slowest possible, torturing the woman who likes to pretend I'm hers. Who likes to think I want her the same way she wants me. If only she knew.

When I pull away, Irene's eyes widen. I smirk, sitting on a chair by the window. "If you want to come, you have to touch yourself."

"Ari-" she whimpers like she always does when I step away.

"Don't call me Ari," I say and Irene sighs. Too far. I am pushing too far. So I soften my voice. "You are too stressed, sweetheart. Your job keeps you uptight. You have been spending your days with lawyers."

"I thought tonight you-" I raise a brow at her and Irene stops speaking.

We both know I won't have sex with her. I explained to Irene nothing would happen while Dorian and I are still married. A few stolen kisses, some groping, but never more. If it's up to me, it won't ever develop into anything more. I am so close. So freaking close I can taste it.

I take Irene's wrist in my hand and guide it beneath the fabric of her underwear. Hope fires in her gaze but soon fades when she realizes I will stand my ground.

"If you insist." She walks to a table in the corner of the room. I watch as she unbuttons her pants and lets them fall around her ankles. Irene leans on top of it, her hands drifting on her body, and I realize she is soaking wet. Then I look away, not being able to keep my gaze on the woman as she calls for me. It's risky, but I don't think she will even notice when she is concentrating on herself.

She moans and arches her back. I mumble words under my breath as I try to ignore the sound of her touching herself. Irene becomes louder. She rubs herself, whispering my name. But I don't go to her. I never do.

Biting down on her lip, Irene reaches her orgasm and I walk to her. I dare a glance and almost breathe in relief when I see her adjusting her pants. Taking her hand and lifting it to her mouth, Irene sucks on her fingers.

She makes it so easy for me. I can hide my true intentions and pretend I am all for this little game she plays.

"Now," I murmur, cleaning her bottom lip with my thumb. "Be a good girl and avoid killing my husband with those pretty eyes of yours."

My hand pulls the door handle, and I sprint down the hallway. Irene stays in the room. She has been pushing my buttons more. Calling late at night, sending messages when I tell her I'm busy. And now this.

I need to speed things up, or she will get suspicious. I don't know how long I can keep her waiting. Irene is growing needy and if she snoops around my life, everything I have worked for, everything I have sacrificed, like my marriage, will be in vain.

When I enter the main room, I hear laughter and cheers from the crowd while I notice where my husband is. Deep in conversation, Dorian only realizes I am by his side when I touch his arm.

He gives me the most charming smile and something in me dies when I realize others are watching. It's the only reason he would be glad to see me. "Where were you?" He whispers, taking my arm in his hand. Dorian places his empty drink on a table. He turns and leads me away as we approach the part of the room where the guests dance.

"I had to meet a colleague."

"I'll pretend I believe you."

He takes my hand and steps away, not even asking me if I want to dance, and guides me to the middle of the space. The crowd parts. Black and gold mix in details, the company's colors. It seems to be what most people chose to wear tonight, and as I let my husband glide us across the dance floor I notice his gaze sweeping over me. Dorian's attention feels like a kiss across my skin. My dress sways as we stroll towards where he wants. Dorian places his arm around my waist, pulling me closer to him. His scent invades my lungs, and I let guilt wash over me.

I could tell him. I could tell him about it all. But he wouldn't understand.

I keep my attention on his shoulder as I speak. "If you don't believe me, why do you ask?"

"I'm trying to give you the chance, to tell the truth, Ariella."

The sound of a snort rests in my throat before he pulls me to him, allowing our bodies to move with the music until reaching closer to where Louis dances with his wife. I become aware of where my husband's body touches mine and Irene's eyes on us.

Her flute reaches her velvety lips as she takes long sips before discarding the empty glass and picking up a new one from a server passing by. If a stare can kill, Irene is slaughtering my husband in her mind.

Two songs later, and saying nothing, Dorian and I step away from the dance floor. He walks by my side towards the bar before stopping and tilting his head back with an exasperated sigh. Louis comes out of the bar, holding a set of drinks, one for him, another for Dana. For whatever reason, this makes my husband upset.

He loses a long breath when Louis stops in front of me, handing me the third glass in his hand.

"I'm sorry Dorian. I didn't know what you wanted so-" my friend starts.

"But you knew what my wife wanted?"

The delicate glass almost slips from my hands as Louis and I turn our heads to face him.

"Dorian-" My voice fails and the words don't leave my mouth when he lifts his hand to stop me from speaking.

Without even meeting my gaze, he says, "If you don't tell me the truth, then maybe *he* will."

He glances at me for the briefest second as I give up the hope that I had about his behavior. Louis frowns, trying to figure out whatever is going on and so, taking a sip from my drink, I tell my friend the truth.

"Dorian seems to think you and I are having an affair."

"He- what?"

Dana approaches us behind her husband, placing one hand over his arm as he hands her the second glass of champagne. He didn't take his eyes away from the accusatory man by my side.

"I don't know why you think that, but we have nothing between us, Dorian," Louis explains. "We are just friends."

"Friends right," my husband replies, chuckling and shaking his head, as if it will take away the thoughts in his mind. "I wonder if friends call at 2 a.m.? Or if friends make their wives disappear for at least fifteen minutes at a party? Even better, do friends often hang out together when they are supposed to be working?"

"What's going on?" Dana asks, her eyes darting from us to Louis.

"Let's go," I tell Dorian, not even giving him the chance to make a scene. Well, a worse one.

Louis will tell everything to his wife. They hide nothing from each other. I drag Dorian away from the curious people around us, to a corner of the room where others seem not to be interested in. My husband stops and stares down at me. His height towering over my smaller frame. I take a deep, long, excruciating breath to hold back my temper.

"You're an ass, you know?"

"Right back at you."

"Dorian, you can't make accusations, especially if you don't have proof."

"I have proof," he states, taking his phone out of his pocket.

He hands it to me, clicking on something in his

email, and a set of pictures opens. Pictures of Louis and I having fun during our dinners. Pictures of Louis and I laughing, smiling, and hugging. Even one where I met him and Dana at a bar and we danced.

"You followed me?"

Something that looks a lot like remorse crosses his gaze. "I didn't. I had someone else doing it."

What the fuck? I watch the handful of photos over and over. I understand without context what it must look like, but it appears whoever this person was, they did not care to take pics of Dana and me. The only ones Dorian has are whenever I was with Louis.

"Why?"

Dorian shifts his weight from one foot to the other. "I realize it's wrong, but I needed to know, Ari. You are so distant and… *merde*." He inhales when looking down at me. Anger sets in my stomach at having my privacy invaded, and I bite on my tongue, struggling to let him talk and explain himself. His accent, however, thickens and I realize words slip into his native tongue as he struggles. "I know it's wrong. I realize it now. I am sorry. But we have to talk about this. Something is off and baby, I…"

"You saw this, and you still don't want to divorce?"

Dorian's gaze glistens as he speaks. His thumb

lifts my chin up so he can look me in the eye. "*Putain,* Ari. I would never divorce you without first trying to make things right."

I fight the urge to throw the device at his head and consider if I want to scold him before or after I kiss him when a voice comes from behind me and I grow cold. My eyes widen as I listen to the smoothness of her voice, but I can't shake the fear in my mind. "Hi Ariella," Irene purrs.

6
Dorian

"Hi Ariella," the woman almost sings, and my wife stops.

Ariella's face changes. Gone is the sassy-ness she was about to throw at me and I miss like crazy. My wife is fearless, determined, and kind of a bitch if needed, but most of the time, the politest woman I have ever met. However, with me, she would never keep quiet. I always knew how to push her buttons and make her snap and although pissed, at least she was talking to me. I could apologize after. I would apologize after. If she wanted me to, I would even kneel and beg for her to forgive me for how I behaved. But we need to talk. This stranger is to blame for our interruption. I notice how Ari ponders whether or not to turn around, how she tries to stay in place, and then gives up before twirling on her heels and looking at me again.

I crossed a line speaking about Louis, but it's the only way Ari will admit what is going on. Even if she isn't with him… something doesn't feel right.

"Irene, I didn't know you had business with us

tonight," Ariella says.

The woman's face softens. "I'm hoping to get the contract to commercialize the new designs you made."

Irene smiles at my wife. This woman, whoever she is, didn't find us by accident. No. She has been watching Ari for a while now. I noticed her strolling around us, trying to find a gap to come closer.

Wrong timing, though.

If she has business with *Wear A Kiss*, the brand Ariella has worked with for years, I am pretty sure this conversation could have waited.

"Really?" Ariella asks. "I didn't know you had intentions of associating with our brand."

Irene's eyes dance between us as if I am the one who shouldn't be here. Every time they do ice-cold emotions swirl in the air. She doesn't seem fond of me. Although I can't understand why, the feeling is mutual.

"Hi. I'm Ari's husband, Dorian."

I extend my hand at her and she glances at it for a brief second, but then doesn't seem to make a case out of it. Who does this pretentious, snobbish woman think she is?

Staying behind Ariella, I try to notice the slight changes in her. She has been losing a lot of weight. The stress has been taking a toll and my curvy wife shows signs of it, especially in this dress. Her waist looks a lot smaller and her arms are thinner. I spotted the other day the jeans she loves, with the ripped holes on her knees, laying somewhere in the wardrobe because they're too loose.

Small things I keep glimpsing and missing. Yet she stays beautiful. She can still take my breath away every time she walks through the door. Tonight, when I saw her in this dress I almost fell to my knees and begged her to stay home with me and work this out. Work our marriage out. The thought of someone else kissing, touching, and looking at my wife… fills me with thoughts no man should have. Thoughts that will get me in jail if I catch the bastard.

When did she fall out of love with me? When did I change my attitude toward her? She said I blame her for Raphael's death, which I don't. Not deliberately, at least. But maybe during the healing process, something happened. Something broke between us.

Trying to deal with my pain, I pushed the woman I love away. While she was unaware of it all, I made her think I blame her for the loss of our child. Ariella was driving when the truck hit them. I, however, will always face the guilt of not being there.

I need to talk to Thea about this.

My mind keeps me trapped for a while, and I almost don't catch Ariella whispering something to Irene about leaving. I raise a brow at the two of them, unaware of the approaching footsteps but welcoming whoever it is from breaking the woman's focus on my wife.

"Ms. Rogers," his voice comes to my right and I almost grunt, displeased to have to deal with Louis again. "You look somewhat acceptable."

It's as if he is one of those weird guys who never knows when to leave or stay away. My gaze almost pierces through him. I don't want to shift all of my anger on Louis, but it seems hard not to when I know he has the answers I seek.

He knows something about my wife that I don't.

"I cannot say the same about you," Irene replies at him with a wide grin.

So, she is unpleasant to all except my wife.

Everyone's focus is on Irene, and I mean everyone. Louis rolls his eyes so hard for a second, I think he despises the woman even more than I do. If this Irene has been around for a while, and if her attitude is always this pleasant and bright, it's reason enough to argue with others. Arrogance can be cute, but only until it gets out of control.

Dana steps aside from her husband, glaring at me before tightening her grip on Louis's arm. I crossed a line back there, and I realize now Ari is not the only person I need to apologize.

"You are trying to distribute our brand, aren't you?" Louis asks. "How long has it been since you people made the headlines? Three months? You must be desperate for some more propaganda. Planning your company's scams cannot be easy."

Irene seems ready to slap Louis. When she

doesn't, I'm not sure how to feel about it. Because the thought of it thrills me.

Ariella takes a step back. Her body bumps against mine, and her hand brushes my leg. For a second I could swear something alarmed her, and she is searching for me, but it hasn't happened for so long. It's my stupid hope.

Louis is about to speak, to part his lips, and continue the fight, but in front of me, Ariella's body becomes tense, and I can't focus on anything else. My heart jumps to my throat realizing she is uncomfortable, so I do the only thing I can to ease her discomfort a little.

"Let's go," I whisper to her.

Ari nods and grabs my arm. She glances over her shoulder at Louis, who gulps and mumbles some apology in our direction. With hurried footsteps, we reach the door. It appears someone had mercy on us since the garden is empty. People mingle inside the manor, trying to enjoy the night. The breeze engulfing the two of us is cool enough. I step closer to my wife to shield her from it. Ari tries to calm down and closes her eyes for a slow second before staring at me.

It doesn't make sense. When she and Louis are together, I don't see it. I don't see why she would cheat on me with him. I don't even see a hint of intimacy. But then Ari doesn't speak. She closes herself from me and wants to deal with her grief by herself. It's as if we stepped back in time and she is once more the girl who refused to tell me her name when we first met.

How am I supposed to help her if she doesn't let me in?

Anger slips through the cracks of my heart and my thoughts become clearer.

"What was that about?" I ask, and she raises a brow. "You whispered something to that Irene woman. Louis apologized to you."

"Dorian," she says, raising her hand, but I gently wrap my fingers around her wrist, pulling her closer to me. I need her warmth, her body against mine to know it will all be okay.

Her eyes narrow. Ariella knows I will let her go if she asks me to, yet she doesn't seem to try. The fire in me is getting out of control and the need for answers takes over. "What is going on, Ari? What aren't you telling me?"

My wife pulls away from my grip and walks around the garden, circling the house to the front where the drivers are. It's what she has been doing for months. Avoiding. Her dress sways as she hurries to leave me behind. My wife tells the valet to call for our car, all the while ignoring me following her close by.

Once inside the vehicle, she turns her body away from mine, staring at the street outside the windows. Shielding the eyes, I can always read. "I want the truth, Ariella. Something is wrong with you."

"Of course it is." I can almost hear her eyes roll.

Mon Dieu. This woman and her stubbornness. "I don't mean it like that and you know it. There is something wrong with us. I want to fix it."

"I have nothing with Louis," she breathes out, keeping her gaze on the darkness outside.

But it's too late. I already struggle with believing in what she has been telling me. I also struggle with the idea of the woman I love, the woman who shares a bed with me isn't the same one I got married to. She isn't the same person I fell in love with.

"How did it start?"

Ariella seems in full control of her patience, not even glancing my way. I know it's wrong. I know I should let it go and sign the papers. But a life without her… how am I supposed to survive it? How am I supposed to survive the loss of the only other person I love unconditionally when I already lost someone I would give my life to have back?

"Dorian, I don't want to have this conversation again."

Ariella stares at me as I slide on the black seat and place my hand on the car's window. My body leans towards her, and she gasps for the sudden action I haven't allowed myself to have for months.

For trapping her.

"But I do. And we are going to talk about it whether or not you want it."

7
Ariella

He stares at me, his eyes filled with emotions I cannot read. Dorian grips the door handle. The leather slides beneath his palm and I am forced to look at him, afraid of where this conversation can take us. I'm not ready to tell him the truth yet.

It's not like I made the right decisions, but I never wanted for things to be this way. To feel this way. Yet again, I haven't been able to talk to him for months. Scared to death, he pushes me away once more. It scares me more to be the focus of his pain than to be by myself. I can deal with being alone. Before Dorian, I had been by myself most of my life even when I had people around me. I was alone despite it all. But what I can't deal with is being the reason for his misery. I cannot deal with the way Dorian has been looking at me for over a year. A mix of fury and pity.

Irene doesn't look at me with pity like other people. The reason is she doesn't know most things about my personal life. But I will admit this neither to my husband nor Thea. I don't keep her around to satisfy my physical needs or because I want a fling. Sometimes I still dream about the first time she kissed me and how I threw up when I was alone. I have something to focus on. I search for my answers regarding the company she works at and distract her while doing so. It makes it easier to deal with the storm in my chest.

But with Dorian it never happens, because in his eyes, in my husband's most pleasant dreams, I was always perfect. Even when I got upset, he would take pride in it and dive into how I felt. He would praise me and cherish every part of my body while apologizing. He loved to tease me and get me riled up because of him. He loved me. The smile on his lips, the spark in his eyes, said as much.

Those memories haunt me in my dreams every night.

I glance at the closed partition to make sure the driver cannot see us. I am not scared of Dorian, but I am scared of the heartache I will feel once he signs those papers.

"Admit it," my husband mumbles a breath away from my lips. "Admit, you were with him back then."

"Dorian-" The eyes I love demand me to stare at him. The green gives way to brown streaks. My husband is so lost in his world that he doesn't see it. He doesn't want to see what's right in front of him.

"Admit you are having an affair, Ari, and I sign whatever you want tonight."

This is it. This sentence almost makes me choke on my breath as I don't dare to reply because I cannot explain it to him. I should. I need to know the truth and let Dorian go. But he still can make my heart beat in different ways. Fast, slow, whole, and broken.

Dorian still has power over me, my body, and my mind. He can still make me forget the outside world exists.

Dorian's eyes let go of the hold on mine. They trap me and travel to my lips, letting me breathe a sigh of relief as I am no longer held captive by his gaze. His tongue peeks out, grazing his bottom lip as sinful thoughts cross his mind.

He leans forward, his mouth hovers over mine as he speaks and it sends a shiver all across my body.

"You can't say it, because it doesn't feel the same," he states, his hand resting on my leg, teasing me and traveling under the fabric, touching the inner part of my thigh. "You are here with me now. Whatever he does with you, whatever casual sex you two have, you still sleep in our bed. You're still married to me, you're still-" he stops. His thumb grazes my underwear, and I am not strong enough to deny him or what he does to my body. "You are still wet when I touch you."

After a year, his lips take mine. In the beginning, it's soft, but as it deepens, as he puts his body weight on me and presses me against the leather seat those butterflies, I thought dead come back to life, and I remember the need whenever we kissed, whenever he would take care of me, whenever he made love to me.

His fingers sink against my flesh as the kiss gets out of control and our breathing fastens. It's as if we hadn't kissed for years, as if we forgot how the other tastes, how the other feels. As I lean against him, he opens his mouth on mine, breathing into my pleasure and the need crawling across my skin.

Dorian's thumb presses against me before his palm replaces it, stroking my core with slow, deliberate movements. It makes me remember how good he always makes me feel. How hypnotizing his peppermint scent is. His taste. His love.

He circles his finger, using the delicate underwear as friction and having me close to the edge in mere minutes. The truth is my soul, my heart, and all of me will never get enough of this. Of how he can break me and bring me to my knees, ready for him.

"Ari," he calls when needing air before dropping his mouth to suck on my collarbone, as he always loved to do.

Ari. Not Ariella. Dorian is the only one who ever called me by it and the nickname means more to me than I realize. I missed it.

His long finger finds its way, pulling my underwear to the side. He strokes my body, rocking me in a wave of pleasure bound to burst from the inside. My hands find their way to his hair, sliding between his dark strands and pulling him closer. I want to scream. I want to tell him how much I missed this. Missed him.

"Toi et moi," he mumbles, kissing my neck letting his lips then glide to my shoulder. "Always."

My phone slips from the end of my purse and lands on the floor and I don't care. Dorian kisses me and groans when I come into his fingers. His lips take mine with all the patience of the world. Then my husband opens his eyes to look at me and notices how flushed I've become.

"Ma belle," he says and my phone rings. He looks at it before I can and bites the inside of his cheek, pulling his hand away.

The absence of him around me makes me whimper, but then I look over and notice what made Dorian change his demeanor. Louis' name lights up my screen.

I am about to turn and tell Dorian it's not what he thinks when he speaks. "I bet whatever it is you two do, he does not make you feel like this."

I don't allow myself to sleep in the same space as Dorian. I'm terrified to break if I do. So I struggle to rest on the single bed, the one with the stuffed toys I never put away. The stars and planet stickers we placed on the ceiling still shine.

But my mind is struggling as I realize the room doesn't smell like Raphael anymore.

It's early in the morning. Shades of purple mix in the deep blue sky, welcoming the dawn as my eyes close. It takes forever to fall asleep, but here, in the tiny bed where I used to lie down with my little boy as he fell asleep, I have serenity.

Dorian's footsteps approach the door. He stands on the other side. A small thud, as if it's his hand or his head bumping against the wood. Dorian mumbles something under his breath. I don't know what happened back there.

We arrived home, and courage evaded me as I considered talking about what happened in the car. But when he came into our bedroom, I did not allow myself to do it. It didn't feel right to lie next to him after witnessing the way my husband struggles when he is with me. It's similar to the way I hurt as well.

I'm hurting about losing Raphael. Hurting for us drifting apart. Hurting for not having answers. Hurting about last night.

I know my husband hurts like I do. But Dorian isn't like me. He doesn't cling to the past. He wants to move on with his life and put the pain behind us, which seems to be the only thing I cannot do.

"Ari," Dorian murmurs.

The nickname he gave me on our first date, the

sweet tone he used to call me for breakfast whenever I slept over at his house. The one he said before kissing me so passionately, and letting me out of breath when I told him I was pregnant. It's always associated with happiness, yet it's the second time he mentions it with such despair it makes my heart break even further than I thought possible.

"Please come to bed," Dorian calls again, a little louder. "I don't like you staying alone in there."

Another thud. This time I am sure it's his head hitting the door. When Raphael disappeared from our lives, I would lock myself in here whenever Dorian got numb enough to barely notice I was around. I would stay in the dark, holding my antidepressants. For a long time, I considered taking them and ending everything.

I know he still thinks I shouldn't have taken our little boy from school earlier to go to the park. It was a day like so many others, and I watched Raphael laughing in the back seat. Because whenever our son smiled like he was doing in those last minutes, it reminded me of his father and how much love we had in our lives. But life changed and, in a moment, my heart burst with joy before they ripped it out of my chest.

I don't reply to my husband. I don't dare my voice to show my emotions as I speak to him. Let him think whatever he wants from me, it will be easier anyway. I'm too deep into this. Too deep into finding the truth. It's better for him if Dorian walks out of my life.

It's easier.

He finds the doorknob and I open my eyes into the emptiness of the bedroom, only to turn on the bed and breathe a sigh of relief when I remember I locked the door. My secret needs to be safe, and Dorian never comes here. It's too painful for him.

I have a damaged heart, and I can't bear to darken Dorian's even more. I won't allow him to whimper like a plant dying from missing the sun. He doesn't speak about it, he never does. Therefore, I took matters into my own hands.

Dorian tries again, and I look out the window by the bed. I can't help asking myself if I knew how the future would be, what would I do?

Would I still marry him? Would I still bring all this pain into our lives? I know the day we lost our son would be different. I would save him even if I had to die to do so.

Sometimes this is the one question I can ask myself over and over again. Why him and not me? It's the reason I cannot believe there is a God out there. God would never bring a child into this world only to take them from it.

"Why did you lock the door?"

Dorian's deep baritone travels, but I don't move from the bed. The answer is obvious, splattered on the wall above the dresser where my notebook rests. Pages scrambled with words, names, and the path I need to take. Newspaper articles about Red & Blue Associates and how the company almost crumbled fourteen months ago. How it all links to the day of Raphael's death.

It's the whole reason I started this, isn't it? Why I never went ahead with killing myself. To find the truth. If Dorian gets involved the plan won't work and I am so close. Almost finding the name I lack. Irene will soon give in. She knows. A month after my son's death, they fired her boss and Irene took the role of Vice President.

My husband curses before his footsteps fade into the hallway. Dorian slams the front door shut as he leaves the house for a few minutes, letting me pick up the pieces of my broken soul.

Hours after I slept, my naked feet step across the house as I prepare to leave as well. After what happened last night, I need to clear my head, to distract and numb my thoughts from the prison they've trapped me in. As I pass by one photo in the hallway, my eyes turn to notice Dorian smiling at the camera.

I wrap the dress around my waist before placing my earrings. Dana is at her office, and if I hurry, I can still catch her and apologize for last night. Dorian will be home soon and maybe when I am back home we can talk about what happened.

"You're going out?"

My husband's deep voice comes from behind me

as I finish placing the hoops on my ears, turning to pick my heels. "Yes."

"Are you meeting *him*?"

I catch the way the last word lingers. Jealousy hangs in the air and I almost tell him it is none of his business. Because once I woke up, the memory of us last night haunted me. The only time my husband touched me in over a year, he tainted it with jealousy.

"I'm meeting a friend."

Dorian stands at the door frame as I turn around, stopping me from walking out of the bedroom. His eyes travel across my body, something he hasn't done for a long time, staying on the low-cut cleavage, noticing the tattoo peeking from beneath my breasts.

His tongue grazes his bottom lip as I tilt my head to draw his attention. Which seems to work when he stares at me once more. I can't deny the tingle it sends across my body from knowing I am the reason for his attention.

"A friend? We still live together, Ariella."

"We haven't been together, Dorian. We are getting a divorce, you said so last night. Why does it bother you I am trying to be happy?" I don't know why I say it. I don't know what happiness feels like anymore.

"Happy?" He snorts and I almost wince at my choice of words. The vein on my husband's neck is visible now, and I suck in a breath, trying to keep my head in this conversation. Because a memory of him apologizing for something as stupid as leaving his towel on the floor while I was a sweaty mess beneath him comes back to taunt me. "Screwing him makes you happy?"

"Screwing him makes me feel pleasure. Fighting with you doesn't," I lie, losing my calm. There hasn't been, nor will ever be, anyone but him. After the way he acted in the car last night, I want to hurt him as much as his indifference has hurt me over the last months. By the guilt I carry every time he looks at me. At this moment, I don't care who it is. I want to break away from the scorching torment my mind trapped me in last night.

The space separating both of us vanishes when he takes the last step. Dorian's 6.2 frame makes me feel so small at 5.5. His green eyes darken. There is a small spark in them from the threat of how he isn't the best at something.

My husband will never touch me without my consent. He knows that if the word no leaves my mouth, I mean it. Yet, last night I had a weak moment. I gave in to a need caused by the emotions trapped inside of me, the ones I try to tame. And maybe because of it, something kindled in him as well.

His eyes light up, adorned by the threat in my voice, while I suppress the wail, wanting to crawl out of my throat. His gaze holds mine for a few seconds. "Then maybe I should remind you of what real pleasure feels like."

He slides his hand around my waist and presses me against the wall, and I place my hands on his chest. "You are still my wife, Ari," he says, letting his lips hover over mine. "You continue to sleep in *our* bed. You still wear the ring I gave you."

"Wearing a ring doesn't mean I still love you, Dorian," I lie. Again.

He grunts at my words. His touch, something I longed for, keeps me in a weird deadlock, as I can neither walk away nor stay still.

"If you don't want me, if you don't want this, then why are you still here with me and not him?"

It's a battle of stares as my husband parts his lips, waiting for me to speak, leaning forward and letting his breath tickle my sensitive skin. I fight the urge to claim his mouth, to get myself lost in the drug, the addiction of his kiss. As I did last night when he caught me off guard and I succumbed to a moment of pleasure.

When his hand slides from my hips to my inner thighs, parting my legs more so he can nuzzle himself between me, the heat on his body makes me forget about staying away from my husband.

"Do you want to leave?" He asks again to make sure he isn't pushing it too far. I bite my bottom lip at the way his fingertip glides on my leg, lifting my dress so he can touch me more. "Ari?"

"No."

The word escapes my mouth as my husband knocks all breath out of me when his lips touch mine. Taking away all my fears even if for a moment. His kiss, fiery yet demanding of my true nature, steady yet soft, forcing me to forget about the world outside.

Dorian deepens the kiss, his tongue sliding through my lips and playing with mine as I forget what was happening minutes ago. His long fingers slip up, finding the lace fabric of my underwear and gliding over me as I grind against his touch.

My husband turns us around, pulling the string of my dress loose and letting it fall on the floor. He then walks me back to our bed, where he lays me on my back as his eager mouth drops kisses on my neck. It's as if flames burst on my skin, spreading through it and heating my entire body.

"Ari," he whispers as his lips touch the top of my breasts.

My hands grasp the strings of his charcoal hair, pulling him where I need him to touch me. I want to say it. I want to let the words fall from my mouth and burst through my lungs. He lets his body hover over mine before his lean long fingers hook on my underwear, tugging the lace panties down.

He doesn't even dare to take my shoes, and I smile, knowing it's the one thing he enjoys the most. There were many times when I would surprise Dorian as he walked into the house, greeting my husband with nothing more than my heels.

I unzip his pants before my brain allows me to think what is about to happen. Because if I do, I will pull away from him. It's been too long. Dorian's thumb presses against my clit in a slow caress, before he dips one finger inside, grunting when he realizes how eager I am for him. He takes his finger out, sliding it into his mouth and tasting me.

The action makes me release a sound from the end of my throat, and my husband grins.

But we are both too eager for foreplay right now, too lost in the lust of our bodies, our breathing molding to each other. His pants slide down at last and the man I will love till the day I die eases himself inside of me.

"Dorian-"

He silences my moan with his mouth, kissing me as he gains a steady pace, a rhythm we both don't want to break. My hands fly around his back as I cling to him, circling his waist with my legs. I meet every thrust, every promise of his still-aching need for me.

He lets his hand slip on my arms, pulling my hands over my head and lacing our fingers together. My body becomes aware of the pulling sensation in my lower stomach.

Dorian has his eyes on me. The sweet way he gazes into my soul makes me swallow the words of affection, wanting to burst from the ends of my heart. But I can't put everything at risk, not when I am so close, so I bite down on my lip to stop them from escaping.

I love you.

The words don't slip from my mouth, but they tip me over the edge as my body shakes with the force of my orgasm. Like a wave hitting a lonely rock on the ocean shore, it hits me out of nowhere. I lift my back from the bed as Dorian kisses me with such passion I get out of breath. The blissful way he moans my name is what it takes for me to push away the hair from his eyes.

I want to watch him, to see him in the rawest way.

And I do. I watch every little detail of Dorian's face. The mole over his brow catches my attention every time I look at him. The scar on his cheek from when he was a teen and always makes me want to graze my fingertip on it as he sleeps. I stare at every tiny mark on him, everything only I can see up close. He rests his head against my neck in silence for a few seconds before lying by my side.

Dorian's fingertip brushes against my skin. Now, lying naked next to him, without being able to hide my emotions again, I become aware of everything. I thought I had it. I thought I was ready to let it all go. Not to think about him in this way.

I was wrong.

The love I have for him, though I push it down, is strong enough to survive the torture it has endured.

It's powerful enough to make me stop breathing as my eyelids close and I let the darkness sink in, remembering the last minutes we both lived.

How Dorian's kiss did things to my heart. How his green eyes made me want to crawl into his arms, let my head sink in the curve of his neck, and crumble. I never felt so exposed as I do now, and it's the second scariest thing that's ever happened to me. Because how do I move on from here? How do I keep whatever it is I am doing with Irene when I will only feel guilty about lying to my husband?

Should I speak? Should I say something? What if he regrets this, but for the opposite reasons? What if this was his way of saying goodbye?

As silence remains between us, my heart tears into pieces. I can't seem to think about anything else than why isn't Dorian talking? He is the chatty one. A word would be enough for me to at least have a glimpse of what he is thinking. But instead, Dorian stares at the ceiling while I allow myself to look in his direction.

I always loved looking at my husband when he wasn't paying attention. Seeing his true self when he wasn't overthinking how to act. Dorian's eyes glisten against the light, the world in his gaze as it always should be, with the emotions I once could decipher. My husband blinks, his eyes coming in my direction as I immediately shift my gaze away from him and try to make my breathing even.

Before we lost our son, Dorian would tell me every day he loved me. He would leave a small post-it inside my bag, for example, or send me the spiciest texts while at work. He didn't have to say it. I knew it. It was obvious in how he looked and touched me every chance he had. But all of those have stopped. First, I thought it was because he was mourning Raphael's death. But now I know we never recovered from it. Trying to cope with the pain, he tore his heart, and, as he dealt with it, as he became absorbed in the mindset he was in, he grew distant. He stopped loving. I do not criticize him for dealing with his grief in his own way. I have been doing the same.

Dorian sighs, the first sound he lets out in minutes. When he turns his head for some stupid reason and I have a feeling his eyes are on me, I grasp the sheet harder beneath my hand to cover my naked body.

I never stopped loving him, but I repressed my feelings in order to figure out the truth about that day. The blood covering my hands; the torment clouding my mind; the tears stopping me from looking at Raphael's angelic face.

My husband stands up from the bed, not giving me another glimpse of his beautiful face, and walks towards the bathroom. He leaves the door ajar, wanting to be alone. I stand and walk towards it, my hand hovering, ready to knock. Something in me says I should follow him and I could, but it will only make things harder if I do.

Dorian wants to be with his thoughts the same way I need to avoid mine.

I need to find somewhere where I don't have to face the ghosts of my past. I pick up the dress and underwear from the floor, get my hair under control, and cover Dorian's doing with his fingers.

The moon is high in the sky, lighting my path as I approach my car, who mirrors the stars above me as if they're in front of my eyes. The stars Raphael loved. The ones my son always wanted to stare at night. I glance at the tree by the end of the garden and almost tear up, remembering Dorian's plan to place a tree house there. He wanted to teach Raphael the constellations.

It never happened.

A gust of wind swirls around me, comforting me in my decision, and I step inside the car, driving back into the city.

Most of the time love is complicated. Dorian is and will always be the only man able to deal with me, the only person I want. I drive without paying attention to where I am going, maybe for half an hour before I stop. I don't want to be here. But she texted. She asked me to meet her tonight, and after Dorian's reaction, I think it's clear things are not returning to what they were. No matter how much I want it. Might as well keep my mind busy.

Irene is at home. She lets me in once I ring. I sigh,

thinking maybe I should go somewhere else. But the idea of facing Dorian tonight… I don't think I'm strong enough for that. I wish I was with him. I wish I was in his arms and not here. I walk through the double doors, making mental notes of the place. It's the first time I am meeting this woman in her house. And it's one time too many. But if I can do this tonight, then it's another chapter of my life I will leave behind.

Almost there.

"You're here," her melodic voice reaches my ears before Irene's lips silence my reply. I turn my face before she can kiss me.

She's eager, especially after I denied her again the other night. Irene's hands drift, ready to feel my skin, grasping my legs and lifting the skirt away from my ass as they roam, inquiring where to touch. She is more impatient than anyone else I have dealt with. Even what could be a caress is harsh. It's so different from the touch I had on my body moments ago when I let my husband take charge.

Dorian's touch still brings emotions from within me, but Irene doesn't. It never did.

I think sex with my husband broke me. When Dorian and I were intimate, he always made sure he would pleasure me first. He would be there for me the same as I was for him, and even tonight, even after fighting, he still did it.

Just like before.

But why did he leave? He had to be feeling some sort of regret… right?

"Irene," I warn her, not in the mood for her to dominate me. "No."

"I missed you," she says, not letting go of my body.

Her hands grip me tighter, a little stronger than what I usually enjoy, but Irene is not an ordinary woman. I push her away and sit on the sofa, watching her. Nausea curls in my stomach.

"You're too impatient today," I say, and she sighs, agreeing. "Long day at work?"

"Dealing with stupid lawyers again for the dull lawsuit."

So close. I can get the name if I distract her. Somehow, whenever this woman is focusing on herself, she doesn't notice the words slipping through her mouth. I pat the seat next to me. "How is the lawsuit going?"

Irene kneels in front of me instead. I don't want to do this, but she won't admit anything unless I do. I try touching her, but my stomach isn't having it. Irene is beautiful. Anyone else would want to have sex with her. I know the me from ten years ago would, but not anymore. I am broken. Dorian's doing. The fact she is involved with Red & Blue doesn't help either. It is the main reason I avoid the woman as much as I know I need her to win this case.

"Well," she replies as I let my fingers touch her

neck. “The lawyers think we can take Adriana down.”

I grip the fabric of my dress and she frowns. Irene has been meeting with these lawyers more and more each day, and now I am intrigued. “How?”

She cocks her brow at me. It's not normal to ask her this much, to ask these many questions in a row. If I'm not careful, she will grow aware of my purpose when we are together.

“They say there is no case, but it seems risky to remember what happened,” Irene shrugs. “Why are you so jumpy today? Did your lunatic husband make you upset?”

I shake away the thoughts of Dorian. His naked body on top of mine as his mouth took me back to the world we once were happy in. I shake off the heavy feeling that creeps over me as guilt threatens to take over and prevent me from accomplishing what I intended to do. At this moment, I'm not Ariella, nor Ari.

So, I look at Irene, wanting nothing more than to ignore how broken my soul is. I summon the will to touch her, but nothing. The only thing I can focus on is what she said.

“Don’t talk about my husband Irene. Never talk about my husband. It’s part of the deal.”

Irene bites down on her lip, her teeth marking the pink skin paler as I make myself comfortable against her sofa. “Are you letting me fuck you tonight?”

I roll my eyes at her blunt question and shake my head at the woman. "I'm too tired."

She leans in to brush her lips on mine, tempting me to succumb to her cravings and desire, which will never happen. It does not matter if it is a man or a woman. To me, this is business. I wish for answers I am sure Irene holds. I can't get intimate with anyone but my husband. I am not able to. After tonight, I know it will never change.

Irene licks her lips before pressing them against my skin. "Ari I-"

"Don't call me that. I already told you not to call me by a nickname. Those are for people in relationships, which is not our case."

Irene grunts, but the desire to please me is too strong, and so she leans forward. "Please have sex with me," she pleads, and I wonder how long I can keep denying her. But she doesn't get it. She never will.

My fingertip brushes her jaw as I stand to leave. "Not tonight Irene. Not tonight."

8
Dorian

The cold water runs through my soaked body as I fight the need to crawl back on the bed and draw Ariella closer to me. I think she needs time and space to process what happened. She didn't move. It was the first time we were in silence after sex. She was holding all the emotions in her eyes, not letting me see how she feels. Ari still loves me, and as I walk out of the shower, wrapping a towel around my waist, the thought keeps playing on my mind. If she loves me, then why is she doing this?

I step into the room and my heart drops into my stomach as I realize Ari left. The front door closes, but I am already running through the house trying to stop her. By the time I make it outside, the only thing I see are her taillights in the distance.

I go back inside and get dressed, texting Josh to meet me at the bar close to the office. I need to distract myself. To be with someone who doesn't ask me how my marriage is. Maybe watch the sports channel over food or something.

The night greets me as I speed my way out of the

house and drive into town, where my friend is waiting. By the time I arrive at the pub, Josh is hiding in a booth at the far end of the room. His presence could be unknown if it weren't for the women lining up and trying to figure out how to talk to him.

"Hey," Josh says loud enough. "Sweetie, what took you so long? I was getting worried."

"Sweetie?" I ask, raising a brow and taking off my jacket before throwing it on the seat next to mine.

"Go along with it. I am not in the mood to be persuaded for casual sex tonight," my friend answers me with a grin as I sit in front of him. "If I need to pretend to be gay, I will. Even if the one I am gay with is you."

"First, ouch. Second, I would rock your world. But what if I don't want to pretend I'm gay for you?"

"Too bad, that's what best friends are for," he dismisses it with a shrug. "Okay, I'm here. What's going on?"

The server arrives. Her eyes shift from Josh to me. The devil sitting across the table taps my hand to stop the persuasive way the girl asks for his name. Her eyes linger on our hands as I try not to laugh. On a normal day, my wedding ring is enough for them to walk away. But Josh doesn't have one, which makes it difficult for him.

"Ariella," I say when the girl walks to get drinks. "We- uh-, see we were fighting and-"

"You had sex. Don't look at me like that. I remember when we shared an apartment, how your fights always ended up. The walls at our old place were thin, you know?"

I blink at him. This bastard never spoke about it before. "Fine, yes. I was giving her space, but then she left. And I think she might have gone to meet Louis… or whoever it is she is seeing."

"And you know this how?" He asks, tilting his head as the server places our drinks on the table. "Did you somehow put another detective following your wife?"

The server gasps, giving me a dirty look before glancing at Josh and mumbling something along the line of, "all men are trash." With a chuckle, I turn my attention to the young man in front of me, sipping from his beer and pressing his lips together in approval after.

"I didn't. She told me she was going to meet him before- well, before anything happened."

"She said she was meeting Louis?"

A frown settles between my brows. "She said she was meeting a friend," I explain. "The thing is, the one friend she occasionally sees outside of work is him. So what do you want me to think?"

Josh stares at me for a couple of seconds. "I understand what you are saying, but Ariella is one of the smartest women I know. Don't you think if she were meeting this guy you say she's cheating on you with, she would somehow hide it from you? She doesn't tell you they're together. He also denied it.

What more do you need?"

"The photos Josh I-"

His hand raises, stopping me from speaking any further or disgracing his perfect image of my wife. Both my best friends love Ariella the same way a brother loves his sister. She was there for them during some of their most challenging times.

For Josh, Ariella was a shoulder to lean on. He never saw her as anything else. When she got pregnant, she chose him to be Raphael's godfather. Then Eli got upset, and that was the reason my son had two godfathers and no godmother.

"She is hugging him, Dorian, not screwing the guy. Ariella isn't cheating on you. If she is doing something shady, Louis has nothing to do with it."

I drink my beer and by the time Josh orders another one, I excuse myself to the bathroom. The bar is not the most ideal place to have this conversation, but Josh is not one of those friends who enjoy deep talk. No. Those conversations I always had with my wife. If I leave now, I can wait for her at home.

We should talk this over. Whatever it is going on with Ari… we should talk. I will even suggest for us to get back to therapy together again. But I am not sure what I will do with my life if she genuinely wants a divorce. The damn word is taunting me.

When I am cleaning my hands in the common space between the bathrooms, a voice stops me, and I freeze.

"Hi, Mr. Vaillant."

The hairs on the back of my neck stand up as I turn around. My secretary stands behind me in a short, tight dress. It leaves very little to my imagination. I remain unfazed and dry my hands. "Hi, Zoe. What are you doing here?"

As soon as her name leaves my lips, she beams at me. Zoe didn't get discouraged after what happened. In fact, letting her be around me the other night only enticed her more. After everything, I don't even look at or acknowledged her at the office. I avoided being alone with the girl again, so as not to reinforce her already out-of-place ideas.

"It's a good hangout spot," Zoe replies with a shrug of her shoulders.

I can't help but smile at her, and my mind gets bombarded by the night we had. The conversation and promise of all the sinful things bound to happen were enough to make me make me question my damaged marriage. What if Ari never wants to be with me again? What if tonight was her way of telling me it's over?

Zoe bites down on her lip as she stares into my eyes. Her hand brushes my leg while the girl leans forward, revealing the white cotton bra she wears.

I am weak enough to admit my gaze stayed on her breasts for more than a couple of seconds.

"I've been thinking about you all the time," she confesses in a whisper. "Especially at night, when I'm alone, in my bed. I've been dreaming about having those hands of yours on my body while I rub myself."

Zoe closes the space between us; with a glance over her shoulder, she checks to see if no one is staring at us before her hand is cupping my front, and I twitch under her touch.

A warning settles in my throat with the sudden move, and before I can stop her, Zoe speaks.

"Let's do it," she pleads sweetly. "You and me on that desk you always have so tidy."

"Zoe-"

The warning in my voice is no obvious threat, as even I don't believe in myself. But Ariella left. Whether or not to meet Louis, she still left. She wants a divorce. Why do I keep fighting for a marriage if she has already given up?

Right now, the girl with big eyes wanting nothing more than a good time is too tempting. The anger builds up again. She leans forward and when she does, I don't stop her. Zoe's hand grabs the knob of the bathroom door and both of us slip inside. Her lips are cold and taste like cherry, and I try not to think of who I am touching.

The cramped bathroom smell burns my nostrils. Holding my breath, my hands clasp on her thighs as Zoe yelps at the sudden touch. My lips part on her, breathing in her overpowering perfume, and the girl takes her shirt and bra off, hurrying to be naked in front of me. Zoe caresses her breast as I stare at her hands traveling down.

Her bottom lip becomes a hostage of her teeth while her fingertip makes its way between her legs. She lifts her skirt enough for me to see her white underwear.

"Do you like this?" she asks. "Watching me and not touching?"

I can't say I don't. Ari would do it so many times, staying in front of me as I watched her reach her orgasm, closing her eyes, parting her mouth, and moaning my name out loud, gasping for air before I took the place of her hand to feel her.

She left the house. I thought she wanted to be by herself for a while and I gave her privacy. But then she left the house. She left me. So what if I indulge tonight? What if I let it happen even if I don't have any intentions of taking this further with Zoe? She is a beautiful girl. She is attractive, and she wants to be with me.

"Yes," I breathe out before Zoe's lips touch mine.

She kisses me, hurried and demanding more while her hands unbutton my pants. It's rushed, it's messy, greedy, as hunger seems to take over the half-naked girl. She tastes like bad decisions and my stomach churns as I realize it's not her lips I crave. It's not her touch I want on my body.

It's when Zoe's hand grazes my crotch that she notices what's happening to my body. Or *not* happening.

"Mr. Vaillant," she mumbles, letting go of my lips. She slides her hands over the fabric of my boxers, and finds the lack of collaboration from my lower half. "Do you need help?"

My eyes stay on Zoe's questioning ones as I can't get rid of the vision of my wife crying out my name as I made love to her. She doesn't want me, but if it's the case, then why was she staring at me like before? Why was she avoiding speaking, and her eyes were shining like stars? If she doesn't love me, then why can't she say it?

Yet, as Zoe keeps touching me, her hand sliding up and down, trying to make something out of the situation, nothing seems to happen.

"I-"

Words get stuck in my throat as I take a step back. My body and my brain seem to punish me in different ways, as I can't understand what's going on or decide what to do.

"Mr. Vaillant, this happens. It's normal. You have been stressed-"

"I can't do this, Zoe," I say and decide those words are not direct enough. "I don't want to do this."

She frowns as I blurt out the words and tries to peer into my eyes. This has never happened, ever. I am always ready or was. Even with Ariella mere hours ago, I was ready for her again as soon as we were done.

"What do you mean?" She asks with a smile that does not reach her eyes.

"It's not happening."

"We can-"

"It's not going to happen Ms. Young."

Zoe seems confused, but when my words sink in, she glides her tongue against her teeth and picks up her clothes. She still glances at me now and then. I open the bathroom door for her and she is about to speak when I shut it in her face. Turning, I lean my forehead against the tiled bathroom wall and all I can do is ask myself what the fuck is happening?

"Adriana?" I ask her, amused, and she laughs at my tone.

"Yes," Ari says as I place a plate of food in front of her while she glances at it, fascinated. "It's what my parents called me when I was born."

"No wonder you changed your name."

"Are you mocking me, Vaillant?"

"Maybe," I confess, sitting in front of her. "What are you going to do, Adriana*?"*

The aroma of the noodles is tempting. Even Ariella glances at the food while speaking to me. She had a long day, her internship will soon be done, and this girl is about to get into the world where sharks swim. They aren't ready for her. Watch some middle-aged man think he can intimidate her and get a sassy reply while she wears the most beautiful smile on her face. She may be shy, but if someone pushes the wrong buttons, she will stand her ground.

"Nothing if you keep calling me that," Ari replies,

swirling the food with a fork, and I snort. "What?"

"You're eating wrong," I explain, walking around the table and picking up the silverware from her hands.

"Wrong?"

"Yes."

She frowns while staring at my hands. "I never ate with chopsticks before."

"Your parents didn't teach you?"

"Takeout was not a thing at my place," she rolls her eyes. "Father made sure every meal we ate was home cooked. By a woman, of course."

Jackass. I know little about her family, but I know if I ever meet them, I will give them a piece of my mind. She is private about her past, but every time she reveals another piece of it, I have this urge to protect her. How could her own family treat her the way they did?

"Well, if you are planning to date me, you need to eat with chopsticks. We don't eat Chinese food with forks at my house."

My hands lift hers as I help Ari, but she isn't staring at my fingers. Instead, her eyes burn a hole in my skin as I dare myself to meet her questioning gaze.

"So, we're dating?"

I don't ignore the glint in her eyes or the proud grin on her lips. The ones I long for every time she is around me. Even right after kissing her.

"Yes. I mean, I invited you to my house tonight and kicked both my roommates out so we could have some privacy-"

Ari silences me with a kiss. I can feel her smiling the

entire time before leaning away and scrunching her nose at me.

"You're cute when you get flustered."

"Get up," he says, shutting the door with enough force for me to wake up.

"Go away, Josh."

"Dorian," he lets out in a breath, not caring about my request. "It's close to 10 a.m. and we are at the office."

My eyes fly open. I walked here after leaving the bar, and instead of dozing off… oh shit. The sun shines in the sky, gracing the fields outside where horses run wild as clouds haze the blue canvas.

Merde.

"What the hell. I thought you left for home," Josh states, still staring at me with a judgmental gaze. "Did Ariella kick you out?" His eyes widen at the thought, and he clicks his tongue, crossing his arms over his chest. "What did you do?"

I sit on the couch, my back hurting from sleeping on it. "She didn't kick me out."

Josh sighs, picking up the chair in front of my desk and turning it to face me. He will judge me if I admit the truth. I fear the way he will look at me as if I killed something in our friendship. Which I may have contemplated. I almost had sex with someone else.

"Ok, let's go through this. Start from the very

beginning, the entire night," Josh says as if we have all the time in the world. "Zoe can delay your appointments."

He doesn't like my secretary. I don't get why, but Josh doesn't enjoy the way she walks around the office. The way she speaks to us. The way she pretends to be something more than she is. I never understood what his problem was with her. Every time I ask, he avoids answering.

"What happened?"

His eyes let go of the hold on mine and travel down my body. He notices how the clothes I wear are all wrinkled and how my gaze doesn't meet his.

Josh narrows his eyes. "What are you hiding? Did you see or talk to Ariella?"

My breathing gets stuck in my throat as the words all crumble before I gather the courage to speak. "No. I bumped into Zoe at the bar and one thing led to another-"

"You had sex with Zoe?" He almost yells, and I shake my head.

The words that left him are only a mirror of the guilt piled on me. Guilt and shame as the events from last night still haunt my mind.

"No Josh," I reply, my emotions clinging to my skin. "The night I hung out with you and Eli, I thought about it. It's wrong, but I did. Then yesterday we kissed, but it didn't progress beyond that."

Josh scoffs, stopping me from rambling on as he stares out the window and not at me. The youngest closes his hands into fists, swallowing his anger before speaking. "Do you love Ariella?"

The question throws me off as I frown in an attempt to reply.

"I do."

"Then act like it, both of you," it's all he says before standing up and heading towards the door. "I swear you two are the most stubborn people I have ever met. And don't worry, I told your wife as much when I talked to her the other day," Josh stops, the muscles on his back tensing as he grasps the door handle. "I'll let you know when Eli arrives for lunch, but maybe you should keep your activities with your secretary between us."

A crease appears between my eyebrows. The three of us don't have secrets. For Josh to ask me this, something else is happening. Josh leaves and Zoe knocks on the door. The sight of her makes me nauseated. From the kissing to what it was leading to... I barely look at Zoe, but it's clear as day that she has something on her mind.

"Mr. Vaillant, your therapist is here."

Thea walks in, not waiting for me to reply to Zoe. She carries a playful smile on her lips, but watches my secretary. I hold back a chuckle, noticing how she lets her gaze linger on the girl's figure as she walks out of the room.

"Something on your mind?" I ask Thea as she walks towards me, putting one arm around my back for a hug. When the sun shines on her hair, it looks almost white.

"The girl has an interesting choice of clothes," Thea replies, her blue eyes shining. "Not that I'm complaining."

My therapist takes a step back, walking towards my chair and pulling it towards the window. "So," she takes her notebook out of her purse. I dread that thing. "Do you want to try to talk about a happy memory?" I shake my head but can see the disappointment in Thea's eyes. "Then tell me what's new."

It has been Thea's idea to visit us at our workplace for these sessions. The pay is higher and I think it has something to do with us being in a familiar environment. It is not helping my case right now. Memories of last night with Zoe undressing, and me falling short of action rush towards my mind. I can't speak about that. There are so many reasons, one of them being shame.

Instead, I take a deep breath, looking at the horses outside and watch as Josh walks towards them. A frown on his face, his lips pursed into a line, and I can almost hear the words he mumbles while stomping in front of the animals. I am pretty sure I saw him mouthing the words "stubborn dickhead."

"Ari and I had a fight," I say, not meeting Thea's

gaze. "A big fight."

"About Raphael?"

My head shakes in a no as the name pierces through my heart. A memory invades me, of my little kid running through the meadow in the back of our house, running from Ari and into my arms. It's one of the happiest memories I have. We were happy. So fucking happy. Until we weren't.

"No. We fought about Louis. Or whoever it is, Ariella is seeing."

Thea takes a deep breath. Whatever it is she is thinking is going to wait till the end of the appointment. This is the best part of her and why we stick with her despite our lives being chaotic. She knows what we need to hear. Our therapist is blunt, and straight to the point. She will force us to get out of our comfort zone. She doesn't give her opinion, despite us knowing she wants to, but she calls things as they are.

"You know this how?" She asks, scribbling on the pages.

Thea grimaces when I don't reply right away, and her curious stare falls on mine. She places the notebook on her lap, leaning forward as if compelling me to speak the truth. Better say it, admit my actions to the one person who can help me let go of all the madness I've been creating.

"I had my wife followed."

Thea nods along as I speak and lets out a long

sigh. I open one eye to catch her writing more on that damn book of hers.

"Why?"

My therapist is trying to force me to understand the reasons behind my actions. Josh's reaction will be a walk in the park compared to the woman in front of me. There is nothing as frightening in therapy as realizing all the wrongs I did.

"Because I needed to be sure," I mumble.

"And are you sure now?"

I nibble my bottom lip, making it hostage to the reply I carry in my heart because the truth is, I am not. Not yet. Not after everything, Josh said. A hug can mean so many things and so little at the same time.

"No."

"Okay, Dorian, what's wrong?" Thea asks, discarding her notes and placing them on top of my desk. "I can see you are struggling to speak, and you have a guilty puppy look all over. This will be easier if you rip the band-aid and tell me."

I glance in her direction and realize she is waiting. Which is great. It means Thea does not know what I did. I let my hands travel up and down my legs with deep breaths, knowing Thea has her gaze set on me. "Dorian?" She asks again, and I catch the warning in her tone. "We can sit here without you telling me what is eating you up. But I guarantee you things will move faster if you talk to me."

"I crossed a line with my secretary," I blurt out.

Thea blinks, leaning back against the chair. She slips a hand through her hair and takes her framed glasses off. Licking her lips to gain time, she places them on the table before resting her elbows on her legs and placing her hands together as if attempting to pray while closing her eyes.

"Let me get this straight. You were worried Ariella was cheating on you, and so you cheated on her?"

"I-"

The words dread to slip from my lips as I recall both nights I saw Zoe. The one where I pushed her away and the other when I caved in. I still don't know if it would happen. Even if I stood to the task, I don't know how it would go. But I kissed Zoe, and worse, I kept her around despite knowing it was wrong.

Call it an ego booster. It's still wrong.

"When did this happen?"

"Well, we were together last night," I try, but Thea's expression gives in to her thoughts before she wipes them away.

"Only last night?"

"No. I mean yes. Well, it's complicated." I lift my hands, attempting to plead for mercy. When my therapist gives no signs of judgment, I continue. "A few days ago, Zoe and I were here, and I was a bit more than tipsy. Nothing happened, she tried… I thought about it, but then didn't do it."

I speak in a hurry, trying to let the sorrow wash away from my body. I don't want to talk about this, but Thea is the one person who won't condemn my behavior. She may explain and say things I do not want to hear, like my wife and I need to communicate, but she won't judge me and turn her back. She won't say I'm an awful person, which is how I feel. She is here to help, and it will only happen if I talk.

The actions from the night before haunt me as I remember how I couldn't stand up for a beautiful half-naked woman in front of me. I have never experienced this problem, so I worry whether it is a physical or mental condition. Because what if God is punishing me for doing something I shouldn't? It's when Thea stares at me and raises a brow that I throw caution to the wind and say it.

"But then yesterday she was undressing in front of me, and I couldn't be ready for her."

"Ready as in?"

My hand gesture to my middle area while I try not to say the words that make me ashamed.

"You couldn't get it up?" She asks and I nod. "Why do you think that happened?"

I shrug. "I don't know. Ari and I had a moment at home but then we stayed silent-"

"A moment?"

I can feel a sigh settling in my throat. "Sex. We

had sex."

"Okay," Thea says and begins writing on her notepad once more. "How did you feel after?"

I recall the way I wanted to hug Ari but feared her turning away from me. It's obvious she still has feelings, but something isn't right. "I felt good. Great even. Complete again. But then… I don't know. It seemed something was off. It was awkward between us. Like she was holding something back."

Thea nods. "You think Ariella has a secret?"

"Yes."

"Have you tried asking her?"

"It's not that simple."

Her watch makes a sound, and she glances at it. "You're a good man Dorian. You did something you consider morally wrong and you are trying to make amends about it," she states. Her eyes soften as we approach a sensitive topic. "You and I know Ariella closed herself on something. I don't know what, and I can't tell you what I think about it either. But I can tell you this much; everything has a solution."

"And not being able to-"

"Why do you think that is?"

I scratch my brow. "I- well, she isn't my wife. I kept thinking about Ari…" I stand again and, without thinking, trap one of my fingernails between my teeth. Words spark in my mind and the memory of the woman I love fighting back her tears comes back to haunt me. "She says I think the accident was her fault."

"Do you?"

"I don't. I never said anything like that either."

Thea takes a sip from her water. Her eyes study me as she thinks about how to voice her concerns. My stomach twists and bends at the whim of my anxiety I know Thea won't break doctor-patient privilege, but I wish she would help me decide on a route to walk on. Something that would help me decide my next move.

"Sometimes Dorian, we don't need to say things for others to catch on to our feelings. You may not think she is guilty, but you should consider that your wife has been hurting for a while. She may see and interpret your actions in a way you don't want her to.

I give her a nod and consider this. The night at the hospital was the worst night of my life. I had lost my son and my wife was fighting for her life. Ari almost died, and yet when she woke up, I had a hard time looking at her. All I could see was the pain and fear on her face. All I could think about was how I failed them both. How I was safe while the two of them were fighting for their lives.

"You need to think this through," Thea says, and I blink my eyes in reply. My therapist stands. "Actions have consequences and you can hurt yourself and Ariella because you can't see what's in front of you."

"And what is that?" I ask, raising a brow.

"That it's easier for you to dwell in pain and grief than accept you hurt your wife."

"Thea-"

"Talk me through it," she continues. "Imagine something broke between you two. Why would she say it? What happened after the accident?"

I look away from her as the shame and guilt creep over me. The overwhelming emotions from the news I had received and not being able to cope with them. I never got instructions on how to react to such things. How is someone supposed to take the worst news of their life?

"I watched her coming back to her senses, and I was relieved, but I didn't know what to do or say to her. She tried to explain the accident to me, but I didn't want her to relive it. Over the next couple of days, it was hard to even say something at all. It's like I was on autopilot. Nothing got to me because I was not there. I knew what had to be done, and I did it. I drove with my parents to the funeral home once to give them instructions, then my mom took it upon herself to organize things.

"Ari went home the day before the service. She was still on bed rest and-" I inhale. "And then we had the funeral. I didn't want her there. I didn't want her to see my pain and anger. I wasn't angry at *her*," I explain and glance at Thea. "I was just angry. At everything. At God. At life. At me. I couldn't speak and I couldn't process anything because all I had was rage inside of me. I felt hopeless. I felt as if I was nothing."

"Then maybe you should tell her that."

Her voice sends a jolt of pain through me as I let the truth sink in. Thea wouldn't call for my attention if she didn't know some certainty about my marriage. This isn't something Ari told her, either. This is what she gets from our relationship. This is what my wife doesn't want to discuss, and Thea tries to force her into it at every appointment. This is what Ariella meant the other night when I got a glimpse into her damaged soul.

Do I blame her?

There's no way I've said it. I can acknowledge I am not perfect. But I never told her I blame her.

"Pain is a complicated thing, Dorian," Thea says. "Some people need help to deal with it. Others close themselves off. The pain you both felt drifted you apart."

"You think she's still hurting?"

"You tell me," Thea tilts her head. "You spend more time with her than I do."

"She wants a divorce Thea," I reason with her and Thea looks away.

"She could have filled in the papers already, yet she didn't."

I blink at Thea for a few seconds, wrapping my mind around this. "What?"

"She doesn't need you to amicably sign the papers as she is trying to do, Dorian. By what you describe, and this is just speculation, maybe she thinks it's easier. She thinks that's the way she won't feel the burden of her pain. Sort of a last act before giving up for good."

Thea heads to the door, leaving me to think. "You sound like my best friend," I snort, turning to face the woman again. Her words, so similar to Josh's, touch something in me.

"Then I guess you have a great friend to talk to," Thea laughs. He is a loyal friend. He is also a pain in my ass on numerous occasions. "You think she is hiding something, and even if she is, you are the one who has to live with your actions. I think you would benefit from coming to appointments together again so we can work on communication."

Thea gathers her things. I need to apologize to Josh, and am about to do it, walking out of the office with Thea. However, I notice him in the far distance by the stables talking to Eli.

Eli smiles as we approach; he narrows his eyes at my accompaniment and hits Josh in his arm. The younger one turns. He eyes me still holding the anger from moments ago. However, when his gaze lands on Thea, his eyes widen.

The girl at my side doesn't make a sound when she notices the man gazing back at her.

"Eli, you're already here," I mumble, stating the

obvious and noticing how Josh glances at the woman near me. "This is Thea."

Josh looks at Thea up and down and takes a long time to snap out of it. Only when I clear my throat does he extend his hand. For the first time since I have known her, Thea doesn't have words to say. I nod at Eli frowning while Thea seems to come back to life. Like a computer malfunctioning.

"I'll see you again this week?" She asks, turning to me. "I can come by tomorrow again. If it's easier for you, I mean."

Thea stumbles on her words and I can't help but smile as Josh awaits my answer as well. With a nod, Thea grins at me before smiling at both men and excuses herself while walking towards her car. Josh still doesn't tear his gaze away from her figure.

"So," I start, but he doesn't even blink. "I'm guessing you are ready to date again?"

Josh shakes his head in reply while we walk toward the parking lot. He grins as if the idea is alluring enough. "No. But she is cute though. I'll admit that."

"Eli, where are you going?" I ask the oldest, who turns towards the building. "I don't need to go back inside."

My friend pouts, glancing over his shoulder at the structure and letting go of a sigh, and I grimace. Josh takes a deep breath, and his words from earlier float across my mind.

Don't tell Eli.

I discarded it, thinking it was because he would get upset if I was hurting my wife. He would react softer than Josh. But maybe, just maybe, there is another reason.

"Eli?" I call him again, and he reluctantly breaks away his focus from my office's front door. The idea seems absurd, but I need to ask. "Do you like Zoe?"

Eli smiles, laughing at the idea, and I know the answer to my question.

9
Dorian

"You knew this?" I whisper to Josh, standing behind Eli as he places his card on the ATM. Josh, however, raises a brow at me, not understanding the question. "About Eli and Zoe."

"Yeah, I figured it out when he started coming by every other day. It's like a 30-minute drive from his office without traffic. How didn't *you* suspect it?"

Eli has surprised us many times over the last few weeks. I never saw this with second intentions.

"I thought he wanted to hang out."

Josh rolls his eyes. "He likes us, but I don't think we are that dependent on each other."

As fascinating as it is, the fact that it's for a girl, especially the one working for me, is also a little hurtful. He could have said something. The problem is, how didn't I notice this?

"Most of the time, he flirts with her while you're inside your office," Josh replies to the question I haven't asked.

"You think it's serious?"

Josh shrugs. "He doesn't talk about it. I tried

asking if something had happened between them, but he deflected the question every time."

Great. Now, not only am I hurting my wife, but I am also harming one of my best friends. I fight the urge to facepalm myself in the middle of the street and let a sigh escape me instead. Eli turns around, staring at us, and places the money in his wallet as we continue to walk down the path, deciding on a place to eat.

He has no clue. I could tell him I kissed Zoe, explain Ari and I have been through a rough patch… or I could take the easy way out. The coward's way is to pretend it never happened.

"How long can you be away from the office?" Eli asks, glancing at us.

"The boss is out," Josh shrugs as if I'm not right next to him. "He won't mind."

A chuckle falls from my lips as I attempt to grasp the shame that has swept over me. The smile on my friend's face only makes it more difficult for me to stare at him, knowing if the truth comes out, it will disappoint and anger him.

There will probably be a few punches in the air, not in my direction anyway. I only saw Eli behaving unusually and getting involved in a fight at a bar when someone insulted the girlfriend he had. There was also one time when we all still lived together when Josh took things too far as they were playing Call of Duty, but they didn't get physical.

"Oh," Eli exclaims, stopping in the middle of the sidewalk, and Josh and I turn to him. "This one seems nice."

This place. I have been to this restaurant before, but not with a friend. This is one of Ari's favorite places to eat during the week. This was where we would meet whenever we wanted to have lunch dates, whenever waiting till the end of the day was too much to see her.

"I-"

The words get stuck in my throat while I fight for an excuse. But nothing comes, not one word leaves my mouth, and instead, Eli strolls inside with Josh following him. It would be easy to blur out the truth, but I prefer to die than to have the two of them staring at me with pity in their eyes.

Slow jazz music travels to the front door as the restaurant's sound comes to life in front of us. I am swallowed by the emotions dancing inside of me while trying not to focus on the familiar smell of some of my favorite dishes.

"Hi," a girl chirps. One of the young servers, her dark hair swaying as she carries a smile. "Table for three?"

"Yes," Eli replies, already following her.

Maybe I can hook him up with someone? The idea is enticing, and I would do it right away. I would set a blind date between him and Thea, if I hadn't noticed how she was drooling all over Josh.

I wonder how unprofessional it would be. I'm sure the answer is very much so.

"Mr. Vaillant," a familiar face walks around the corner. His lips lift into a grin as he walks in our direction. "I haven't seen you in a while. I'm delighted you are here."

"Good to see you too, Paul," I reply right away, not without having a glimpse of Josh and Eli eyeing me.

"Will you be joining Mrs. Vaillant and her colleague?"

Everything in my body turns cold while Paul's words hit me like an iceberg coming out of the blue. Ari is here.

"Yes," Josh replies before I can.

I am going to kill him.

Paul nods, turning around and leading the way instead of the petite girl. As soon as we walk around the corner, my eyes are on one person. Ari sits at a table, her legs crossed as she sips from a glass of orange juice. Her beautiful skin shines in the places the sun kisses it, and when she tilts her head to the side, sliding her long fingers through her golden strings. A group of dormant butterflies caresses my stomach.

I still love her. Although I am hurt at how things are, even angry, my heart still aches for her. My soul still longs for her words, for her smile, for her love. Every cell in my body draws me to her, to be with her.

"Hi," Josh almost yells at Ariella.

Her lips curve into a beautiful smile, one I haven't seen for months, and my wife places the glass on the table again before standing up. She throws her arms around the youngest. Then she notices Eli and lets go of Josh, who pouts at the act but smiles when understanding her excitement. Eli, however, takes a step closer, and his broad back cuts my vision of her.

"What are you guys doing here?" She asks, and I can't help but grin at the joy in her tone.

"Eli is paying for lunch. Dorian suggested something around here," Josh replies.

At the mention of my name, my oldest friend steps aside, and my wife's brown eyes fall on mine. Locking and speaking apologetic words, I want to yell at the skies. However, she discards them, breaking her gaze from me and tightening her lips into a smile.

No happiness, but a pool of emotions I want to drown myself in if it means I understand her. Her lips part, and Ari tries to come up with a word but fails at it, motioning for the others to take a seat, and they do.

"Louis," she calls the man sitting across the table. "These are some of my closest friends, Josh and Eli."

They introduce themselves. Eli takes the seat next to Louis as Josh sits at the head of the table. Ari doesn't even blink, letting them share the table with her, and I snicker at myself, knowing my friends left the spot next to Ari for me.

Like they always did.

I breathe in deeply as I settle on the chair by her side, the aroma of a field of orchids fills my lungs.

Louis stares at me, still upset about what happened, and I can't blame him.

Josh speaks first. "What have you been up to?"

"Working," she shrugs. "New York's fashion week is coming. You should get your invitation soon. You too Eli."

Josh groans and I smile. He doesn't like the fancy nights, as he calls them, but attends because it's important to Ariella. My wife pulls back her chair, her hand brushing mine as she does.

"I have to go to the bathroom," she mumbles under her breath, letting only me know.

I dip my chin and Josh leans forward. A smirk on his face as Eli talks about the races he hopes to attend. It appears Louis is interested in my friend's explanation of cars and the classic he intends to buy. Meanwhile, the younger one appears to want my attention, glancing at the other two men, and when he sees they are not listening, he speaks.

"You have to stop being stubborn," Josh whispers in my ear. "Your wife may have a secret. I am not saying she isn't doing something behind your back. But she isn't cheating on you with Louis."

I raise a brow at the same time Josh leans back in

his chair. Eli talks to Louis. I study my wife's colleague and Josh's words sink in. It doesn't add up, but something is still wrong with my wife and me.

Ari comes back after a few minutes and I realize this is not as bad as I thought it could be. The tension between us is something we can work out. Louis stares at me as if he wants to stick the fork in his hand right in the middle of my forehead. His eyes narrow every time our gazes meet, and somehow after fifteen times of this, it gets a bit unsettling. I am not intimidated, but I don't enjoy having people look at me the way he does.

But sitting next to Ari gives me the opportunity to understand how my wife and her colleague are when together. With Thea's and Josh's words trapped in my mind, I am drawn to the idea I have been debating.

A secret. Ari is holding on to something, but she and Louis are not involved. Maybe he knows who is the one my wife spends her nights with, but he isn't the one bedding her.

The issue at hand now is not even who Ari is cheating on, but if I can live with it? We both did so many wrongs…

"Have you two worked together for a long time?" Josh asks, and I fight back the urge to kick him under the table.

"I'm not sure. How long?" Ari tries to make sense

of time. "Three years, maybe?"

Three years.

I didn't realize it was that long. When Ari got pregnant, Louis was the one joining the company to fill in for her. Still, he was great. When Ari came back after her maternity leave, she was so impressed by how well he did, and how her work seemed to be easier with him around, she asked the company to let him stay on her team. When Ari talked more about him, jealousy spread over me instead of admiration.

Then, after the accident, my jealousy got the best of me.

"Yeah," Louis replies, staring at her. "That's how long I have been saving your reputation. I deserve a raise."

It's easy, almost simple, to notice she is having a battle in her head, but unlike before, I can't figure out what my wife is thinking. Last year it was clear, I could read Ariella like an open book. But not anymore.

We have changed; we were distant for so long, adamant, trying to prove we were right in our pain and being wrong at the same time.

Everyone stands from their seats, the awkwardness settling in, as I have no clue how to act with Ari. Do I hug her? Kiss her?

The tension between us seems to have settled down. Even so, my heart aches for the way I have been acting. Yesterday I did many wrongs; one of them was turning my back on my wife after sex. I walk ahead of them and, despite Eli's complaints, pay for the lunch bill for all five of us. All the while listening to their conversations behind me.

"We should do this again," Ari says, hugging both of our friends. "I miss you guys."

"Yes, we have to. Plus, it's a good excuse to force your husband out of the office," Josh agrees.

Ari's gaze softens, glancing at me behind the youngest and thinking my eyes are not on her. Not directly anyway, but the reflection on the window allows me to see her. How the curve on her back looks in the outfit she chose for today. Her hair falls against her skin as she glances at me, and for a split second, I consider taking her hand.

"How bad is it?" she asks Josh.

"Bad," Josh replies, turning his back as they walk out of the restaurant. "He has been killing himself with work."

My wife peeks in my direction, grabbing her coat from the girl by the front door. For a second, I could swear I saw the same worried expression she always had before. The one she would throw at me if I came home later than usual, or if I missed family time by taking a call.

"I'll call you to make plans for next week," Eli tells her, leaning forward and kissing my wife's cheek before Josh hugs her.

Ari nods, stepping aside and stopping in front of me. All three men seem to be busy on their phones and give my wife and I some sort of privacy in the crowded street. Louis drifts away, taking a call. I know no one is calling since his phone rings with an incoming call.

"I had a good time Ari," I whisper so only she can hear, and the hurt expression on her face doesn't go unnoticed. "Maybe we can do this again? Tomorrow?"

"Tomorrow," my wife frowns, checking her phone. I can see she has a Mrs. Garcia scheduled. "I have a meeting tomorrow at lunch. You know how it gets the week before NYFW."

Hope fades away as her words cut through me. I remember all the years before when she would work for hours at night. Before Raphael was born, I would fall asleep in her office waiting for her to be done with work.

Tomorrow is also the 17th, but we don't talk about it.

"You're right. It's been a big week. So maybe I can drop by someday and eat with you at the office. I'm sure you will be too busy to eat at the restaurant."

Ari's mouth parts and I fight the urge to lean forward and kiss her lips. I fight with every cell in my body that tells me she still wants me.

"That would be nice," she lets out, and I almost jump out of happiness.

But because I'm weak for this woman, I let my lips touch her cheek, inhaling her scent before pulling away. It will be enough for now. "I'll see you at home."

Ari's eyes sparkle. "I'll see you at home." She leaves, walking with Louis towards her car as my friends join me to go back to the office.

Josh chirps next to me. "What did you tell her?"

"Nothing. But you're right, Josh. I need to act right. I need to show her I still love her."

"You're going to try again?" Eli asks.

"I am."

10
Ariella

"We have to go," Louis whines for the third time as I place my pen and notebook down on my desk.

I am taking my time on purpose.

The day has been long. Dresses required adjustments. Most pants needed fitting and to be trimmed. The models were not the ones I asked for. I need variety, diversity, and shapes. I want every woman who will see my clothes walking down the runway to identify with at least one model. If it was up to me, we would have Jonathan Van Ness closing the show in a wedding gown. However, my bosses think that is taking it a step too far. They already struggle with my choices in the models for the show. Somehow diversity is offensive. I think it's most offensive if we are not inclusive and stick to the same thing over and over again.

Then there was Olivia, a friend from college who called to let me know she was pregnant. It scared her to give me the news. Not knowing how to tell me about her pregnancy because I lost Raphael. I called her an idiot and then purchased a gift for her baby.

As we prepare for the last meeting of the day, the

sun setting outside and flickering against the white furniture and glass around me. I survey a little more of the sketches displayed. I switch back into work-mode trying to figure out what will please this new partnership.

"If we leave late, I will starve," Louis almost shouts from the other side of the room.

"If we leave late, I'll buy dinner," I snort. "You can invite your wife to join."

"You can call your husband and do the same," he talks back, and I stop.

My foot touches the wooden floor of my office as I stare at my friend, trying to comprehend his sentence. Or trying to tell myself he isn't saying what I think he is.

The men in my life are stubborn as hell.

"Louis -"

"Don't even try Ariella," he interrupts, placing one hand in front of my eyes, motioning me to stop. I walk around the desk, gathering everything. "You were so obvious about it yesterday at lunch, sitting next to him. I saw how you glanced at him whenever you thought he wasn't paying attention. I noticed how you had your hand right by his so he would touch you whenever he moved."

My breathing becomes irregular, as my emotions rise to the surface of my chest. I try to come up with something to ease the pain and worry of judgement Louis may have about my husband and my marriage. He knows about Irene. He knows what I am doing and why I have to do it. How this was the only way after months of trying. I didn't tell him Louis figured out the only time we bumped into Irene at an event. He called her behavior with me odd since she was so polite.

This is the only way I can find out what happened after the accident.

My friend knows all of this, and he has made it clear he doesn't agree. He doesn't believe I can follow through with something as cold as getting involved with Irene and then discarding the woman.

"I can't involve him."

"You can. You can give up on this idea of a vendetta you have and have a happy life with your husband."

"My husband," I sigh, picking up the folder and heading towards the door. Lunch yesterday felt amazing, and even when I got home, Dorian had already bought dinner for us. We ate in silence. I don't know if he was fearing a fight as much as I did. But it was obvious we have a lot to say. "My husband doesn't care-"

"He doesn't look at you like someone who doesn't care," Louis tries walking by my side, and my blood grows colder with the nerves. It's not what I was intending to say and yet his words land with a punch. "He doesn't look at you like someone who doesn't love his wife."

I want to believe this so badly.

Maybe not to the untrained eye, but I recall his eyes filled with anger at the hospital. I remember how he stared at me with nothing more than resentment. I remember me reaching for him in the middle of the night, listening to him crying and my husband pushing me away.

I remember his love for me dying, shrinking like a petal from a flower that no longer needed it.

"You just can't see it, Ariella," Louis adds, softening his voice to my understanding. "Because you are so far along in this insane plan of yours. You can't see it, but your husband loves you."

"My plan is not insane. It's needed."

"There are other ways to achieve justice for Raphael's deat-"

As soon as my eyes land on him, the words Louis was about to pronounce fall short, and he gulps. He almost said the word. The one I don't allow anyone around me to pronounce.

The one I can't even think about.

I am not delusional. I know my child is not here. But I still have a hard time hearing the word as much as I have a hard time saying it. It's as if someone is pressing on my already bleeding wounds.

My feet are fast, turning me around and heading out of the office, knowing Louis is close by as we pass the seamstresses. Fabrics unveiling creating my designs that will close the runway on the day we are there. With deep breaths, I walk in front of my friend, who tries to keep up with my pace.

"I'm sorry, Ariella, I didn't-"

"I am doing what I have to so I can sleep at night, Louis," I hiss as we reach the meeting room, stopping so this conversation stays outside. "Whatever it takes, I will find the right culprit. Not me, not the driver, but the people who are behind the money. The ones who framed the driver and the ones who dared to accuse me of being a part of the accident."

"I didn't mean it like that."

"I know what you meant. And maybe you are right. Maybe Dorian still loves me, even if it's just a fragment of what he once did. But I don't want him hurting. I don't want him being dragged into a battle where I am the only one to blame. If I have to sacrifice my love for him, I will. Dorian accepted what happened a long time ago. I have not."

Louis nods, knowing there's no point in having this conversation now. I wrap my hand around the lever and pull the door to reveal the board members already inside. They stand close to the far windows looking out over New York.

It's one of the busiest cities in the world. Full of life. Lately, it seems gray has replaced the things I grew used to over the years. The city that took me in when I was nothing more than a girl running from her past.

Life here was easy, and simple, but busy at the

same time. Now, it's incomplete.

"Good, Ariella, you're here," my boss says, and I frown, noticing a female figure shadowed by all the men. "We are meeting with the VP of the company that will distribute our brand."

Stating the obvious as usual, he motions with his hand to the gathering of people at the end of the room. Louis glances at me.

My blood gets as cold as ice, becoming numb to everything, and all color leaves me as I notice who the other woman is. The men step aside, allowing me to see her, and when her eyes spot me, she is already smiling.

"Ariella," one director introduces. "I believe you've met Ms. Rogers."

How formal of her to be introduced to all the men in the room by her last name. But how smart of the woman, as usual, to be here before me. If only these horny older men knew their persuasive manners to this woman wouldn't matter. Trying to seduce her into a good fuck, thinking maybe it will give them leverage over her business, doesn't mean a thing to her as she will toy with them for her own pleasure.

Like I have been doing to her.

With her hand extended to me, the woman smiles as I take a deep breath. After the gala, I was hoping she would back off with her proposal to work with Wear A Kiss. I was certain my boss would not accept it. I was wrong.

"Ariella," Irene chuckles. "Always a pleasure to see you."

I can sense Louis rolling his eyes as I step aside and pretend to talk to Irene more privately. No one suspects. Of course, they don't. "What are you doing here?"

Irene brushes her silky red hair away from her face. She glances at the pleased men at the end of the room who seem unable to contain the grin on their faces. Except for Louis. My friend won't smile at Irene, even if his life depends on it.

They share a past. Louis worked for Red & Blue Associates before being recruited by Wear A Kiss. He never told me what happened between them, only that Irene would intrude on everyone's job even if she wasn't from the same department.

"I told you this deal would be good for my company, Ariella."

Her tone is smooth as if this were just business as usual. As if my questions are absurd, and I shouldn't even be asking. As if I haven't told her to keep her distance from my private life.

"And I told you not to do this, Irene. I told you to stay away."

I wrinkle my nose as Mr. White walks around the room. The expensive perfume he has on, and the clothes he wears are all for show. This man may have money, he may be rich, but his soul is dirty and rotten.

I don't like this man one bit. He doesn't care I may not enjoy having Red & Blue Associates involved in my life once again. He knows about the accident everyone I work with knows. He also knows the truck was from Irene's company, and now he has made Irene a sort of partner for the brand. Men, at least most of the ones I have worked with, have this weird notion that they are superior to women. To me.

How wrong they are.

"Good," he says a little over our conversation. "I am happy to see you two are getting along already."

I want to roll my eyes, yet I can't. Maintain professionalism, only for a little longer. Until Irene says what she must. Then I can do whatever I want. I can even quit. I love working here, but this company restrains my creativity sometimes. Like the fact, I may not design a bride's line, although we are expanding into the area.

It's my favorite thing, wedding dresses. To make someone smile by wearing the one thing, others love to see. Even if it's for only one day. I designed my wedding gown and Dorian's tuxedo. It was worth it, as I still remember the grin on his face watching me walk down the aisle.

"Sir," I call, tilting my head. "Can I talk to you for a second?"

Irene eyes us, but Mr. White turns his attention to me. Louis calls for her, so we have some privacy. She leaves with a reluctant sigh, fearing that denying it t will crack the mask she wears.

"What is it? Is there something wrong with the designs for NYFW?"

"No sir, all coming along. I wanted to ask if it is necessary for me to be at these meetings?" He raises a brow and I add. "Considering my history with Red & Blue, I mean."

If I have to explain it further, then I might as well draw him a picture. But he seems to understand what I mean. Mr. White's gaze sharpens, and he leans forward. For a second, I allow myself to believe he will dismiss me and put Louis in charge of everything by himself. My friend is qualified.

But then Mr. White leans and whispers as if conspiring. "I know it must not be easy for you right now, but don't hold grudges, Ariella. These people have nothing to do with the unfortunate events of your life. It was an accident and they are not to blame for it. The drunken bastard who worked for them is."

Don't hold grudges. Don't. Hold. Grudges.

It stuns me in silence. Among all the things I was expecting, this was the last one. This man's lack of empathy reveals one thing only. His money has risen to his head. I am so baffled by it, I don't even notice Irene stepping next to him again.

"What?" I ask when she talks to me.

The woman gives me a devious smile. "I was

explaining *Mrs. Vaillant,"* she says as if my husband's surname gives her nausea, "my plans for distribution."

"You two are amazing. Always working," my boss says. It doesn't matter who the creator is; if the money comes from someone else, they dictate the rules. One of these days he will also have what he deserves. "Maybe you could give Ms. Rogers a private tour of the building."

Irene smirks, knowing she had her way, and I entertain the thought of locking her somewhere. All I want is to leave this room. "I would love to," I say, nodding with a fake smile. "Louis-"

"Will stay here," Irene says over my voice." He can discuss the strategy I already established with the board and inform you after."

Fuck, she thought of everything, didn't she? This woman tries to stay one step ahead. I wonder if she is taking a sniff at what I intend?

"Sure," I say before heading out of the room.

Irene follows closely. I am not showing her anything, yet she giggles as I rush us through the floor, heading to the one place no one will hear us. My office.

People glance, whispering words to the ones next to them as we hurry through the crowded hallways. Irene isn't thinking straight right now; in her mind, lustful thoughts spread, clouding her judgment.

"Get in," I demand, pulling the door open.

The click of the lock being shut has me sighing as

I try not to show her how pissed I am. Irene is pushing me against the wall, wanting something I told her since day one I can't give. Something I don't want to give her. She is a means to an end, and I was always honest, saying we are not together. It is casual, and she was okay with it at first. Of course, I don't tell her why I started all of this. It would make my life a lot harder if Irene knew I am trying to figure out how much damage I can imprint on the company that shredded my life apart.

I want to know the name of the person who paid the police to keep everything quiet.

I did not mean to get involved with Irene, but I had been struggling for answers for over a year. The day I met her she was reluctant, but after a little forced affection from me she opened up. She spoke about the lawsuit. It's not an excuse; I cannot say what I have been doing is justified. I'm a cold-hearted woman when I have to be. And if it will bring justice to my son's death, I will be as cold as ice.

"What the hell are you thinking, Irene? Didn't I tell you that this was off-limits?"

"Ari I-"

"Don't call me that," I snap at her. "I already warned you about the terms of this arrangement. I am there for you, but coming after me at my workplace is too much, Irene. This," I say, gesturing between us. "This is too much."

She walks the short distance between us, her tall figure towering over me for the slightest, and I raise my chin. Irene thinks she can snap her fingers and have me ready. Her position at Red & Blue allows her to be blunt and direct, saying whatever she wants to get her answers.

"Ariella," she purrs, letting her lips come to rest on mine. "I have missed you. I know you said tonight you couldn't see me, but I was wondering if we could hang out after whatever it is you are doing?"

If only she knew how overwhelmed I feel with all the wrong emotions whenever I am in her presence. If only she knew how much I despise myself from even talking to her.

"I can't, Irene, and I cannot meet you for a while."

Not tonight. She won't take this from me.

Tonight is the only night we stay in silence, staring at the flickering lights against the sky. I always ask myself if my little boy is looking down on me, and I always apologize for who I have become. Tonight is the only time Dorian and I get together, no matter what. We make time for this every month.

Irene inhales a long breath, trying to lean forward and kiss me, but I pull away.

"Please?" She pleads tasting the words as if they are wrong. "Work has been crazy, and all the lawyers are giving me headaches. I need you."

"Then maybe you should have thought about it before making this kind of decision," I state, pacing towards the door. "I told you, Irene, my work and my private life are out of limits."

"Does this mean no sex?"

For crying out loud, everything is carnal to the woman. "We never had sex."

"Because you don't let me-"

"Go, Irene."

She tries again, her hand attempting to grab a string of hair, but I pull the door open, and she frowns. Irene walks out, turning to face me Instead of looking at her as she pleads, I shut the door in her face, remembering her request to stay with me tonight.

But I can't.

Tonight, it's the 17th, and tonight I am allowing my demons to surface.

11
Dorian

"I heard you yelling," I say as soon as Josh is in front of me. "What happened?"

"One of the new guys kept walking around the horse. I warned him when I saw him standing behind the mare. He got kicked, then complained about it." Josh shakes his head. "Here. I have some papers for you to sign."

Josh tilts his head to the side, checking to see if anyone else is in the office. He stretches his arms to me, trying to make me grab whatever documents he holds. He glances at my notebook on top of my desk, and the meetings I have lined up.

"Josh?" He hums in reply. "These papers are not for me."

"Oh," he says, but still doesn't look my way. "Sorry."

"She isn't coming today. It's tomorrow," I let out, handing him the documents again.

"Who?"

His eyes widen, as if realizing I was in the room all along. Funny how neither of the two entertains the idea of dating, and yet they seem to want to know more about the other. "Thea. You heard us talking about doing the consult the other day, but she rescheduled the session."

"I-"

"I noticed you were eyeing her. Stop making this harder for everyone."

Josh rolls his eyes at me, but a smirk spreads on his lips.

There are people in this world made for each other. Right now, the guy who always tries to act tough around me is the perfect match for the girl who always has a point. Two people who are liable, strong-minded, and can listen.

The sun peeks out from behind the window as the day is coming to its end, cascading over Josh's hair and making it appear lighter than its usual color. "I can give you her number," I say, following Josh as he walks around the office, trying to peek out the window.

"That would be nice, thank you."

"But there's a price."

Josh turns to face me. He crosses his arms over his chest, narrowing his gaze to me, and a scoff escapes his lips. "Which is?"

When I muster the courage to ask what my curiosity demands, my mind goes into overdrive. "Maybe, just maybe, you could talk to Ari? Figure out how bad-"

"No."

"I don't want you to meddle," I explain. "It's not up to you to clean the mess we made. But I want you to be there. For her. Ari is hiding something, and no matter what it is, I need you to be there when the time comes."

Josh nods, resignation spreading all over his face. "You don't even have to ask for that."

All I want to know is what Ariella thinks when she looks at me. But only she can tell me as much. Her eyes can plead for mercy when her lips don't allow the word to fall from them. My wife is stubborn, perhaps even proud. Especially when hurt, and all I want to know is the depth of her wound. Pain can make us behave in ways others cannot understand.

Last night I wanted to talk about the divorce papers, and how she sees our future. But we had a great time at lunch, and I feared if I mentioned anything, it would break the little bubble around us.

"I know things don't make sense to you right now," Josh explains. "And whenever I talk to Ari, she still doesn't open up much. But I can tell you your wife is hiding how she still feels for you beneath an ice curtain."

"She is?"

"I believe Ariella is still madly in love with you. She is beyond hurt, does not trust people anymore as a defense mechanism, and no talk will make her feel better. The talk is what you two should have done if you weren't so stubborn all those months ago. Now you need to act on it."

"What do you mean by months?"

"Remember how she was hurting? How broken you were after Raphael's death?"

I do.

I remember the excruciating pain in my heart, the way my wife's eyes defied life. Haunts me still. The way I wanted to kill the truck's driver, seeing my family being shattered to pieces, seeing the love of my life crumbling on a hospital bed, my son's skin usually the same shade as mine, as pale as the moon.

His image still haunts me when I close my eyes. I still have nightmares about it.

"She tried to reach you, Dorian, and you pushed her away."

"I didn't Josh I-"

"She tried Dorian," Josh states. "Ariella wanted to go to therapy. It was her idea. You said as much. She thinks you blame her."

Blame. It's as if it still crawls on me, as if the pain and sorrow, the misery of the moment, still lingers on my soul. I blamed her not for his death, but for the events surrounding it.

I blamed her for picking up Raphael, and for taking him from school earlier that day. Even if I never voiced it, if I never shared this with anyone, I resent my wife for this.

As I did to myself.

I blamed myself for not being with them when all my wife wanted was to go to the park with our son. I blamed myself for not being there for them, for not being with her, for not saving my kid. The what ifs or what I could do if I was there rarely let me get a full night's sleep.

"Try Dorian," Josh suggests, and I stare at him. "She is still there."

"I'm trying. I-"

"None of you is to blame here. None of you two is to blame, yet you are so consumed by the pain you don't see it."

I grit my teeth. "I want to try, but I did her wrong, and Ari is-"

"Even if she is cheating on you," Josh admits, stopping me once again. "Even if she is, ask yourself if you can live with it. If both of you can forgive each other. I am telling you to reach out to her. Tonight, it's the 17th. Share her tears and hold her hand. Be there. See her pain, Dorian. See who she is when the walls come down."

Be there. I haven't been there for her for so long. I wonder how lonely it has been for her as well.

My wife was the one who approached me with the idea. She doesn't want to miss the 17th of each month and I feel the same way. Despite it all, we sit and stare at the sky, watching the lanterns gliding in the air until reaching the stars and blending with them. Our minds, the pain, everything becomes too much, and one of us leaves so the other doesn't see the tears falling.

Most of the time, I leave first.

"She loves you." Josh steps closer as if trying to prove his point. "You love her, but along the way, you both got lost. Now you need to be there for her, as she needs to do the same. If she wants this, she will act on it. She will reply."

I step towards my desk, searching for the small yellow pad and scribbling a number on it. With a twirl of my feet, I grab my jacket by the door, not before noticing my friend's curious gaze as I appear to go on automatic pilot. I stand in front of him, handing him the small post-it. Josh grins at me.

"What's this?" He asks, already knowing the answer.

"Thea's number. She is out of the office by seven."

"Where are you going?" Josh asks, amused, as I grasp my hand on the doorknob, pulling it open.

"To get my wife back."

Zoe opens her mouth to speak as I pass by her, but regrets the idea right away when I don't even acknowledge her presence. I will deal with her soon. One mess at a time. When I am in my car, I am already dialing Thea's number. "Yes?" she asks, uncertain on the other end of the line.

"The other day you asked me for a good memory and I refused to talk about it. Do you remember?"

"I remember you said you weren't ready."

Traffic is slow and I sigh. "Well, I'm ready now."

The laughter behind the house is the first thing I see when I walk around it. Raphael runs to his mom, wraps his arms around her, and both fall on the grass. She yelps on purpose when he puts something on her open palm and laughs at her again. I have been missing these moments. It's the first time in over a week I made it home in time to see my son still awake.

None of them notice me until I speak. "What are you two doing?"

"Papa!" my son yells and runs towards me.

My arms open as I lift him, kissing his cheek. He looks so much like his mother in these moments that it overwhelms my heart. Ari stands and cleans her jeans. She smiles, showing me her hand and what Raphael gave her seconds ago. A grasshopper. "He caught it. I was explaining we should let him go."

Raphael is ready to say no when I speak. "Maman is right. He has a family who will miss him if he doesn't make it home soon."

I try my best to hide the smile on my face when I see resignation settling in my two-year-old. When he acts like this now, I can't even imagine how his temper will be. Ari tells me not to think so far ahead. To enjoy these moments with him. My lips meet Raphael's forehead. "Have you had dinner?" He nods.

"I was waiting for you to put him to bed," Ari says. I recognize the heaviness laced with frustration in her voice

at how much I have been working. "He wants you to sing him his lullaby tonight."

Slowly, I put Raphael down once more and sit next to my wife. At the same time, Ari lets go of the grasshopper. We watch our son running down the lawn after it. "He's so big," I say and Ari grabs my hand.

I bring it to my lips. This woman… God, I would give her the world if I could. I don't think I ever realized how much I needed someone like her in my life until the day I saw her at the bus stop. I fell in love right then. I fell in love and I keep falling further each day. Her hair sways when she turns to me, her eyes speaking more than she lets anyone know. "We should take him to the park when the heat subsides a little. Do you think you can take an afternoon off in a couple of weeks?"

"I can. This revised contract should not go any further than the 5th."

Ari struggles to hide her thoughts and I kiss away her pout. "I promise I will make time for us," I mumble against her lips.

"You better. I don't like how much you have been working, Dorian."

"I know. It's just a hard client."

"And I don't enjoy falling asleep in our bed without you."

"This is the one thing I hate most," I say, sliding my arms around her waist and pulling her to me. "I will make time for the three of us, and I will also make time for you and me."

"Promise?" She asks with a raised brow.

I nod and Ari sighs against my lips. "I'm going to put him to sleep," I say, my hands traveling to Ari's back beneath her shirt. "Why don't you go to bed and wait for me?"

As she grins mischievously, I become half-hard knowing what she is thinking. She kisses me, a promise of what is coming. I pull away and run after Raphael, lifting him over my shoulder. Despite my son's protests, he gives in. We walk into the house, Ari following us. She gives Raphael a goodnight kiss and heads to our bedroom while I walk with our son to his bathroom. "Brush your teeth," I say, kissing his head. "You need help?"

My son dips his chin and I help him as much as he lets me. If there is one thing I learned is despite his young age, I need to let him do things by himself. After what feels like half an hour, and Ari yelling across the hallway for me to tug our son into bed and stop messing around with him, I cover my little boy and sing him his lullaby.

When he was born, no one told me I would feel my heartbeat outside of my chest. No one told me the things I would love the most would be these quiet minutes when he is falling asleep and I can watch him.

No one told me how much I could love someone as I love him.

12
Dorian

Night surrounds the house. While leaning on the passenger seat, I grab the bouquet of colorful papers and begin my plan. My wife's favorite flowers rest there. White camellias. The ones she would always fill the house with. Taking a look at my empty entryway, I hope tomorrow morning she has set up a small display on the kitchen table like she used to. I walk inside, but Ari isn't anywhere to be seen.

I head to our office. I open the cabinet behind the desk and allow my shaky hand to grasp around the lantern. With a long breath, I close my eyes, tune my emotions down and remember I have to be there for her tonight. Not only present but also there for my wife if she needs me.

The 17th is never easy for us.

From the corner of my eye, I notice the white wool blanket resting on the armchair, the one my wife uses to cover her legs when she is reading, and I grab it. The nights are getting colder. I don't want Ari to get sick.

Before I leave the house with the folded bag in one

hand and the blanket in the other, I pass my son's bedroom. I try opening the door once more, knowing it's still locked. Ari isn't inside, but it's torturing me not to know why she always locks it. Does she think I want to change the room and undress it from anything related to Raphael? Shaking my head away and trying not to overthink, I walk to the back door and open it. The first thing I see is my wife sitting beneath the willow tree in the back.

Raphael's favorite place to play.

The memory of arriving home to find Ari sheltered in the tree's shade listening to our kid's laughter as he played around her fills me before I allow myself to drink in the broken image of my wife tonight.

Ari hugs her legs and rests her chin on her knees, staring at the white paper lantern already lit up in front of her.

It's the only light that allows me to see her figure, her emotions, and the way her face scrunches as she closes her eyes. I open my lantern as I approach her, making my presence known not to startle the woman I love.

I sit next to her. Close enough to feel her warm body beside mine. Close enough to wrap my arms around her if she is willing. I light up the ring inside my lantern, watching it burn next to Ari's before she leans forward.

Her long fingers encircle the fragile piece. I notice

she has drawn a heart on the side before she lifts the object toward the sky. I do the same. The lanterns fly together, swaying in the air, illuminating the blue canvas above us and reaching the stars beyond our reach. I watch them until they disappear and wonder if heaven exists and if my little boy is looking down at us.

A sob erupts from Ari's chest, and I turn my head and stare at her as she rests her forehead against her knees, hugging herself to calm down. With shaky hands, my eyes hover around the small frame of my wife. I am attempting to understand if she will push me away before I give up and hug her close to me.

She stiffens but doesn't push me away. I sigh in relief.

Ari falls against my chest as I tighten my arms around her. A cry of pain gets stuck in her throat. She clasps her hand against my shirt. The fabric crushes beneath my wife's hand while my hand caresses the back of her head.

"I'm here," I breathe out. "I'm here, Ari."

Ari lifts her face to mine, tears streaming down her cheeks, tainting her beautiful skin as my thumb caresses them away before leaning enough to smell the perfume of the woman to who my heart still belongs to.

I rest our foreheads together, noticing how she closes her eyes and when my lips brush hers, my wife parts her mouth, waiting. The softest, slowest kiss possible. I try to make her see what I can't say out loud.

I pull away and Ari watches me. Her fingertip comes to the corner of my eye, dismissing a tear threatening to roll down my cheek. I sniffle my pain, swallowing the remains of it, wanting nothing more than this.

Her. I only want her.

"I'm here," I repeat, and she takes a deep breath.

Ari shifts her body so she can see the lanterns in the sky but rests her head on my chest, her hand searching for mine. I hold her as close to me as I can.

She sleeps.

Next to me, wearing a small pajama set I love, and it was the first night in months, she came to bed while I was still awake. She saw me reading and crawled beneath the sheets, her hair down, and hugged her pillow tight. Maybe what happened after we released the lanterns did something to her. Cracked a bit of the wall she kept lifting between us.

I watch her, my fingertip inches away from her skin, so close I can sense the heat from her body against me.

I want to kiss her. I want to hold her in my arms and tell her I will take all the pain away. I will make her happy again. But I have to go slow. I know my wife. Whatever is happening, I can't scare her away, and if I go with all my strength after her, I will only make her drift from my reach.

She has a hard time letting go.

Understandable, considering her past. When your own family turns their back on you for the way you are, and for whom you love, it leaves a scar. The woman I love has a big one in her heart.

Small rays of sunshine make their way into the peaceful bedroom, cascading against my wife's skin, allowing me to appreciate her beauty.

She has been working hard. There are dark bags under her eyes, and I even notice that her bottom lip has some blood marks on it from where she tugs the skin.

It's time for me to grow, for me to mend us. I am not the only one to blame here. However, I am the one who doesn't want to give up. I won't let my marriage with the most wonderful woman I know break apart because of our stupidity.

If we can survive the most heartbreaking moment of our lives, we can survive anything.

13
Ariella

"Where are we going, maman?"

His tiny hand wraps around mine as we stroll through the parking lot. Raphael is excited. It's rare for me to pick him up this early, but I couldn't ignore the way the sun is so bright today. I can see a slight breeze swaying through the trees and know we are not getting too many days like this. Summer has arrived, and it's been scorching, too hot to walk in the streets. But today, the heat seems to have relaxed, letting the people in the city enjoy the best of it.

"We," I let out with a chuckle, picking him up. "We are going to the park."

A cheer leaves my son's mouth. His excitement strikes me in the heart, sending a warmth through my body as I take my keys and put Raphael in his car seat. Dorian hasn't texted yet. He should have by now.

Raphael keeps asking about him. It doesn't help. I am running out of excuses.

"Papa?" The gasp makes me frown as I purse my lips together, nodding.

"Dad is a little busy." I let out a sigh. "He will come."

With Raphael in his seat, I check the straps as I always do. These things are as hard to lock as they are to unlock. Dorian lost five minutes last week thinking it was stuck. Fortunately, it wasn't, but it needs a bit of thought and a soft touch.

I glance at Raphael, noticing he resembles me more lately; his hair is not as dark as my husband's, and his nose is similar to a rose button. Still, there's one thing that always makes me think of his father.

His eyes.

No matter how much our son looks like me, his gaze, his sweet green eyes are the same shape and color as his father's is enough to melt everyone. His smile also helps. I swear this kid can get away with anything by smiling. He even crooks his smile like Dorian.

My phone rings as I close Raphael's door and walk around the car to take the call, not even caring to check who it is. Louis wouldn't call. I can count on my colleague for that. He won't let anyone from the atelier call either, so it can only be one person.

"Yes?"

"Ari," Dorian starts.

"You're not coming."

It's not a question. I know by the sound of his voice. Dorian is once again too busy to meet us. He has been for the last three weeks, and although we never meddle in each other's work, this is too much.

The other night, he came home for four hours to change and eat before heading out once more.

So I open the door on my side but stand outside, not

wanting to fight in front of our son.

"I'm sorry."

"Dorian, you know what day it is, right?"

"July 17th," he replies. "I didn't forget the promise I made, Ari."

"I know you didn't," I continue. "But that's all the more reason why you should be home early at least. You said this deal would take a few days; we are reaching the three-week milestone now, Dorian. You promised you would be done with this by the 5th. You told me you would take a few days off from work... it's been over a week."

"Ari-"

"No, don't Ari me. What are you going to do if this client says he won't sign the papers? The man doesn't care about your time zone and forces you to call him during the late hours of the night. What if, at the last minute, he decides he doesn't want the horses? You've been neglecting your family for your work-"

Dorian stops my rant. "My work puts food on the table. It's not like you don't prioritize your job, either."

He wants to go there, doesn't he?

I lick my lips and take a deep breath while glancing inside the car for our son. He sits as I left him, with his favorite stuffed animal giggling with the slight breeze coming from the open door.

"You're right. I prioritize my job, but I also know when to put things aside and be with you two," Dorian sighs, knowing I am right. "I have fashion week in less than two months. We have started everything and I am

still here. I made time for him. For you."

"I'll be home early," Dorian says, ready to end the call in a tone that doesn't suit me.

"Great. You can also grab dinner before heading home."

I intend to stay in the park with the little one for as long as I can. NYFW is around the corner; Dorian and I always make sure our agendas don't clash, so this work of his is dragging, and that's what is making him anxious because it's about to overlap the two-day trip he has scheduled for Morocco in August, plus our Paris trip in November.

Although I'll be there for work, my family is coming with me.

Dorian ends the call and I sigh. Raphael is 2. I don't want him growing up and looking at pictures, wondering where one of us is. He has to have his parents there for him. At least for what matters.

My husband hasn't been present for over two weeks now, and the little one is missing him.

"Papa?" Raphael asks as soon as I slide into my seat, grasping the steering wheel.

"Papa is meeting us at home," I smile at him, glancing from my seat. "Now, let's go to the park."

My body is sore as if I ran a marathon. As if the crying last night left a mark on me. The pain in my mind is turning physical, fading away from my thoughts as anger vanishes a little from my soul.

I dreamed of the day of the accident and it is one

dream I fear the most. Being in Dorian's arms yesterday is the reason for it. I wipe away my tears and glance around the room.

The bed feels empty, and I notice my husband isn't on his side of the bed. Nor anywhere else in the bedroom. I sit, peeking at the bathroom, noticing he isn't there either, and scolding myself when sadness hits me straight in the gut.

His kiss last night, the words he whispered in my ear, had an impact as big as the first time he said I love you.

I turn on the bed, letting my bare feet touch the floor. There is a scheduled meeting after lunch with Irene's company, and I am not excited about it. I dress as professionally as I can with a black suit. The pants hug my figure before flowing over my legs, paired with an old rosy silk blouse.

All I need to do is make her speak, make her say the name of the person who made her company get away with this. A board member bribed the police into presenting the report as an accident. A lie they crafted. The road I was coming from was clear enough to see, and the truck couldn't step on the brakes in time. They never inspected the Red & Blue Associates vehicle. The accident was so long ago, but I still remember everything.

I remember people screaming on the street. I remember the driver's face in panic as he couldn't stop the truck. I remember yelling at my son to bend in his car seat before turning to face him.

It wasn't an accident caused by a lack of visibility and a drunk driver, like Red & Blue, wants the public to believe.

It was the product of irresponsible, greedy people who don't want this crime they have on their hands to taint their names further. The newspapers didn't even acknowledge the company as being the guilty party in the accident. They didn't even talk about it other than saying two vehicles collided and a little boy died. I did not want our names involved. Dorian talked to his family, and they helped us. But I was at least hoping someone would call out Red & Blue on this.

I pull the bedroom door open to be graced with the smell of fresh cooking. With curious eyes, I walk around the house, stopping as soon as I spot Dorian in front of the stove. He is sliding greens inside a pan and humming his favorite song.

"Good morning," he says before turning around with a smile adorning his lips and his green eyes sparkle.

I missed that.

His eyes and smile. I missed this and the sweet words he could whisper in my ear as I would rant about my day.

"Good morning."

I love him. I will always love my husband and what we once were. But I am not sure I am right for him. Dorian deserves a life filled with laughter and joy. I still struggle with letting him go. About calling it all out. It is the right thing to do, but after last night, I want to be selfish.

"I made you breakfast," he sings, approaching the round table and sliding an omelet inside my empty plate. "Your favorite with scallions."

"Thank you," I say, trying my best not to let the words fail me.

Dorian sits at the table. My eyes notice the mug with orange juice as I caress the words I haven't heard for so long. He waits for me, as he used to do, so I am the first to try his food. My words from that night so long ago linger on my tongue before I mumble them with a smile.

"Is it poisoned?"

My husband chuckles, leaning forward and cutting a piece from the food on my plate. He then eats it so close to me, moaning at the taste. I try not to let the emotions show in my eyes.

It's the night he bought me a cupcake all over again.

I cut my eggs and chew on them with a happy sigh. "I was thinking," he admits, and I lift my gaze. "Let's have lunch today."

"Today?"

"Yes."

"Dorian I-"

He reaches out for my hand. "Ari, I don't want us

to fight anymore. I know something is off, something is stopping you, and although I'm not sure who it is, I don't want us to go there right now. We are both right and wrong, but I only want us to try. I don't want to give up yet."

Try.

Trying to be with the man I love. The lawsuit is close to taking place. Soon the court will ask us to be present at a hearing. When it happens, I won't be able to hide behind my former name anymore.

When it happens, Irene will know who the invisible person her company is fighting against is. The same one she has been talking to for weeks.

"Lunch," Dorian says again, interlocking our fingers.

I nod and my husband tilts his head, encouraging me to continue eating. Dorian chuckles, not before standing and taking his cup to the dishwasher. He walks to me and crouches. This isn't helping my blood pressure to come down. His peppermint scent lingers around us, enticing me to give in to this man.

"I'll be by your office at 12," he says, leaning to me and taking my lips into a kiss. Teasing me is more likely. He rests his hands on the curve of my ass, barely touching it. His tongue meets mine and I swear I don't melt to the floor because he is holding me.

"12," I reply, opening my eyes to the two sweet green ones already looking at me with pure adoration.

I watch as he leaves, wanting to hug Dorian and apologize for everything, but fear grips my heart and keeps me in place. Not yet. I still need to hold on to this for a little longer, and I will do so as I fix my marriage.

Only the idea of ending this with Irene lingers as I turn my attention to the mug in front of me.

The one with the word mom that Dorian bought the day he found out I was pregnant.

I leave the house soon after my husband.

The hours go by too slowly despite my busy morning. I would lie if I said I didn't check my watch every ten minutes. This lunch almost feels like our first date. I'm biting my nails because of the uncertainty around it, the make-or-break feeling.

"You seem to be in a hurry." Louis's voice travels across the studio as I pack my things and head to the privacy of my office. A quick glance at my watch tells me it's almost time. "That looks new."

My colleague's eyes stay on the string around my neck as I lift my fingertip to caress the flower on the pendant. The one from my birth month Dorian gifted to me all those years ago during our first Valentine's Day.

"It's something I had lying around."

Louis narrows his eyes. "There's something different about you today," my colleague says again. "You smiled the entire morning. What is it? Come on, tell me. I'm curious." Louis stays with his eyes on me as I pick up my purse. "You're not staying for lunch?"

"No. I'm having lunch with Dorian."

It falls from my lips as so many times before. It was a normal thing for us. My husband would meet me once or twice a week so that we could have some time for ourselves.

But now, it's so much more exciting. From the corner of my eye, I catch my friend's expression changing.

"Oh my God. You guys are having lunch. No, wait, you're not leaving this office without details. I need details, Ariella," he shouts as I am opening the door to the studio, and the face I woke up to smiles back at me.

His almond eyes study my dumbfounded expression before Dorian speaks. "Hi."

"Hi," I say in a breath, not oblivious to Louis's giggling behind me. I'll take care of him later. "I thought we were meeting at the restaurant."

"No," Dorian states, tilting his head. "I said I would pick you up at 12, it's-" he glances at his watch for a brief second to make sure, "11:56."

He is still wearing the same outfit from this morning and it still takes my breath away. My husband's hair parts at the front, making almost a small heart on his forehead. His shirt clings to his chest, and the green is the same dark shade as his eyes.

He is here, and it is still difficult to believe. Dorian is a busy man, which makes me realize he had to move his schedule a little to be with me today.

"Good morning Louis," Dorian says.

"Yes, hi," Louis replies, not making a big deal out of the situation and leaving the office.

As I watch him leave, I realize the frown on Dorian's eyebrows while he speaks and scratches the back of his neck. "I was wondering if you want to meet for drinks this week?"

Louis stops in his tracks, turning to face my husband. "Drinks?" Louis asks to make sure he didn't misunderstand. "You want me to have a drink with you?"

"I am meeting the guys, and I thought you should join us. You seemed to get along with them at lunch the other day."

Louis glances in my direction, and I shrug, not knowing what to say. It would do them well to get it out of the way. Maybe bond a little over guy talk. It's my husband's way of apologizing to another man; if only he knew chocolate also works with Louis, he wouldn't be offering to pay for alcohol when the guy drinks like a sponge. Impressive how he drinks as if there's no tomorrow whenever we go out, waking up with no signs of a hangover the next morning.

"Will there be food?" Louis asks, and Dorian's

lips turn into a smile.

"Yeah."

"Then I'll be there. Text me the address."

Dorian lets go of a chuckle, warming the ends of my heart before tilting his head towards the door, and we walk in silence. The restaurant isn't far, and as we step into the breeze of New York streets, I try to calm myself down.

I want him. I want him so badly it hurts.

It's weird, stupid, and idiotic, but I love the man walking by my side. Every piece of him, even the broken ones, he tries to hide from me.

I already said I am selfish, but I lost someone I loved before. I know how it feels, and I don't know if I can do it no matter how hard I try.

"Thank you," I whisper, staring ahead and spotting the restaurant in the distance.

"For what?"

"Asking Louis to join you with the guys."

He laughs, this time a loud laugh that has me on the verge of stopping him in the middle of the street and crashing my lips against his. It would be perfect, and warmer than standing in front of the fireplace on a cold winter night.

But I need to take it slow. It will be better if I don't jump headfirst into this. I want it to work.

"I figure I owe him an apology," Dorian shrugs. "What better way of doing it than with food and drinks?"

"He will love it."

We arrive at the small door, and my husband holds it open for me. The server greets us, accompanying us as we head to our table before Dorian sits across from me, holding the menu and deciding what to eat.

"What do you think about the mushroom risotto?" Dorian asks, glancing at the menu as I lift the corner of my mouth into a smile. "I know it's your favorite."

"They have the best one in town."

"We will have two," he says to the server. "And two lemonades, please."

The server leaves us, her ponytail swaying as she walks, and I become aware of the silence creeping in between my husband and me. I avoid looking at him because I know if I do, my heart will go into overload.

"How's work? I noticed you had new sketches on your desk."

"The-"

"The gowns and wedding dresses," Dorian finishes with a grin. "I'm happy you're working on them again."

The word happy makes my heart swell. Dorian knows it's a dream I still hold, having my own couture line. Where I can let my creativity flow and explore designs, my contract doesn't let me. Be different.

"Thank you," I mumble under my breath,

avoiding his gaze and staring at the window next to us. "I was just putting some ideas down. It's not like they are letting me sell them. How's everything at the office?"

Why in the world am I asking this? I don't want him to speak about it. Especially considering Zoe still works there. The first time I met her when everything was still okay in my marriage, I noticed how she eyed me. Trying to figure out what my husband saw in me she didn't have?

I have a brain and know my place, but that's another conversation.

The first time, I noticed her mumbling something about me as I passed by. But I couldn't make out the entire sentence, so I have no proof. If I did, she wouldn't still have all her teeth in her mouth.

Yes, I can get aggressive, jealous, and overall possessive with my husband. Not in a toxic way. But if I was to walk with him across the street and someone stared at him as if he was their favorite meal, you can bet I would make sure the same person knew he was mine.

"It's fine," Dorian replies, still staring straight at me, and I meet his eyes. "I have been thinking about promoting Josh and I need your opinion on it."

"A promotion?"

"He has been working hard, and we need someone I can trust to run the place when I am not there."

This doesn't add up. Not the Josh thing. The idea has been on Dorian's head forever, but I don't think I like the way he says he will be absent from the office. My husband loves his job. He loves spending time with the animals and runs everything according to his wishes. There were times I had to drag him back home and assure him his work would still be there in the morning.

These were times when he wanted to think about anything but his problems. After Raphael disappeared from our lives, he would spend nights buried in paperwork to avoid feeling the pain.

"Are you going on a trip?" I ask, with the idea spreading through me and tainting my thoughts like wildfire.

I don't want him to go. As a matter of fact, I don't want a divorce. But I also can't force him to stay. If Dorian leaves the city, or more likely, the country for work… It will be harder to see him. His work is important, and I would never force my husband to choose. He would sometimes spend weeks abroad trying to negotiate with other breeders, only calling late at night.

I never complained.

The girl who took our order comes back with the drinks. When she leaves us for the second time, I become aware my husband still hasn't replied. Instead, he stares at me, an amused smile on his lips as I scold myself from how obvious my question was.

"No," Dorian shrugs, leaning forward and picking up his glass before tilting his head and taking a long sip. I wait for him to speak again, sliding to the edge of my seat. "I want to spend more time at home, and I can't do that if I'm always working."

Smooth son of a bitch.

Dorian always liked to leave me speechless. Sometimes succeeded, other times he wouldn't. Sometimes he would just say the words for the sake of it and leave me upset as well. The teasing was common with him.

Right now, he is letting me know he is in this with me. I cannot deny when his eyes light up and he deepens his voice doesn't do things to my body.

"You want to spend more time at home?"

"*Oui*. I told you I wasn't signing those papers, Ari. We need to talk and come to an understanding. I don't want to lose you too," his voice softens with the last word.

My heart breaks as the tears dread falling from my eyes with the confession, and I need a moment to recompose. A whole hour, an eternity. I wasn't expecting how much pain would strike me from hearing the hurt in his voice.

"I-" The words fail to come out of my lips. I decide to drink the lemonade in front of me, trying to gather time to stare back at him.

"I know," he says, reaching for my hand. His

thumb glides against my skin and sends electricity throughout my body. "Let's go to therapy together again, at least once per month. You keep your sessions with Thea. We both need private sessions, but let's try Ari."

The damn word again.

It weighs on me. Like a trapped man in a cell, staring at the street outside and wondering when he will experience freedom again. Knowing how it tastes, how it feels against his soul. I can try. I want to try. Irene's company has taken a lot from me already, and I know I can fight both battles.

The one with myself and the one with Red & Blue Associates.

"I know you're scared," Dorian pleads again as I grow silent. "But we got this Ari."

I lace my fingers around Dorian's long ones, staring straight into the two green pits that hold my gaze as if he is climbing from the darkest cliff in search of light.

"Let's try."

Lunch turns out to pass too faster than I wanted it to. Dorian asks me about Louis, about what I want to do during the days I have off from work soon. I have yet to inform him that those days will be the same ones I have to be at court for the hearing. Maybe once everything is stable and Dorian and I are in a better place, I can explain.

Dorian pays the bill as I greet the server with a

generous tip. When my husband looks at me from the front door, I swear my legs turn into jello. Because it is the light of pure adoration shining in his eyes, as he thinks he is lucky I am there, when I am the lucky one.

"This plan of yours to leave the office earlier. Does it start today?"

Dorian tries to hide the smile that wants to crawl on his lips and show me I entertain him with my question, yet he fails. I know it because he presses his lips together, staring ahead as we approach my office building, and my husband takes a deep breath before wrapping his long fingers around the door handle.

"Yes."

One word, but it's enough for my body to appear to be electrocuted as energy runs through me. I try to figure out how long it will take me to drive from the office to the store I like, grab whatever is needed to cook his favorite dinner, and head back home. It's been months since I cooked for him, and I miss it.

I have missed a lot of things, but I was so fixated on letting go of Dorian that I didn't realize maybe what I missed the most was having his attention.

We head towards the elevator, and as we step inside, my husband's hand brushes mine, and I stop breathing while his fingers grace my skin. Dorian glances at me before staring ahead once again, and I take the hint to wrap my hand in his.

If I want him back, I need to act on it and meet him halfway.

The music coming from the speakers as the elevator rushes through the floors is my distraction before his baritone invades the silence like thunder sounding in the distance. "I'm sorry."

I watch Dorian staring back at me. His eyes hold the entire universe in them. Eyes that want to make me crawl into his arms and embrace him as mine once again.

"Dorian-"

"I'm sorry, Ari, for how I behaved that night at the gala. I never properly apologized for it."

The distinct sound from the bell signaling we arrived at the right floor brings us back into reality as I tilt my head, letting him know we can continue this conversation inside the safety of my office.

Louis smiles at us when passing by him. I know Dorian's eyes are on me, his hand still holding mine like a safety in a storm. Never in all the years I've worked here have I opened the door so fast. Dorian steps behind me. I take a long breath, gathering the courage to turn and face him.

"Dorian I-"

I love you.

I'm sorry.

I made a mistake.

I hate myself.

I'm in pain.

All the thoughts I have been facing over the last year swim in my heart as I push them back to say the only thing he needs to hear. "We could both have handled things better, Dorian."

He smiles, so beautiful and unaware of the torment I face as I fight with myself, saying I can make the plan work without getting involved with Irene. At least in a physical way. It will be challenging, but it's possible.

The only reason I got involved with her was because she would talk faster, and I was running out of time. From delivering the lawsuit papers in court until being called, it would be a matter of a couple of months. By then, I thought Dorian was ready to let go of us. I never wanted to hurt him. I never wanted to be with Irene, to kiss her.

"I know something is up, Ari," he says, lifting my chin with his fingers as his words stab my heart. "But I can forget it. I made mistakes as well. We can let this go. We can-"

My heart burst as I tiptoe to reach his lips. I allow my body the torture of the bliss of my love taking shape. "I'm sorry," I breathe out as a tear slides down my cheek and Dorian wraps his hands on the back of my head, sliding his fingers through my hair and pulling me closer.

He silences me with a steady kiss, eager for more than a sweet moment, twirling me around and walking us toward my desk.

My husband lifts me, helping me to sit on top of

the desk. I part my legs so he can nuzzle himself between them. This kiss is different, not so much as teasing, trying to lead to something else. The man I love slows down, tasting me as if time means nothing.

Taking his precious minutes with my lips and molding his body onto mine.

"Ari," he says into my mouth as I open my eyes. "I missed you."

"I missed you too."

I missed every moment we were in silence. I missed him the most, especially when he wouldn't look at me. When the accident took place, I didn't just lose my son. I lost myself, and I lost the man I love. None of us knew how to be around each other.

Dorian gives me one final sweet peck on the lips, pulling away with the most dashing smile before brushing his thumb over my cheek.

"I'll see you tonight," he mumbles, walking to the door as I stand on my feet and rearrange the desk. The moment the door is open and I turn to watch him leave, my heart drops to my feet by watching someone already there.

She scoffs, looking at my husband, then at me as if the words she can say are not enough of an insult. I try to push the creeping panic away, clearing my throat and approaching Dorian, who glances in my direction.

"Irene, what are you doing here?"

My question sounds more like an accusation than curiosity, and both of them notice.

The woman smiles at me for a second, then turns to the handsome man at my side. Irene frowns, her gaze setting on how our hands are almost touching, our bodies so close to each other.

"We have a meeting in half an hour," she replies. "I thought I should drop by first and see how you are."

"Hi," Dorian speaks. "I think we met before, at the company gala. I'm Dorian Vaillant."

I am not scared of her, but this is still my workplace. She still needs to respect me and the others around here, even if it's to maintain her image. Irene is a client, someone who wants to do business with us, and I can ruin her if needed.

I dislike the idea of a collaboration anyway, at least with her company. The only thing I want from that place is to see it burning to the ground and dance on its ashes.

"Irene," she amends, extending her hand. "The soon-to-be ex-husband, I suppose?"

Avoiding rolling my eyes, I catch a smirk on Dorian's lips when he doesn't take Irene's hand in a handshake. I can almost hear the growl traveling up her throat.

My husband's gaze, however, seems uncertain of the lingering silence creeping around the room. He knows how I act toward the people I work with.

Even if I have to be strict, I never treat them the way I treat Irene.

"Not quite," Dorian grins, and Irene frowns in reply.

"Dear God," a voice from outside carries a hint of disapproval into the room. "You're already here?"

Louis steps closer as we watch him. His tall figure shadows the woman the focus of his annoyance.

"Yes," Irene replies. "I see you are already being your usual disgruntled self."

He smirks. "Disgruntled? Look at her learning new words to impress us. No, sweetheart, I am not displeased, only surprised to see you here before time. In fact, I don't know why you are so keen on being around. Seeing no one at this company enjoys your presence, your business, or the scandals it comes with. I am pretty sure as the Vice President of such a big company you have some subordinate who can attend these boring meetings."

Irene lets her fingers travel through her hair, pulling it away from her eyes with a nasty chuckle. This is about to turn into a bloodbath. I don't want my husband to know the details of this woman's life before I have to tell him.

She eyes him with enough displeasure to make anyone else's stomach turn. "Your boss disagrees."

"My boss needs the money," Louis shrugs. "The old man never has enough of it." He adds, placing his hands inside his pockets. "Nor does he ever stop thinking with his dick, which I am sure you have noticed by now. But you don't care, right? It's not like you have any morals. I heard you pay the women who work for you to keep quiet whenever they want to present charges for sexual harassment."

She smirks. "Hypothetically speaking, how much of a victim can someone be if they accept money for their silence?"

They are going to turn this into a heated fight soon. All the while, words are being exchanged, Dorian watches us. His eyes are going from both Louis and Irene to me as I stay silent, something abnormal, and my husband knows it. His fingers caress the back of my hand and I smile at him. I don't want Dorian to know who Irene is, where she works. At least until the right time comes.

"I'll be home soon," I whisper, turning to him, who grins at me.

A smile I love, yet it vanishes from his handsome face once someone mumbles behind us.

"Ariella, could you please stop the inappropriate behavior? This is a workplace. I am sure you don't get paid to have your husband around. I need to talk to you about the time it will take to have the outfits ready for sale," Irene calls, and I allow a grunt to escape me.

Keep it together, Ariella, only for a little longer. "Sure," I tell her, and Dorian sighs, kissing the top of my head before leaving.

"I'll see you at home." He stops in front of my colleague, who still sends death glares to Irene.

"I'll walk you out," Louis says. "I have to go downstairs, anyway."

They leave, walking towards the exit as I permit the relief I held for so long to leave my lungs. My secret is now safe. For the time being, at least. It's a one day at a time thing, and it will still take me a couple more weeks to figure it all out.

Especially if Irene keeps behaving the way she has been. There's no way I will keep quiet about the way she treats Dorian and Louis. It's not that she was always this unpleasant; with me, at least she wasn't.

Irene steps into my office. I grasp my hand on the doorknob, tired of her crap, especially the smile she wears on her lips. How can she think she won this round when I have done nothing over the past weeks but stop her advances?

"You need to stop that shit," I blurt out as soon as the door shuts.

"I did not lie Ari."

"It's Ariella for you, Irene."

She makes a noise, not enjoying the tone in my voice. She can make my entire plan fall into the trash and ruin my entire purpose of keeping her around. The main people at Red & Blue keep their cards close to themselves. Close enough, they hide whatever immoral things they do from the rest of the company. Paying the police to clear their reports it's only one of the many things they do.

"You need to behave, Irene," I warn, making the threat in the tone of my voice clear. "I don't like the way you speak to Louis and my husband."

Irene shrugs, touching her hair and twisting it around her finger in a playful manner. As if the scolding coming at her isn't worthy of her concern. "You mean the husband you told me you're divorcing?"

"I never told you I would divorce Dorian," I throw at her, raising my chin. "I said I couldn't be with you because I was married. But I never said I was going to leave him."

She rolls her eyes. "Oh please, Ariella. Everyone can see how wrong you two are together."

"I didn't ask for your opinion on my relationship Irene. My personal life is not for you to meddle in, and my husband is out of your reach. So stay away."

She licks her lips biting on the soft flesh right after, but I catch the twist of her eyelid. The way she lets her gaze linger on me, knowing my words are final and whatever she thinks is happening between us will stop if she so dares to cross the line once again.

Not that it will continue, but I need to lead her in the direction it may.

"I'm sorry. I thought-"

"No, that's the problem. You don't think. You

never think, Irene. Not about other people anyway."

"What do you mean?" She laces her voice with a warning.

It's the threat that has people shaking whenever the woman passes by in the hallway. The tone she uses diminishes what others consider important, like Louis or even some of my superiors. She uses her charm, and her presence to be polite, then lets small words slip from her lips, knowing they will have an impact.

She shows one face to the people she wants to impress and then another to the ones she thinks are beneath her.

"Do not come here and insult my husband and my marriage."

"You have to be fucking kidding me," she interrupts, laughing. "You mean to tell me you don't like how I treat the man you are cheating? How hypocritical can you be, Ariella?"

Fair enough.

Yet, this is not something she should even try to comprehend, not when I was nothing but honest with the way I see the two of us. In the same way, I am tired of trying to pretend it can happen.

"I don't think we should do this anymore." I blurt out.

Irene becomes still. Too still. The silence lingers between us and the only sounds reaching my ears are the ones from outside the office. She frowns for a few seconds but then shakes whatever emotions troubling her away. Irene takes a step closer to me and extends her hand as I pull back from her touch. Her eyes stay on mine and I can almost see the venom dripping from her lips as she straightens herself.

"Is that your decision?" She asks, and I nod. "It's the wrong one, darling, especially with everything I can tell your husband."

14
Dorian

I stroll inside the empty house, surprised to arrive before Ari. The meeting she was getting ready for must have taken longer than she thought. I pace towards our room to change into comfortable clothing and then go to the kitchen, rolling up my sleeves. When I open the fridge, I am greeted with a lack of vegetables and protein.

I should have gone to buy groceries before coming home. Ari used to keep a shopping list on the wall, to write everything we needed and then order during the weekend. Now, the list is gone, as are the drawings from our son. I took them down and put them away one night after finding Ari crying in front of them. The sound of her car arriving at the back of the house makes me turn around. By the time I arrive at the backdoor, Ari is already carrying two grocery bags in her hands.

"Give them to me," I tell her, and she slides the heavy bags into my arms with a shy smile. "You went to buy food?" I ask, already taking things from inside the bags as she picks up her hair in a messy bun.

The shorter tips fall around her neck. I gather the strength to look away from the skin that seems to beg for my attention. From the corner of my eye, I notice a small mark adorning her collarbone, something I did the other night, and a grin makes its way to my face as I watch the woman I love, grabbing her apron and sliding it over her head.

She's even more beautiful than the day I met her.

There's something different about Ari today. Something in the air around her appears to lift the mood of the entire room. Maybe it's the way her lips turn up whenever she glances at me. Maybe it's the way she thinks I don't notice how she keeps peeking now and then as I walk by.

Maybe it's me falling in love with my wife all over again.

Ariella takes the knife out to cut the vegetables. I watch her and help in any way possible. It doesn't take long for the smell of the goodness she cooks to fill the entire kitchen and make my mouth water.

Something in me lights up as I watch her gaze focusing on the food, and fight the urge to wrap my arms around Ari, pulling her towards me.

We are not there yet.

"Dorian?" she calls, and I shake my head away from the thoughts taking over my mind, realizing my wife has been watching me, watching her.

"Yes?"

"I asked you if you want to taste the food?" She snickers. "Were you listening to me?"

"I was. Of course I was," I lie my way out, knowing she doesn't believe in me. "Taste yes. Let me try."

As soon as the spoon lifts to my lips and I swallow the meat twirling in my mouth and invading my taste buds, my eyes close. It's as if angels sing in my ears.

"So?" she asks, her voice wavering the slightest. "Salty? Not enough salt?"

"Perfect," I whisper, leaning forward without even realizing.

Ari's lips stay a breath away from mine. She glimpses at my mouth, sliding her tongue in anticipation over her plump peach skin. I close my eyes, letting my lips caress hers. When my mouth closes on hers, Ari breathes a slow moan into me. My hands wrap around her, mirroring the thoughts from moments ago as I let go of the caution I held onto and show the woman I love how I still feel about her.

"Dorian-" she murmurs into the kiss as I press her against the counter.

Ari's hands slide to my shoulders, making a route until finding the hairs on the back of my neck and tugging them. I deepen the kiss. She wants more. She wants me to reassure her I am here. I won't let go of her again. And as I realize this, the kiss slows down.

It's the best part of being with someone for so

long. I can understand what she wants by the smallest reaction.

Opening my eyes to meet her soft gaze and promising myself the next time she gives herself to me like this, I will make things right. I know my wife. I know if I get too eager, she will doubt everything that's happening. This woman likes to have things taken slow, and I have always respected it as she always respects when I need my space, for example.

It's when I notice the struggle in her teary gaze. "I'm sorry," she whispers, and when I lift her chin, a tear slides from her eyes, touching my hand.

"I know. Ari, I know."

"I never wanted for it to happen, Dorian. I didn't want to hurt you."

My arms pull her closer, embracing my wife as she fists my shirt and fights the pain spreading through her. The pain she has been feeling for over a year. I have accepted mine. I have accepted our fate. It still hurts, and sometimes it almost tears me apart, but I know how to deal with it.

She doesn't.

We all can be a little too absorbed in ourselves, and I won't ever blame Ari for drowning in the silence of her excruciating thoughts. None of us battles the other to know who hurts most, but we both know we carry our grief, and sometimes I'll admit we can become selfish because of it.

"Whatever we both did is in the past," I murmur to the top of her head. "Let's not go there anymore. Let's be happy."

"Louis," I call, lifting my hand and he looks in our direction.

Eli was the first one to arrive. How he drives out of town and is at the bar before Josh, I have no clue. It makes sense Louis is half an hour late with the traffic over the bridge. Josh once told me he thinks Eli has some sort of tele transportation power. I explained our friend most probably tells the office he is going to a meeting out of town and walks out earlier.

"Sorry for being late."

Josh nods and Eli lifts his beer. "Ari's keeping you busy?" I ask and Louis smirks.

"I don't bad mouth my boss to her husband."

"Smart," Josh adds. "Why isn't your wife here, Dorian?"

"She has some sketches to go over tonight."

"Our gang is growing," Eli speaks, gesturing to the server with his empty wing basket.

"Don't call it a gang."

"What do I call it?"

Josh shrugs. Eli glances between all of us. "Anything but a gang. We are not five."

"Why aren't they coming to take our order?" Eli grunts and stands from his stool. "I'll be right back."

We all watch as the oldest goes into the bar. He seems happier today, and I hope his mood stays this way over the next few weeks. I hope I can get everything done before Eli visits us at the office once more.

Josh sips from his beer. Louis orders one from a girl passing by. I feel Josh's gaze on me before I ask. "What?"

"You're overthinking. I can smell it."

"You can smell me overthinking?"

Both men nod. "What is it?"

I bite the inside of my cheek, still looking at Eli. A thought lurked in my mind earlier today, but I need to be careful. I checked and Zoe's contract ends soon. I instructed the company's lawyer to write a document for her to sign up stating we release her from her duties and we will not be renewing it. Of course, there will be money involved. I cannot fire the girl without warning and not pay. But what is making me reconsider it all is Eli. Not the firing Zoe part, but how to break it down to him when he asks. Because he will ask.

"I am waiting on the lawyers so I can let Zoe go," I confess, and Josh's eyes widen.

Louis, who doesn't know who Zoe is, looks from Josh to me.

"You're letting her go," Josh says, and I notice it

is not a question.

"Seems fair. Ari broke off whatever it was she had going on, and Zoe still hits on me from time to time. I already have someone lining up to take her job."

"Okay…"

My eyes meet Josh and he frowns. A sigh escapes my lips as I lean and rest my arms on the table. "I need to make it happen when Eli isn't around. He cannot know what happened between us."

15
Dorian

I stare at her. My eyes don't leave her figure as I walk around the car. Ariella smiles while her gaze drinks in the outfit she chose for me. One she designed with all the care in the world. All black with emerald remarks, a color we both love and my wife always says, brings out my eyes.

Ari stands in front of me, grinning as she fidgets with the lapel of my jacket, pulling it into place. "You look sharp as always," she says, brushing her fingers on the blazer, admiring her work, and sending a spark of need through me.

I have promised myself for the last few nights to take it slow, knowing we need time to get everything into place. Still, the way she is behaving, her hair pulled up cascading around her exposed neck. The thin fabric of her dress clings to her chest and curves, falling straight over her hips. This leaves nothing to my imagination. It's not helping. I can feel myself getting hard every time I think about undressing her.

I want to lock us in a room and take all the time

in the world to worship her body.

"It's easy to look sharp when I have the most stunning woman in the room next to me."

This makes my wife lick her lips with satisfaction. "Smooth, as usual, I see," she says.

"For you always."

We walk up the stairs. Ari gives small glances at the cameras but doesn't interact much. My wife has kept our lives away from social media and the press as best as she can. She never gives interviews and stays hidden in her office for most of her work.

"I'll try to leave as soon as possible," she whispers. "I know how hungry you get at the end of these things."

"We can pass by the drive-through on our way home," I mumble, leaning closer to her and letting the flowery fragrance of her perfume invade me all over again.

"Sounds like a good plan. But I don't think eating junk food in this dress is a good idea."

The corner of my lips turns up, and Ari frowns, staring up at me.

"You're having dirty thoughts, aren't you, Vaillant?"

"Maybe."

"You know," she mumbles, staring straight ahead as they instruct us to walk further into the venue. Stepping inside the massive building where paintings and artwork adorn the walls. One of Ari's favorite places in the city is beautiful and has people swooning over it. Yet my wife stands out in the room as the most beautiful woman attending. She could stand out anywhere. "It would be a shame to ruin your suit as well."

"Are you implying I should take off my clothes to eat, Mrs. Vaillant?"

It's been so long since I referred to the love of my life using my family's name, yet, as a small shade of cherry adorns her skin, my heart beats faster, waiting for her reply. "You look better without them, anyway."

My tongue grazes the inside of my cheek as I try not to give her the reply I want. Not in public, at least since it would end up with Ariella back in the limousine and me undressing her. It is a work event, and I will sneak her away after the show. I carry her arm in mine, proud of the gazes sneaking their way at us. Ari pats my hand, calling for my attention as I stop noticing one of her superiors talking to someone. A sigh leaves her lips before my wife's body stiffens.

My gaze follows hers. I clench my jaw when spotting the woman with red hair smiling with her hand on Ari's boss's arm.

"Irene, I did not know they invited you."

"Mr. White asked me to tag along with him," she chirps. "I thought it would be nice to see the magic happening."

"Irene will be around for a while," Mr. White instructs us both. His words almost sound like a warning. "It won't hurt to see a little of what we do backstage. I am aware our brand is a little more… expensive than the others you have under your company."

"It wouldn't hurt for her to keep herself informed at all," Ariella admits although reluctantly, stopping her boss as I clasp my hand on hers, pulling her to me. "I hope you enjoy it."

The conversation soon drifts into less troublesome topics as the three discuss business, and Ari only speaks whenever she has to. I let myself admire the room we are in, a painting at the far end. Le Bassin aux nymphéas. A Monet. I think my father gave it to the city a while ago so people could admire it. We had it in the library, hidden from the world since my mom says it doesn't go with any of the furniture.

I miss my parents. They love Ariella as their own daughter, but the distance makes it difficult for us to visit. Ari's boss walks to the opposite direction and I still don't pay attention to whatever conversation she is having as her voice fades away.

Until a name I never want to hear pulls me to the present.

"What did you say?" I ask, staring down at Irene to make sure I didn't mishear.

My question startles her as the woman blinks

while staring at me before turning to face Ari and Irene. She seems to realize I am here. At least in front of her.

"Red & Blue Associates?"

My entire body stiffens. Ari's hand brushes mine, trying to take hold of me. Red & Blue Associates, the company-

I glance at my wife, discarding her pleading eyes before taking a step further, facing the snob woman who narrows her gaze in my direction. Tension builds up while I try to muster the right words to say, but my mind becomes blank. Only rage runs its course in my blood. Louis seems to understand something is wrong and glances over his shoulder.

"You work at Red & Blue Associates? The same Red & Blue that kills innocent people and gets away with it?"

Louis approaches as confusion mirrors his thoughts. Red & Blue Associates, the only company in all of New York I despise and would love to see falling apart, is the same company trying to gain steps into Ariella's work. To have a hold on something dear in my life once again.

"That topic isn't any of your concern," the wrench says. "The driver was to blame for the accident because he was drunk. Not my company."

"If the driver was drunk, you are still to blame for employing him," I say through clenched teeth. "And his drunkenness is not the only thing to blame for the accident."

It's what they want us to believe, anyway. Somehow I doubt it. Money is involved. Money buys silence. I have personally witnessed people getting away with murder because of their own wealth.

I want the truth, yes, for so long I've been dreading to know. Still, I was moving on. I was letting go of this, since it was of no use. Knowing it won't bring him back.

Red & Blue could fight their karma for the rest of my life, yet my son will never be back.

People around stop talking. My hands close into fists, my mind becomes dizzy with the stress clouding my judgment. It's my wife's work, and Ari prepares for this week for an entire year. I want to be on my best behavior.

But it still pierces through my heart, knowing she will be in the same room with this woman or anything associated with the scum from that company.

Irene snorts and crosses her arms over her chest, now gifting me with her attention. "Apparently, anyone can have a say in this.

"People have a say when you get away with murder," I shout, and Louis takes a step forward.

His eyes turn to Ari before she mouths something I can't understand, and her colleague leans toward me. "Not here, Dorian. Please."

Ari's hand touches my arm. Her eyes plead

mercy, something I can't quite comprehend, since we are not at fault in this situation. But then Irene speaks again, and I almost lose it.

"You seem disturbed," she taunts. "Maybe you should go home and let others enjoy the party."

"Dorian," Ari stops me from speaking. My wife parts her lips. One tear travels down her cheek and then I notice how stiff her long fingers are grasping the thin fabric of my shirt. "Don't. Please don't."

"Ari-" I frown at her, trying to see what I am missing, and Irene shields us from the rest of the crowd.

"So, he can call you Ari, but no one else can?"

"Shut up, Irene," my wife mumbles. "Just shut the fuck up."

Her forehead rests against my chest, taking deep breaths. Irene treats her as if they know each other as if they are acquaintances, but I know Ari would never be friends with someone like her. She wouldn't be able to. Not with all the things this woman represents.

"Guys," Louis calls for our attention. "Let's talk outside. People are staring."

"Let them stare," Irene shrugs. "Maybe we can put on a show. Maybe *Ari* here has something she wants to confess."

Ariella turns and faces Irene. Her eyes would burn a hole in Irene's head if they could. Her hand closes into a fist as her body stiffens. It's intimidating enough for people to stop staring. I've seen it happen before.

"You can't keep your mouth shut, can you?"

Irene leans forward and says the words loud enough so I can hear. "I am not the one cheating on him, am I?"

"No," Ariella tilts her head, her body pressed against mine as I pull her away from the woman. As if it's enough to protect her from any danger. "And it's none of your concern. It's *my* marriage, which it does not include you in."

My hand searches my wife's, and I am about to walk us away from Irene, heading to the gardens. The sneer on Irene's face stops me.

"And whose fault is that?" Irene says as we are about to turn around. "Maybe your husband would like to know what you do behind his back. How you look on top of me as I make you come in ways he can't."

16
Ariella

My eyes get dry when I don't blink while facing Dorian. Time stands still for everyone but us. He narrows his gaze in my direction, and I notice the storm in his mind. The venom dripping from Irene's lips taints everything around us.

"*Her*?"

The word is the only thing my husband allows himself to ask, and when I am preparing to reply, Irene does it for me. "Yes. *Me*. I fucked your wife, frenchie."

"Not true," I say as tears gather in my eyes. My hands touch his chest as I try to shift his attention back to me. "We never had sex. Dorian I-"

"You don't need to have sex to cheat on someone," Irene adds.

Louis grabs Irene's arms to shut the woman once and for all, using his weight to drag Irene across the room and away from us.

Nothing can compare to the threat of the silence as I wait for Dorian to speak, to say something and stop the overwhelming fear creeping up on me. The way he is quiet, the way his eyes plead me to lie, is shredding my heart into pieces so small they are like sand slipping between my fingers.

"With all the people you could have cheated with," Dorian says so low it cracks another piece of my heart. "You had to cheat with that woman?"

"Dorian." I lift my hand to touch his arm, but he pulls away from my touch.

"We will talk about this at home."

My husband walks away, leaving me alone in the middle of the room. I turn, watching as he doesn't seem to notice the people looking at him and if he does, Dorian doesn't care.

Someone calls my name, but by now, I can't look away from the man I love whose broken heart is on full display. I can't look away from the hurt I have caused him when securing my truth.

I can't look away from how my past and my future seem to entwine, forcing me to stay glued to the floor. Dorian leaves and I still don't move. I don't think I even breathe.

After what seems like forever, I turn around, searching for Louis. I find him with Irene in a secluded corner. If I am letting my emotions take over, if I have to rant, I will do it on her. I consider tossing away my heels so I can move faster. I want to run after Dorian, wrap my arms around him, and plead for his forgiveness.

But I was never one to beg, and he was never one

to talk when angry.

Funny how people say things like "you should talk" when we all know very well it doesn't work on all of us. For one to talk, the other has to listen and reply without irritation in their voices. They have to speak and not let their emotions take over. If I go after him right now, it will be a disaster. I need to at least give my husband a few minutes to process everything and calm down.

"Finally," Irene mumbles as soon as I am in front of them. "Tell your bodyguard to let me go."

"Thank you, Louis. I'll take care of this now."

Louis nods, still glancing at Irene and mouthing a word I don't dare to repeat in front of anyone. I want to leave. I want to go home and explain to my husband why I cheated on him. Mr. White glances in my direction and I shift my back to him so he doesn't notice the way I struggle not to wrap my hands around Irene's throat.

"Why?"

Her stupid frown has me clutching to my patience like a life vest. "Ari, I was trying…"

"I swear to whatever God you pray to Irene, if you try to call me a fucking nickname, I will drag you across the room by your hair."

She scoffs at my words while I look around. Some guests whisper giving the two of us curious glances. People want to know what's going on. It is no secret there's animosity when Irene's company is involved in any business. Their shady ways, and how they manipulate and use whatever means they can to walk away from the consequences, are a big reason why their stocks keep falling. Red & Blue Associates cares about one thing and one thing only. Money. They still have no clue who I am. Or what they did to me. They didn't even try to learn who was involved in the accident. All they have is a name I don't go by anymore. My boss is aware it was a truck from the other company that hit my car. Hence why it's still hard to understand why the company involved in so many scandals is luring the one I work for.

How much of an idiot can my boss be?

Wait, I shouldn't answer that.

I try to hold back a sigh and fail. "I told you we are over. Dorian is not your business."

"Being a third party in this relationship, and the reason you are leaving me for, I think he will want to be informed of your extra activities."

"I was never yours to begin with. We are done, Irene. I have told you before, I don't want this. I don't want your craziness in my life-"

"Now. You don't want it *now*."

"I never did. You knew from the start it was never going to happen."

Irene takes one step, but I don't move. "I can destroy your entire career if I want to, sweetheart. Test me, and you will never work in this city again."

Her threat feels empty and I turn around, giving

her my back. Someone calls my name, but I don't look. When I turn to the door, I spot Louis stopping Irene from following me. I am missing the fashion show, but to hell with it. I have another priority now and I have given more time to this company than they deserve. The valet calls for my driver, and the car soon arrives. Inside the vehicle, I take my heels and let my head fall against the leather.

"Can you please go a bit faster?" I ask the driver as nicely as possible. "I'll pay for whatever speeding tickets you may get."

As the man nods at me, pushing his foot against the pedal, he doubles the speed on the highway. My gaze lingers on the empty road as I bite down on my lip. A mist is spreading across New York where people walk with no care in the world. They stagger on their feet returning home after a night out.

We pull around the corner at the house entrance. I thank the driver and take a deep breath before stepping into the chilly night. The trees shake as the wind torments them, their branches looking fearful. I can relate.

We were getting there. He was mending, healing. Now I am scared to death that's all over.

I open the front door and the silence swallows me. The air is heavy, I don't know what to fear more. A fight with Dorian or his silence.

I don't want to lose him, not now.

The times I said it would be easier for us to

divorce, this is what I meant. Once all the cards were on the table, I knew it would hurt him more. But I have to be honest, this was my decision, and I need to explain to my husband the plan. The details, the secrets, I need to tell him as much as I can and hopefully not lose his trust.

"Dorian?" I call into the empty hallway, trying to ease my desperate heart and mind, which tells me he left. "Dorian?"

Nothing, no sound, travels through the walls as I take cautious steps into the unknown. It's like slow torture. When I don't blink anymore, I can feel my eyes burning as I keep searching for him.

My hand glides against the wall. The light of the one room I always keep close shines like a beacon in the night. My breathing becomes shallow, my legs threaten to give in at any second with the realization that Dorian is in Raphael's bedroom.

The drumming of my frenetic heartbeat echoes in the house as if it's the principal focus of everyone's attention. I come close to choking for air when spotting a screwdriver still hanging from the lock.

Dorian is sitting in the small bed, holding the notes from the papers I left on top of the dresser. The ones where I plan everything about the day when my soul shattered into pieces. The day I have two prominent memories from it.

Our son dying and my husband's eyes as he asked me what happened.

"You knew," he breathes out. "All this time, you knew who she was."

"Dorian-"

"Tell me, Ariella." Dorian lifts his face from the newspaper article he holds, crumpling it beneath his large hands, and lets it fall on the floor. "Were you with her knowing she's linked to Raphael's death?"

His eyes, the ones I love to watch, beg me for an answer I dread to speak. Tears adorn them, fighting to leave and roll down his cheek, but Dorian does his best not to cry.

He means to hurt me, and I am aware this is the beginning. As soon as I open my mouth to explain last month's events, everything will become worse, harder to realize. Still, I have to try. He is worth it.

We are worth it.

"It's not like that," I tell him as I raise my hand to plead. "Irene is just a means to an end. I never had sex with her. I-"

"Oh please," he scoffs. "You were still with her. When I realized you were seeing someone, I thought it was a random thing, but her? The woman who works at *that* company?"

"I-"

Dorian stands, and I stop speaking. He steps the small distance from the bed to the dresser, opening the notebook.

"She was the killer's boss, Ariella."

The killer. It's what he calls the man who went to

jail. There is a difference between Dorian and me. He blames the company but mainly the driver, believing the police did the right thing and the man did not step on the brakes in time because he was drunk. The only thing Dorian blames Red & Blue is how they got away with it without a reprimand. He knows there's more to it, but stirring that pot will only make things worse, will only build up our pain. But because I remember the events of that day, and I remember the driver screaming at the top of his lungs for help, I don't think like him.

"You think I don't know that? You think-"

"Then why the fuck were you with her?" Dorian asks, raising his voice and I flinch.

My father yelled at me every day. He would use his physical assets and strength, for example, to keep the women of his family at bay. He would scream, knowing I didn't like it. It was a means to an end. A scream from my father meant whatever he wanted got done. He ruled with fear. Having Dorian losing his temper, no matter how right he is, brings out something inside of me.

"I am not," I say, doing my best to hide my emotions in my voice. "I was using her, I needed to know-" My voice breaks at the same time my lungs give in and breathing isn't an option. He wants to know, so be it. Let's see how well my husband can deal with what I keep locked inside. Let's see if he will pull back once he realizes how dark and twisted

I can be. "I need to know who is the one to blame for the accident, so I can finish them in court."

My husband's green eyes study mine for an instant as I try to catch my breath. Dorian parts his lips as if he were going to tell me his thoughts. I can't explain what I mean until he is ready to listen.

Until the man I love is in the right mindset, nothing will get in his head.

"You are taking them to court?" Dorian asks, his voice softening.

"I am. There's a lawsuit already happening. Red & Blue Associates is a well-known company, but my lawyer kept my name hidden for the most part. She hinted them with the name my parents gave me. They have been trying to get in contact with me, to silence whatever I have to say."

He falls onto the chair. I notice his eyes searching mine for answers to the questions he hasn't asked yet. Dorian takes a deep breath, running his hand through his hair and looking down at me.

"And you couldn't tell me this?"

"It's my burden to bear Dorian, not yours-"

"I am his father too Ariella," he raises his voice over mine and interrupts my explanation. "I lost my son as well, not just you."

"But you weren't in the car. You didn't see him die. I did. I closed his eyes."

He inhales and throws the piece of paper back on the bed. "No, you're right. I didn't."

Dorian stands pacing out into the hallway and into our bedroom. I listen to him stepping into the closet and follow the sound, only to notice the bag on the bed as my husband grabs clothes from the shelves. He walks around at a furious pace, picking up a few things and throwing them into the bag.

"What are you doing?"

"Leaving."

It's like a slap in the face. My eyes become numb from the suppressed tears before the pain in them only mirrors the torment in my heart. I watch my husband, the man I have failed to show my love for the last year, grant me what I wanted weeks ago.

To be alone.

"Leaving?" I ask again as Dorian sighs and stops with his hand on the top shelf.

"Yes. Wasn't that what you wanted all along?"

"Dorian I-" my feet take cautious steps before he glances in my direction.

"Leave me alone, Ari," my husband warns, the evidence of a threat I am not familiar with hanging in the air.

"Now you want to be alone? This is the exact reason I said it was better for us to divorce. I knew you wouldn't understand-"

"That you are fucking the woman who helped to make our lives miserable?"

"I didn't have sex with her."

"But you kissed her, you touched her in some

way and she tainted you."

My husband turns to face me. His eyes pierce mine with the accusation shooting from them. Tainted. If it were anyone else, I am pretty sure Dorian could let it go. But being Irene makes things a thousand times worse. Words seem to trap themselves inside his mind and when I take a step closer, my husband shakes his head.

"I need to leave," he says, taking a deep breath. "Before I say something, I will regret."

Dorian passes by me, throwing the clothes in the bag and heading towards the bathroom to pick up his toiletries. I bite on my tongue and all the pain I have been pushing aside for the last days surfaces. But the pain is coming like a wave, bringing an emotion it wasn't supposed to tag along with it. Fury invades me by my husband not understanding. The words he just spoke reverberate in my mind because I know the meaning behind them.

"Say it," I yell towards the bathroom. "Whatever it is you're not saying, at least grant me something this time. I am being honest with you, but you can't do the same. Don't just look at me as if I am the reason for everything that is wrong in our lives."

Dorian walks towards me as the words pierce through him. He steps beside the bed, standing at an arm's reach before I speak again, this time staring straight into his eyes as I want the words to sink in.

When you fight someone, sometimes you want to

hurt them with what you say, but it's not the case here. I don't want to hurt him. I want him to be honest with me as I am being honest with him, and running away isn't the right thing to do.

Not anymore.

"Right," I sigh when he doesn't speak. "You won't say what's on your mind. You never do."

"I don't fucking care what you do with her anymore," Dorian says. "I don't care if you cheat with some random person. I don't care about what you want to do, and if you want to bring Red & Blue Associates down, so be it. What I care about is why you are doing everything without letting me know. I *care* you got involved with her. Out of everyone, you got involved with someone we both despise, Ariella. As usual, I am not as important in our marriage as I thought I was because you want to do everything by yourself. Just like on that day, when you weren't supp-"

My husband presses his lips together as I close my hands into fists while lifting my chin in his direction.

"Say it, Dorian," I whisper to him, and our gazes lock. "Admit you blame me."

"For taking him to the park without me? Yes, I do. Happy?" He continues over my voice, and my heart sinks.

I swallow my emotions and press my tongue inside my mouth to stop the cry. But it's no use. I fight it, but tears fall down my cheeks. As soon as they do, I wipe them off with more fury than necessary. He doesn't need to see me cry. He doesn't need to see how hard his words struck.

Dorian's face softens and regret spreads all over his features as he parts his lips, lifting his hand towards me.

"Ari-" he tries stepping closer, but I take a step back.

"No," I say as my husband tries to touch me, but I don't let him. I place both hands on Dorian's chest and push myself away from him. "I asked you to be honest, and you were. I just need a few minutes."

Not wanting to hear anything else, I step away, knowing my shattered heart will have a hard time healing after this.

17
Ariella

When I walk back inside the house, my eyes burn with the tears I shed for the last hour under the willow tree, but I don't see *him*. Dorian's car is outside. However, he isn't anywhere in the house.

So, I tiptoe into our bedroom, laying on the bed and allowing the emotions I kept at bay for a year to take over me. My body succumbs to the sobs. I close my eyes at the unpleasant thought of fear. If there's one thing I dislike is being alone at this house. When it happens, when there's no sound coming from the hallways, I swear my memories betray me with my son's giggles.

Footsteps approach and I clasp my hand harder against my mouth while a cry crawls to break free in my throat. I fight the urge to scream at myself. If I could have died last year when the truck hit us, I would. This type of pain is new, but at the same time, it's not. It's the type of pain when I know there is nothing else I can do. Life will still suck when I open my eyes tomorrow.

This is why Thea wants me to speak, why she

insists on me sharing my pain, which I never do. My emotions are all inside of me, and it's dangerous.

"Ari," his baritone sounds uncertain behind me before the bed shifts under Dorian's weight. "Please look at me."

I can't allow myself to crumble in front of him, to let the man I love see my darkest state. Dorian moves, laying behind me as his arms wrap around my body, and when he whispers three words into my ear, all I have been holding onto, all the pain I try to suppress rushes over like a wave drifting to the shore.

"I am sorry."

My body shakes as a wail escapes my lungs, and my husband turns me around. I hide my face in his chest. I do what I wanted to do all these months ago, but the fear of rejection didn't allow me to. I rely on him to help me with this. Dorian kisses the top of my head, his fingers crawling between the strings of my hair before I lift my gaze to his.

"I'm sorry," I mumble as best as I can. "I'm so sorry."

"Ari, don't…" he breathes out.

"I should never have picked him up earlier. I should have come home like you wanted us to," my voice breaks. Dorian lifts my chin, pulling our faces closer. "I'm sorry."

"*Non*," he mumbles, holding my gaze. "I don't blame you, baby. I can't blame you for it, and I should never say it just to hurt you. I shouldn't have said it, but I- I will always feel guilty for not being there with the two of you."

His eyes sparkle as the tears rush through them. For over a year, it's the first time we speak about our emotions, about what happened, about how we have been hiding from each other.

"No, I shouldn't-"

"You went to pick up our son because you wanted to see him smile. He loved feeding the ducks at the park. You did nothing wrong, Ari. I can't even think I could have lost you, too."

His gaze stays on mine before I close my eyes and part my lips. I wait for the man that can take my pain away to claim me as his. It's all I want now, to lose myself in him, in his touch.

Dorian kisses me, closing the distance between us. He lets the kiss we share be the way we speak, how we apologize. How we forget, even for a moment, that this conversation still has a long way to go.

"I'm sorry," Dorian breathes out.

He sits on the bed and takes me along with him. My legs wrap around his waist and I feel the ache of his body between my legs. My husband unbuttons my shirt before sliding it away from my skin.

It doesn't take long for us to be closer to each other, physically and emotionally. For my husband to make love to me, in a way he hasn't for so long.

For me to thrust down, staring at his green eyes while Dorian guides me with his hands on my waist. He makes promises with his kisses, he speaks words with his touch, and we both confess our emotions to each other.

"I love you." I allow it to come through my lips, reaching the desired climax. Dorian smiles before kissing me, and in a minute, he joins me into the blissful confession of his heart as well.

"Je t'aime, Ari."

The sun is not out yet as we lay in bed, and my mind is free from the torment it faced hours ago.

I cling to my husband as his fingers caress my naked back. Dorian presses his lips against the top of my head. I suck in a breath, still trying to assimilate time and place. My husband and I always knew how to solve our problems and decrease the stress in the air after a fight, usually by being intimate. But now there is so much more happening every time Dorian touches me.

It's the way his eyes plead for mine to complete him.

Intimacy is more than sex to us. It's the little things and how we act towards each other. Sometimes a kiss speaks volumes, as words cannot fill the void left by someone. I am a person who needs actions to know things are coming as I want them. Words fail. They lie and deceive. Actions don't.

Dorian stops, his fingertips grazing a part of my skin I always keep hidden even from him. He touches it as if it is the most delicate thing ever. My husband caresses the scar I carry for over a year. He leans in, pressing a kiss against it.

"You never showed it to me," he says. "I am surprised it's this big."

"The doctor said they had to do a larger incision because of the debris."

Almost three inches of a line at my right side, beneath my lung. I blacked out in the car as the paramedics were rushing to us. The next time my eyes opened, I was in a hospital bed, and Dorian was already in the room.

This scar reminds me of the loss I carry.

"I have been angry at myself all this time," I confess, and Dorian shifts on the bed to stare me in the eyes. He wants me to continue, and I realize this is what will either make us or break us. There is no point in me hiding this piece of me from the man I love. "I survived."

"Ari," he breathes out, swallowing his pain. My husband's hands lift my face as we both sit on the bed, the sheet sliding from my body and exposing every part of me. "Don't even say it."

"Dorian, I shouldn't have survived. Not after that day. Not after Raphael died. It should have been me, not him."

My voice breaks, and my vision becomes fogged with the tears threatening to break free. Dorian pulls me closer to him, allowing his arms to hold me against his chest and humming a tune into my ears. I calm down from the pain that threatens to swallow me whole one day.

"If you died," he whispers, leaning away so he looks down at me. "What would it be of me?" A tear falls from the corner of my eye and he kisses it away. "I already lost him. We already lost our son, Ari. Don't let me lose you too."

His fingers brush a string of hair from my eyes. My lips find his on a whim as all I can say, all I can do, is expose my broken heart to the man I love. When I fall asleep again in his arms, despite the tears staining my cheeks, I fall asleep smiling.

The sizzling sound of a pan makes me stir on the bed before the smell of food wakes me up from my slumber. My eyes pop open as I sit on the disheveled sheets searching for a clothing piece, only to find my husband's shirt on the floor.

I slide Dorian's shirt on, covering my naked body while strolling towards the kitchen. My breathing catches when I find Dorian in sweatpants mixing ingredients inside a pan and being soaked by the first sun rays coming from the window.

He glances in my direction, grinning, before letting his gaze travel to the pan.

"Did I wake you?" My husband asks, and I notice how his eyes linger on my figure as I sit on one of the kitchen island stools.

"No. The smell did."

Dorian turns, holding a wooden spoon and lifting it to my lips, so I taste his cooking, and the savory flavor punches my taste buds.

"You woke up early," I say, glancing at the window, then the clock, realizing I have less time this morning to be with him before leaving for work.

"I only have one thing I need to attend to today at the office."

"Is everything okay?"

Dorian shrugs. "They do not need my presence all the time." He moves around grabbing more ingredients. "I want you to take your lunch to the office. So, I cooked yours and Louis 's-"

"You cooked for Louis too?"

There is a beat of silence before he speaks again. "I know you eat with him," Dorian mumbles, turning around from the stove. "Is it wrong?"

"No. It is not wrong at all. Thank you."

He turns the stove off, placing the still hot food on the recipient for me to eat later. I step out of the stool, walk towards him, and lace my arms around his waist, letting my face rest against his exposed back.

"I can skip work," I confess.

"No," Dorian replies, facing me. Green eyes borrow mine while he speaks. "You have to do this thing with Red & Blue. I don't like knowing she is in the same room as you. But it's work."

"I won't be alone with Irene. Louis will be with me the entire time, and if you didn't notice, he despises her."

"I noticed," he laughs. His thumb brushes my cheek and he becomes serious. "I am only asking you to consider letting this go, Ari. For us."

"Dorian… I want to know."

"I get it," he says, taking my face between his hands. "But it won't bring him back. You want revenge from someone who does not care and wont ever face the consequences of their actions. They won't ever be at fault for hiring that man baby. All this anger you still feel about it needs to be directed somewhere. But ruining them will not bring our boy back. We can talk about it later. Just promise me you won't act on this until we figure out what to do."

I dip my chin. Dorian leans forward, his lips brushing mine before allowing a kiss to be shared. My hands drift on his back, pulling our bodies closer. As the kiss deepens, my husband's hands seem to lose control of the hold on me, drifting from my waist to other parts of my body.

"How long till you have to be at the office?" He

asks with a mischievous grin.

"I can arrive late."

I part my lips for him and my husband slides his tongue into my mouth. My hand is already sliding beneath the waistband of his pants and wrapping around him. Tingles spread all over my body when Dorian groans into the kiss. His mouth brushes against mine, traveling down my neck sending sparks all over my skin. He bites on my shoulder and lets his hands drift beneath the shirt I wear forcing a moan out of me as his fingers glide down. When my husband realizes I am only wearing his shirt, he lets go of a sound from the back of his throat. It brings a smile to my lips.

Knowing his eyes are on me, I fall on my knees and tug my husband's sweats down along with his underwear. My mouth waters at the sight before I wrap my lips around him. He hits the back of my throat and when I glance up, the praise in my husband's eyes only increases my need for him. But I don't touch myself. Not yet.

"Fuck," he hisses, and I know he is trying to hold on the best he can.

Dorian fists my hair, thrusting in and out and when I know he is close enough, my husband pulls away. I almost whimper, but when I look up the promise of what is about to come spreads all across his face. I bite down on my lip as the man I love grabs me from the floor and places me on top of the counter. He slips his shirt off me so fast I fear he ripped it.

My nipples perk at the cold and Dorian pinches one between his fingertips, dropping his mouth on the other before he continues to kiss down on my body. My husband parts my legs and looks up at me. His eyes meet mine and at the first lick of his tongue, it's as if my body becomes alive again.

"Dorian," I moan. Loud enough to have him humming against me in approval.

His lips suck on my clit and my body heats up. Sweat drips from his back and by the time I can feel my orgasm building up Dorian grabs my thighs to keep me in place. He thrusts one finger inside me. Then the second. Then a third and I bite down on my lip.

I love everything about this man. Even his damn fingers.

My body trembles, but my husband doesn't stop. His kisses slow down, but I don't have time to complain about the loss. Dorian flips me around and leans me against the kitchen counter. He looks at me dripping, my ass rubbing against his crotch. His gaze, the way it caresses my body without even touching me has me falling in love with this man all over again.

"*Ma belle*," he says kissing my shoulder and positioning himself at my entrance before ever so slowly completing me.

"*Putain*," he hisses, taking the words right out of

my mouth.

My husband kisses my back. It's sweet and slow, and I feel his entire body wanting to touch mine. My legs almost fail me, but Dorian grabs my waist from behind. "So beautiful," he murmurs against my shoulder. His fingertips caress my skin as he keeps his hold on me. "Let me hear you, Ari."

And I do. With every touch, with every kiss, I let him hear what he does to me. When Dorian leans forward and kisses me, when he pinches my nipples, when he rubs my clit, I call his name. He ruins my body. He ruins it with every caress.

When he feels me close enough, my husband goes faster. Harder. Giving me every inch of his need. He grasps my skin and I hold on to the counter as both of us reach our orgasms.

Panting and a sweaty mess in the kitchen, I open my eyes to find him already staring at me.

"How the fuck am I focusing on work today?" Dorian confesses. His lips touch my shoulders and he mumbles against my skin. "When all I can think about is having you naked in front of me?"

"You will have to manage," I say, and the smile that takes over his face is the most beautiful thing I have seen.

Dorian's lips meet mine once more, but this time it's as if they are talking about a promise. Something we both crave. I get away from him long enough to put some clothes on while he cleans the kitchen.

“See you in a bit,” I say, and he tugs me by the wrist.

Dorian gives me one last kiss before I leave the house. I swear one kiss alone almost makes me call in sick for work while I drive into the city. Something tells me I should enjoy and spend all of my time with him.

I hum my favorite tune, strolling into my office while greeting everyone who's already working. It's a little past the hour I usually arrive, but I'm sure no one is going to notice. I can always say I had to go to the store before coming.

My hand pushes on my office door, and I open it, sliding inside the room, realizing someone is following me.

“You're in a good mood,” Louis states as I drop my purse and bag on my chair and rearrange what they left on my desk.

Arriving late has its perks, but it also means I have people who drop their work to be checked on my desk. A new sample of fabric catches my eye and I swipe it into my hands. It's green. Like the dark olives from our trip to Italy. Maybe I can design a shirt for Dorian using this one.

“I guess so,” I let out, not being able to stop the smile from spreading on my lips.

Louis tilts his head. He glances at the bag I left next to my things, and before I can wrap my hand around it to place it inside the minibar, my colleague is already taking one recipient out and frowning.

"You brought lunch? I thought we were going to eat at the new Chinese place."

"Dorian cooked," I reply, still not able to hide my happiness. "The second one is yours."

He blinks. "He made lunch for me?"

Louis's eyes almost gleam as he lets go of my gaze and stares with utter fondness at the food prepared by my husband. My colleague makes a surprised sound and I wonder if something is wrong.

"Oh," Louis chuckles. "I guess this is for you."

His fingers hold a small yellow post-it, yet my friend appears amused by its content as I take a few seconds to realize what this is.

He wouldn't.

Louis places the paper on top of my desk, walking away, still smiling, and putting the food in my fridge for later. My eyes, however, are absorbing the words written in front of me.

Starting over means I am taking you on a date tonight.
I love you.

I pick it up, reading the word love, trying to make it sink in. It still feels unreal, even after so many years. The phone at my desk beeps. "Yes?"

"Mrs. Vaillant, I have a representative from Red & Blue Associates here to see you."

I almost roll my eyes before catching myself. "We

don't have a meeting today. Please tell Ms. Rogers I am busy. Whatever she has to say, she can send me an email or she can take it upstairs to the board."

I end the call, promising myself I will give Patricia, my secretary, a bonus next week. Even through the walls, Irene's voice travels as she demands Patricia to come into the office and tell me it's important. Which we both know it's not.

If she isn't giving me a name, I can get one at court. It will be harder, and my chances of winning drop by a considerable amount, but today I won't care about it. Knowing that I still have the love of the man I call my husband makes me feel lucky. Dorian wants me to drop everything. He wants me to forget this, but I don't think I can. I will forget the idea of seeking answers from the source. However, as far as taking them to court, Dorian and I need to talk about it.

"She will not stop," Louis warns. It wipes away the smile on my face. "Irene is used to having what she wants Ariella. You know this better than anyone, and what she wants now is you."

"I know."

Screams come from the hallway and soon enough they fade. Patricia must be urging Irene out. She is getting a bonus and a spa day.

18
Dorian

It's been a few days since Ari and I went back to our routine. I did not come to the office this week, working from home and waiting for Ari.

The sound of my phone buzzing on my desk alerts me to a text. My wife's name appears in bright letters, and I smile. It's lunchtime, which means she has a bit of time to herself.

She must have seen the post-it I slipped into the pocket of her jacket today.

Ari: **Are we going on another lunch date?**

I nibble on my bottom lip, trying to reply, as a knock on my door interrupts me. If there is something I never enjoyed is being interrupted when the subject is the woman I love. It's the only reason I almost don't reply to whoever is outside.

"Yes?"

My eyes don't lift to see who enters as I type an answer, yet the heavy footsteps let me know it's the same person who comes to disturb my peace whenever he has nothing better to do.

Dorian: Yes
Maybe you should take a long lunch break today
I don't know for how long I want to keep you

"You seem happy," Josh's voice travels to my ears, and I can almost see the grin on his lips without even lifting my eyes from my phone. "What's happening? Why aren't you the usual gloomy self you seem to parade around here?"

"I am meeting Ari for lunch," I announce, and Josh freezes in his spot, eyes wide and tilting his head in question. "What?"

He shakes his head in response to the intrusive thoughts he was having, a large grin appearing on his thin lips as he continues walking towards the window, slumping on the sofa as if it were his own. Sometimes I wonder how carefree he can be. Then, I realize I don't want to know the answer.

"You are calling her Ari again."

The nickname was always something easy for me, something I would call her whenever I was in a happy mood. I sit in my chair as Josh takes out the file for the horse arriving today and the preparations needed so the seller doesn't make a last-minute decision and pulls back our deal. It wouldn't be the first time.

But it's the minor tune coming from Josh's lips as he taps his foot on the rug beneath my desk that has me asking. "Something on your mind?"

The younger furrows his brow at me. "No."

"Did you take Thea out on a date already?"

Josh scoffs, flipping the pages of the folder with a little more force than intended, and I chuckle at his discomfort. The most carefree guy I know, Mr. "No strings attached" now, can't even ask a girl out.

"She asked. I said yes. We're meeting for drinks tonight."

I am about to speak my mind about his dating life when the sound of a fist hitting my door alerts me. "Yes?"

Zoe peeks inside, her eyes darting from me to Josh, who takes his phone out. They don't like each other, and it's fine as long as they can maintain a proper work relationship. Something tells me, however, it's harder on my friend than my secretary.

"Do you need anything before I head out on my lunch break, sir?"

"Yes, I do Ms. Young. I need to talk to you about your contract."

She frowns, and so does Josh, who stops typing on his phone. His thumb hovers his screen. I open the first drawer of my desk and take the folder with the document the lawyer sent earlier.

"What about my contract?"

I motion for her to sit in front of me. Josh does not stay around while I deal with stuff like this. However, considering everything that happened with Zoe, plus with his recent promotion, it is fundamental that he deals with the rest of the staff. Laying people off and hiring them are things he needs to know how to do.

Zoe glances over her shoulder at Josh, who doesn't spare her a second of his attention. "Sign this," I say, handing her the folder.

"What is this?"

"It is a document stating we will not renew your contract. You will receive financial compensation, of course."

She scoffs and glances at me before resuming reading. The lawyer and I talked it over. Despite us getting involved, Zoe pursued me. The legal document Zoe is reading states as much. If she takes legal action against me or the company, I will do the same.

"I'm not signing this shit," she throws the folder on top of my desk. "You harassed me as well."

"I could have stopped your advances. Ms. Young, what happened the other night between us was a mistake. One I regret deeply. Therefore, I think it is for the best, and for both of our protection, we do not work together anymore. The company will pay your salary until the end of your contract period, plus a bonus for compensation.

"But-"

"Let it go Zoe," Josh sighs.

"I am a woman," she snaps at him. "Who do you think a judge is most likely to believe? You, the boss, or me, the secretary who pushed you away?"

A slow grin spreads on my lips. "I see you forgot about the surveillance cameras we have installed at the office all those months ago." Zoe's scowl doesn't seem to subside. "I asked our lawyer. We can use the images from the night you tried to seduce me if needed, as well as this sweet confession of yours. It's decided Ms. Young. Please pack your things until the end of the day."

19
Ariella

Her footsteps are soft as the door opens, and I smile as my therapist paces inside my vast office. Thea has been here before, although I have been avoiding our sessions like a healthy person avoids the plague.

But I am tired of running away.

"Your office is way nicer than mine," she says as her eyes take in the surroundings. "Apparently, I went into the wrong business."

"I get by," I chuckle, standing to greet her. "It's nice of you to come here."

"If I didn't, you wouldn't ever come to see me this week. One works with what she has."

"I'm sorry, I don't have a hot guy walking around the stables," I reply, motioning her to the chairs in front of my desk.

Thea quirks a brow. "I see you and your husband have been sharing some information."

"Have you called him?"

"Who-"

"Josh."

"We're meeting for drinks."

My smile gets wider as I sit in the chair, knowing she is getting uncomfortable with the switch of roles.

"Is it a date?"

"Aren't you curious?" She laughs. "I'll answer all your questions, but only after today's session."

Well, I tried. Her life is way more entertaining than talking about mine. I know Thea is trying to help, and we were scratching the surface of my issues when my walls lifted, and I closed myself all over again.

My fingers tap against my leg. "What do you want me to talk about?"

"Let's talk about how the date with your husband turned out," she tilts her head and waits for this to be a comfortable topic for me.

"Dorian did everything right. He has been there for me whenever I need him."

"And you?"

"I have been trying my best.".

Somehow it doesn't feel my best is enough. With all the affection he has been giving me, especially with being present when I cry in the middle of the night, it doesn't feel I am doing enough to show him I still want to be in this marriage.

"He is happy with your best," she assures me when I raise my brows in shock. "The other thing you had going on?"

"Extinguished," I state, staring straight at her.

My emotions tangle, and it's hard for me to notice which one is the one choking me into a tight deadly grip—leaving Irene behind has been letting me breathe a bit more. I know revenge can blind people, but feeling it gripping me is different.

"Have you talked about Raphael?"

"Dorian did, not about the accident itself, but about how we felt for the last year. He says he doesn't blame me."

"I bet it took a weight off your shoulders."

It did. Even so, I'm waiting for the shoe to drop since everything else in my life never seems to be easy. It never seems to give me the ending I need.

Is not bringing justice to my son's death.

Thea takes it easy on me. Her questions are not too harsh, and I take my time answering them. She gives me a few hints on what to do when dark thoughts haunt me, and I listen, wanting nothing more than improving.

"It's progress. Even if you don't see it, each session is progress," she tells me, placing everything inside her bag.

"I'll see you next week?"

"You probably won't," Thea smiles, and I frown. "Since I am dating your friend, I think it is time, Ariella."

My hands sweat and I glance away from her. Thea and I have an agreement. The day she thinks our relationship is becoming too personal, she will redirect Dorian and me to one of her colleagues. Despite conflicts of interest, I convinced her to keep me as a patient. This time, however, I can see the resolution on her face.

"But-"

"It's time Ariella. We both know it. You want me around, but not as a therapist, and I am too involved. We had this conversation before," Thea explains as gently as she can. "Don't worry. I will pass the case on to my colleague. I think you will like her. She is very capable. You can begin your sessions next week."

"Is there no other way?" Thea shakes her head.

I wish there was because I don't know how comfortable I will be with a new stranger. We walk towards the door as Thea tilts her head, turning to face Louis. He approaches, not pleased with whatever was said in the meeting he is coming from.

"Well, your office has a marvelous view as well. Although it's not Josh," Thea admits.

Louis smiles at Thea but doesn't give me the opportunity to introduce them as someone approaches behind him.

"Irene is here."

Louis stares at me while Thea cocks a brow when she realizes I am not pleased with the name slipping through my friend's lips. Irene, the one person I don't want to see today, decides to drop by.

From the corner of my eye, I notice a minor commotion coming towards my office and the heels I have grown familiar with approach. My secretary carries a vase in her hands, the flowers on it covering most of her upper frame as Louis turns to look in the direction I am gazing. He rushes to help, knowing the smaller girl struggles to see the path beneath her feet, becoming a walking hazard.

"What's this?" Louis asks, walking towards Patricia and taking the flowers from her small hands. She sighs in relief and hands me the card attached to the gift that now seems to be the floor's primary focus.

Watching from a distance, Irene crosses her arms over her chest. Her all-black attire, a pair of high-waisted slacks that hug her tiny waist, pairing with a blouse that has the last button open to display the slightest hint of her underwear.

"Dorian's?" Thea's voice makes me snap my head at her as we follow Louis through my office.

"Yes."

It's a bouquet of camellias, in shades of pink and white, swimming in small accents of green displayed between the flowers. As my eyes absorb its beauty, the sound of Thea clearing her throat makes me chuckle.

"You still haven't read the note," she admits, her curiosity too strong to hide.

"Because it's private," I let out, glancing at my curious friends. "You're not my therapist anymore. I don't have to share what you ask me to."

Also, because this feels like some sort of movie

where the other girls are waiting for my confirmation to squeal and mock me till the sun fades outside. I don't want to be mocked, especially by the man that can shove an entire meatball in his mouth during lunch.

Maybe introducing Thea to Louis was not my brightest idea.

But it's also because as soon as I read this note, my feet will sway by my husband's love, and I will lean to him once more. No matter how much I want to run into his arms right now, I still have work to do here; he is at work as well.

As soon as you get home, I want you naked and ready for me. I want to lick every inch of your body.

"She's smiling," Thea mumbles with a giggle, leaning toward Louis. "He either wrote something sweet or sexy."

"You think he wrote a sexy note for her to read at work?" Louis asks, amused. "I mean, do they-"

"You know nothing, sweetheart," my new friend says, waving her hand in the air. "I learned recently that these two could go at it for hours no matter what was happening."

"Is the source of your gossip Josh?" I ask, cocking my brow and peeking at the woman. "Because those words sound a lot like his."

"My sources are private."

"So is my card."

They both whisper behind my back as my focus shifts to the bouquet. Nothing in this world can explain the feeling, the emotion of being the center of Dorian's attention. No matter how confident I am with how I look, Dorian always knows what will make me smile knowing he is looking only at me.

No one else.

Not in the way I can get lost in him and lose myself. More of a *I see only you and no other woman* kind of thing. Those feelings are coming back all over again.

"Flowers? I am more of a wine woman."

I turn to stare at Irene, not waiting for an invitation while lazily strolling into my office.

I am more than uncomfortable with Irene in the room and with Thea here, my anxiety spikes. I am not one to be read easily, but Louis is. Irene, although her eyes are cold as ice, sometimes the way she stares at me can give it all away. The only reason Dorian didn't figure it out was that he was so fixated on Louis he could not see what was right in front of him.

Dorian knows about my sexuality. He knows what happened in my past and why I came to New York. He is the only one I ever told.

"Everyone has a taste," I reply, not sparing her a glance and smiling at the flowers now resting on my desk. "It doesn't mean it's the right one."

Irene smirks at my comment. Thea glances at both of us. This is how it started, how the two of us got involved. I was seeking information about her, but she saw it as a game. She would chase, and I would put up a fight. It was a challenge for her. One Irene grew fond of. But one I never knew how to deal with.

It seems she never had to fight too much to get what she wanted. Because I wasn't feeling intimidated by her presence, job and personality, it enticed her to pursue something I couldn't say no to, or so she thought.

The more I push her away, the more she wants to stay, and every time I gift her with my attention, it seems her wall crumbles further down.

"Why are you here?" My voice cuts through the tension in the office.

"We have a meeting about the end of the year campaign. I thought I should drop by."

"The meeting you forced on us? I gave the approval of the campaign last week."

"Don't be like this Ariella. You know I am needed. Someone from my company has to approve whatever it is you do here."

Not for long.

"I'll take you to the meeting room," Louis says, and Irene ignores him. "Mrs. Vaillant will join us as soon as she is ready."

Thea's gaze follows Irene as she leaves with

Louis. Her head tilts as her eyes narrow before she turns them to me and speaks.

"That's the person you were cheating on Dorian with, isn't she?"

I heave a sigh while walking towards my desk, letting my fingers glide through my hair and pushing away the strings of hair falling over my eyes. Thea follows close by, sliding to the chair across the desk, the same one she used for our session.

For reasons greater than my pride, I owe her an explanation. Dorian already knows, and if this is going to work out between us, then I should take the weight out of my chest.

Or at least some parts of it.

"Irene and I weren't together," I say, exhausted from the topic. "I wanted to know more about her company, about some of her work."

"Why her company?"

"She is the Vice President of Red & Blue. She got a promotion a month after the accident," I explain, not meeting her gaze but knowing the small gasp hanging in the air comes from her lips. "The same company responsible for the car accident."

"Ariella-"

"I know what you are about to say, Thea. But I am already too deep in this."

My eyes lift to meet hers, and Thea's expression mirrors mine. Fogged by suppressed emotions, I don't allow to show others. This woman was the one who helped me during the darkest time of my life; she was the one who walked me through my pain and accept it.

Literally, since we used to avoid her office during the first sessions, preferring to be outside, as if we were just two friends chatting.

She is also one reason I can cope with it now.

"Does Dorian know?"

"He knows I was seeing her. He knows there's more to it as I am searching for answers. But he doesn't understand how deep this is. He wants me to let it go, but it's too late. I already filed the lawsuit."

I can see her processing it all. Thea shifts in her seat, staring back at me and I do my best to remain unfazed when I am anything but.

"You're still seeing her? Do you have feelings-"

"No," I reply right away. "But I'm still not done finding answers. The court is setting a trial date. Irene doesn't know I am the one suing her company, nor that I am Raphael's mother. I did not mean us to become tangled like this, but she wouldn't speak otherwise… I know my actions were wrong, but at the time it was difficult to understand it."

"And do you have them? The answers?"

"Irene doesn't like to touch the subject of the accident, let alone who paid the cops. They nominated her Vice President after they fired the last one. She has to know."

Thea presses her lips together. “She hasn't told you about the accident?”

“Bits and pieces. She admits her company received backlash, and she tells me about the trial and what her lawyers are doing, but not much more.”

My friend taps her finger against her arm, folding one over the other while following my train of thought and my case. “Have you considered maybe it was her paying the police?”

20
Dorian

The clatter of Zoe placing her belongings in a box gives me peace. Josh doesn't even hide his grin. Earlier today, he interviewed a couple of new candidates, and I left the decision to pick one up to him. If I spend less time at the office, he will be the one dealing daily with whoever we hire. Zoe has until the end of the day to clear her desk, and as I pass by her, followed by my friend, I notice how she pouts.

It's for the best. I could keep her around until the end of her contract, but it feels wrong. Ari and I are in a much better place. We started couples' therapy again. Thea called me to give the info about our new therapist. My wife and I also sleep in the same bed every night. We almost never fight, and even when we do, it's small things like who didn't load the dishwasher. And it still ends up in a steamy make-out session at the kitchen table.

The fire in my wife is back. The attitude that made me fall in love with her is still there, and I am enjoying every moment I can with her.

Josh closes the office door behind us, waiting only a moment before letting his voice fill the silence. "I can't believe you did it. I mean, I knew she was bound to go, but still."

I sit down in my chair, waiting for peace. Ari sent a text that she was heading home as soon as she finishes the last piece she was working on. I am waiting for the clock to hit five so I can run and meet her.

"It had to be done," I reply.

"The one I hired will keep his hands to himself."

"Josh-"

"I'm just saying," he raises his hands to the side of his head. "The girl was always too eager to have sex."

My gaze narrows as I turn in the chair to look at my friend. His fingers fidget with a pen, twirling it in the air as if it's nothing before his curious gaze lands on mine.

Josh raises a brow. "What?"

"Did she hit on you?"

"I-" he stumbles on the words but gives up and sighs. "Hit on me is a mild way of putting it. It was a long time ago. I think she was working here for a couple of weeks. Zoe told me she was ready for us to get *acquainted*."

As soon as word got out that she was leaving, a couple of people came to my office, saying she did the same to other employees. Like groping one of the younger guys without his consent. But I did not know about Josh. It leaves me wondering how many people get away with stuff like this. It is usually someone with power over others who takes things too far.

Harass is harass. I do not accept it. No matter the assaulter's and victims' gender. Men and women need to report stuff like this so the offenders can get the right punishment. But it's not like the system helps the victims. It's not as if the ones who should help never fail those who need them. It's why so many people are quiet about it. But it won't happen again under my roof. If I can stop it I will.

I want Zoe to get out of the office peacefully, but after everything I learned today, I will drag her out myself if I have to.

"I have nothing against meaningless sex, but sex with people from work… Not fond of it."

"What about sex with your best friend's therapist?"

My question makes Josh choke on air as he stands and heads toward the door. He then gives up, turning to face me, and pointing a finger in my direction. I lean back in my seat, waiting for the fury to subside. I am not willing to know if he and Thea have reached that point yet. But I want to make him as uncomfortable as I can. Think of it as revenge for every prank, every time he calls to annoy me, or even when he takes my wife's side during fights.

"*Former* therapist. And it's-"

"None of my business," I interject with a cheeky grin. "I know. Still, both of you seem quite happy."

A loud commotion comes from the hallway. Eli's voice. He is asking something, his tone raising, but not in anger. Frustration laces it instead, and Josh and I share a glance before walking towards where the sound comes from.

Madam Luck evades me every time I need her. It's like she enjoys toying with my life. Of all the days Eli could visit, today is not a good one.

I open the door, not wasting any time, and my eyes meet my friends. He stands in front of Zoe's desk, waiting for the girl to reply to him. Zoe answers the question we couldn't hear clear enough.

"I am leaving."

"I can see that," Eli says. "But why?"

Josh glances at me as I mouth the words, "take him out of here." Eli is someone who doesn't act on rage, but he doesn't enjoy being caught off guard. I don't think his feelings for Zoe were that deep, but I don't want to take chances.

"Eli, can I talk to you outside?" Josh tries placing a hand on Eli's shoulder.

Zoe is the one who catches my attention, as she doesn't seem to realize what is happening. I don't think she even sees Eli interested in her as more than just the girl he enjoys teasing. If she knows he likes her, she doesn't give away any hints about it. "Mr. Vaillant decided it was best for me to leave since I was messing up his personal life."

I glare at her before Josh whispers a "be quiet" in the girl's direction. Zoe shrugs at him. She doesn't even get bothered by what is happening, and yet Eli is about to ask for more explanations. I try to come up with something, but as Zoe walks around her desk, I gulp when she glances over her shoulder.

"I am leaving now," she declares, and I nod, thinking it was long gone. I should have done this months ago. "I hope firing me is worthy. Maybe now your wife can stop being jealous."

"She is not jealous of you, Ms. Young, nor am I firing you because she asked. You are leaving because I want you to. And refrain yourself from speaking about Mrs. Vaillant. She has my last name for a reason."

Zoe's face reddens, and she looks away. With the box close to her, she passes by my two friends. Eli watches her go, but when his eyes turn to me, they are cold as ice. "What did she mean by that?"

I don't stare at him.

Mostly because I don't seem able to be able to do it without guilt showing across my face. First, because I cheated on one of his best friends. Second, the person with whom I got involved is the girl Eli is interested in.

"I don't know," I lie.

"Well, you must know something," he tries once again as I turn around and head to my desk, ready to wrap things up for the day. Eli still wants to find answers for Zoe's actions, and even though I want to leave, he doesn't seem inclined to let me. "What did she mean, Dorian?"

I lick my lips, searching for an escape from the situation I put us all in, and let my head hang low. It doesn't matter what I say. Eli is like an older brother to me. He knows when I am not telling the truth.

Like the time he asked me if I had ruined his favorite jeans. I lied my ass out of it only to be asked for the 50 bucks they cost him so he could buy a new pair. This man is like a lie detector when it comes to Josh and me.

My phone rings, and my wife's name appears on the screen. I bite my lower lip. Karma is indeed a bitch.

"Just fucking answer me." Eli's voice grows louder as I close my eyes to the sound of his tone. "Because this makes no sense. I came here to ask Zoe on another date-"

"Another?" Josh asks over Eli's voice.

"Yes, another. We went out a couple of times. The first was last month. A few days before Dorian got drunk," Eli gestures towards me and I swear I never felt so dirty. "Don't change the subject, neither of you. Just answer my damn question."

"Zoe," I sigh, daring a peek at Josh, who stares at me with empathy in his gaze. "Zoe and I… we sort of got involved."

"Involved how?"

"Eli," my eyes meet his for a brief second, and no matter how much I don't want to show my emotions, it's no use. "I'm sorry. You never said anything about her. If I knew..."

My oldest friend takes a deep breath and takes a step back. An unamused chuckle creeps from the back of his throat. It's not something good to see, and it pains me to my deepest bone to notice the hurt in his eyes.

"You slept with her?" He asks, making sure of what I mean, needing affirmation from me. "You had s- you-" the words stumble from his plump lips as he scratches his head. He scoffs as if the entire sentence seems a disturbed thought out of our reach. "You cheated on your wife with Zoe?"

"We only kissed," I confess.

"How many times?"

"Eli, don't." Josh tells the oldest.

"You knew this too? You Josh? The one person I confessed I was interested in the girl Dorian had fun with? The one who I told I was making a move on her and was going to ask her out?"

"Josh is not to blame here," I say, coming closer to them.

"Yes, you're right," Eli agrees right away. "It's you and your ways of not being happy with anything you have. So, answer me, how many times did you fuck Zoe?"

"It was never like that. We didn't have sex. The first time I was drunk, she was here, and we only talked."

"Sure," Eli laughs, with no hint of humor. "Talk."

Josh lifts his hands to his face, brushing them over his skin. In all the years we have known each other, Eli and I never got into a fight. It's not in his nature. It takes a lot to bother him. But this is not the type of guy to show interest in every girl, and Zoe played him. And the most embarrassing part is I allowed this to happen.

"I didn't know you liked her," I reply. "If I knew-"

"You would cheat on your wife with someone else?"

"Don't bring up Ari's name in this," I warn. "If you are trying to guilt trip me, it's up to you. But you would do well to keep my wife's name out of your mouth."

Josh seems ready to intervene at any moment, but then Eli nods, poking his lower lip out and strolling closer to me. "Guilt only comes to those who made something worth feeling it," he says through gritted teeth. "You were running around whining about how Ariella cheated on you and then, being the hypocrite you are, you did the same. Maybe Ariella knew better when she cheated on your sorry ass-"

I clutch the collar of his shirt, but Josh steps between us. Eli glares at me. I don't know what Zoe told him, but right now I couldn't care less. I let go of him, pushing Eli back while Josh seems to want to slap both of us.

"Talk about my wife again and I swear it will be the last thing that comes out of your mouth," I give him a final warning. "I apologized for getting involved with Zoe, but maybe you are not angry because I did. You are angry because you don't have the balls to ask a woman out. It took you what, over a year with Zoe?" Eli takes a step closer, but I scoff. "Leave before I force you to. We're done here."

21
Ariella

I leave the office early and walk out of the building. My skin prickles as it always does whenever I sense someone's gaze upon me. Like an eerie feeling I am being watched. When I lift my gaze, I spot the man across the street. He is wearing a suit, an expensive one, and staring back at me with hate spread all over his face. My stomach sinks.

It's been over a decade, but the man still looks at me with the same aversion. He doesn't give me time to think or even react. My body tells me to keep walking, but before I can even reach for my phone and pretend I am busy, my father is standing in front of me.

"Adriana," he says between his teeth.

I almost flinch at him using my old name. "Sir?"

"I see you made a name for yourself," he adds, glancing over my shoulder towards the building I came from. "Albeit not the one your mother and I gave you."

"Not with your help."

The man clenches his jaw. I take my time noticing

the changes in him. It's been a long time since the last time I saw him. The white hair and the wrinkles around his eyes are more prominent. His mustache was dark gold but now it's gray. Father and I had the same hair color, but it was where our similarities ended. I look a lot more like my mother. Which I am sure always infuriated the man standing in front of me.

It dawns on me that I feel nothing as I talk to him. No fear. No anger. Nothing. He tried to break me so many times. He tried to bend me to his will. A satisfied grin spreads across my face before I can stop it. I'm free… from this trauma, at least.

He clears his throat. "Your husband?"

"What about him?"

The man cocks a brow. "I didn't know who he was at the time you were talking to your mother about your engagement."

"You mean you didn't know he was rich?" I correct him. "When did you figure it out? Seven years ago when I got engaged? Or last year when you got the news about my son?"

When Dorian and I got engaged, I called my mom. As I always did once a month after leaving. It was not her fault how father treated us, but I couldn't stick around. I tried for years to help her get away, but she wouldn't.

The call, of course, didn't end well. It lasted for about five minutes. Father did not attend my wedding, not that I wanted him to, but he also didn't allow mom to come. Since he has a hold on her finances, she cannot use money without his permission. I offered to pay for her to be there. I offered to pay for her entire divorce, but she wouldn't let me.

My phone calls with my mother became less frequent. I don't even remember the last time we spoke. It was probably when I was still in the hospital after the car accident.

"You were a plague as a kid. My reaction after you left was justified. I had no idea you had married into a proper family."

"Your reaction after I left?" I snort. "What about your reaction when I came out as bisexual? Or your reaction when you saw me kissing a girl? Because I remember both occasions. During the first one you called me a lust seeking whore to whom sucking dicks was not enough, and the other you beat the crap out of me. It took me weeks to heal all the bruises. The physical ones at least… sir."

My father clenches his jaw. "It caught me off guard."

I nod. Okay. I can reply without losing it. "You don't have to worry about it ever again. I don't intend to talk to you, therefore don't look out for me. You didn't when I married, and you especially didn't when your grandson was born and worse, when he died. Neither of you did."

In his defense, the old man seems uncomfortable. But then he opens his mouth and all the sorrow I could have flies out the window. "Your mother and I were sorry for your loss. But we couldn't fly across the country to cater to your needs."

"You never did. And it took me a long time to realize that neither did she. If any of you wanted to be a part of my life, you would try." I take a deep breath and look away. "Are you here on business?"

"Yes."

"Good. Keep it that way. Whenever you come to town, don't even search for me. If you stumble on me again, don't talk because I won't make time for you again, sir. And also tell mom I said hi, but explain to her I will not call anymore. I think she can understand why, since she doesn't make the effort."

Turning around, I enter the company's waiting car telling the driver to take me home. All the time calling Dorian. He isn't picking up, and my heart is going crazy because of it. It's not like my husband to ignore my phone calls. Even when we were barely speaking, he wouldn't give me the silent treatment. It only makes me think something is wrong.

I fight the urge to call his office and listen to that raggedy brat taking my call as I ask her about my husband's whereabouts. It will only give the girl ideas, and I don't want her to think something that's not true.

Especially on her last day. I know I would rub it

in her face.

The next thought is to call Josh, who I'm sure is still there. My phone rings as a text pops up on the screen, and my heart settles in my chest.

Dorian: I'm heading home now

Something is definitely off.

Maybe he didn't get through with the deal he wanted for this week. I know a lot of money and time goes into his business. Sometimes people pull the cord at the last minute, and things don't happen as we want them to.

But I try not to overthink what is going on with the man I love. He will tell me what is happening whenever he is ready. I keep myself busy with cooking since it will distract my mind. I cut Dorian's favorite vegetables and place them inside the pan as the sizzling sound of olive oil fills the kitchen with an inviting aroma.

Memories from my childhood rush as I drop the spices inside with the rest of the ingredients and recall my grandmother in the kitchen. Dorian loves it when I talk about her. He knows all the stories, especially the ones about me leaving against my will.

That part of my past barely haunts me anymore. I'm happy, and I eat when I am in a good mood. For the last days, I have been eating a lot more. Which, if I think about it, it's something Dorian enjoys. I could notice his eyes lingering on me whenever I would walk into the bedroom wearing less clothing, but not in the way he should stare. Not with lust in his eyes, but sorrow for my curves being less than what they were before.

My husband enjoys filling his hands with my body.

Dorian drives into the garage. He doesn't get out of the vehicle right away and I take a deep breath, not to get caught in the worry settling over me.

He enters the house. I hum my favorite tune, noticing his footsteps approaching before his hands circle my waist. The man I love pulls me into a back hug, resting his lips on my neck.

My husband sighs, without saying a word to me as I stay in silence, gathering my thoughts and emotions before turning to face him. Knowing I can't feel overwhelmed with whatever is troubling his spirit, I twirl on my heels, and my eyes lock on his.

Whatever it is, it is not good. It's something as big as the secret I kept from him for over a year. My hand lifts, taking the strings away from his eyes. The green today mixes with sparkles of brown. Dorian's lips turn up as he takes my hand and presses his lips against my palm. It is a fake smile. One he wears trying not to disturb our peace.

Dorian leans to me, his forehead resting on mine as our breathing gets tangled. Our eyes close, and my husband's lips part mine into a slow kiss matched by the rhythm of our heartbeats. My hands explore the strings of hair at the end of his neck as his lips grow hungry, throwing caution to the wind.

He turns the stove off and guides us both to the bedroom. He passes by our bed and turns the bathroom lights on as our hands explore each other's bodies and clothes come off. Dorian is avoiding whatever concerns him, as I did all those months ago.

My husband turns on the hot water and we both undress before stepping inside, barely breaking contact between our bodies. He closes the shower door. My senses become numb by him when the man who owns every piece of my soul leans me against the wall and lifts one of my legs, straddling it around his waist. While staring into my eyes, he pushes inside of me, making both of us lose focus on the foggy bathroom.

"I love you," he mumbles against my lips before sliding his tongue into my mouth.

I moan out loud and cling to him as my husband stares down at me and the mess I become under his touch. "Please," I whisper, pleading for him to go faster.

And he does. He thrusts without mercy, grasping my ass with both hands and holding me close. I am his. All his.

My heart. My mind. My body. There is not a piece of my soul that does not belong to this man. I come undone around him and Dorian parts my lips with his, feeding on the moans and gasps I let out.

"I love you too," I confess, and feel him smiling into the kiss as we both come apart.

As I open Dorian's office front door, I am greeted by a brand-new face. Zoe isn't here anymore. I tilt my head to the side inspecting the place. The cute bundle of joy who smiles back at me has my lips turning up.

"Good afternoon Mrs. Vaillant," a young girl impeccably dressed greets me. "I am Marcie, Mr. Vaillant's newly appointed secretary."

I like her.

I like her because she introduced herself to me. She takes her time to walk around her desk and greets me, which is something the other one never did.

"Nice to meet you, Marcie," I say, extending my hand to her. "How did you know I-"

"Mr. Vaillant has a photo of the two of you on his desk."

Observant as well. Now I *really* like her. With a smile, I nod my head to the door, and Marcie dips her chin, understanding what I am asking. As I knock on the door, ready to end my day and head home with my husband, my eyes catch sight of Dorian resting his head in his hand.

Dorian peeks through his fingers when he hears

the sound of the door being shut. He tries to hide the worry in his eyes while I approach him.

"I wasn't expecting you here today," my husband confesses as I walk around his desk, pushing his chair back.

"You looked upset when you left this morning. I thought we should go home together."

"I love that idea."

His eyes don't hold mine for more than two seconds as I sit on his lap, lacing my hands behind his neck and kissing my husband's lips. Dorian sighs into the kiss.

"Do you want to talk about it?" I ask, placing his hair behind his ear and allowing a smile on my lips. "You almost didn't say a word yesterday."

"I do," Dorian confesses. "But I'm afraid we will fight if I tell you."

"Dorian-"

"We are in a good place right now, and I don't want to ruin it."

He could never ruin it. If there's someone who fucks things up in this relationship, it's me.

"Tell me. I promise I'll try not to get upset."

Dorian clears his throat, helping me be closer to him after his eyes stay on my collarbone while he speaks.

"You may have noticed I fired Zoe-"

"About damn time," I say aloud, interrupting him and gaining a chuckle from my husband. "I like

Marcie better anyway."

"Let me finish," he asks with a soft grin. "When Zoe left, Eli dropped by as he often does. A couple of months ago, while we were still on bad terms, I- well, Eli liked Zoe, and they were dating. Or something like it. He got upset with my decision to fire her."

"I guess the reason you fired her wasn't something that pleased him, either."

Dorian stares at me as guilt crosses his features and my hands fall on his cheeks. I force my husband to look into my eyes, knowing he needs to hear the words from my mouth. He won't voice them, not when he is avoiding the problem.

"I know," I breathe out, letting my lips hover over his. "I have known for a while that she wanted what wasn't hers, and I am sorry if my behavior pushed you in her direction."

"Ari, why are you apologizing when I was the one who acted wrong?"

"Because I did too," I confess. "If we had talked, if we weren't as stubborn, we wouldn't be in this mess, Dorian. I am not happy to know you cheated, let alone with that peacock of a woman. But I am not a hypocrite to watch the guilt eating you up and not say something about it."

"I didn't have sex with her I promise."

I kiss the corner of his mouth. "I believe you."

There's something that crosses his gaze for a second before vanishing.

"I love you," he acknowledges with a sad smile before taking my lips. "I'm sorry."

"We are both stupid. But we are trying, remember?"

Dorian nods as I make a note for myself to send Eli a text later tonight. My husband doesn't keep many people close to him. Knowing he hurt one of his best friends sent him to a dark place.

We kiss for a little longer. None of us want to go out into the world outside, but know we have to face it. I will talk to him about the case, explaining all details and informing the man I love about my plans. Some parts he may not like, but I am well set on this.

The disturbing sound of my phone beeping inside my jacket has me sighing before I notice the name of the call I am about block.

Until Dorian laces his fingers on it and takes the call before I can stop him.

"What do you want?"

Dorian leans the phone away from his ear as I attempt to stare at him with a blank expression. Attempting being the right word because I doubt the success behind my thought. My husband presses the speaker button on the scream, my insides wanting to come out through my mouth, forcing me to fight the nausea that dwells.

"I am going to ask again," he says through gritted teeth. "What the fuck do you want, Irene?"

"Put Ariella on the phone," she demands, out of

her comfort zone, as I glance at Dorian, knowing his patience is growing thin as the seconds pass by.

"She can't pick up right now."

"Just put your soon-to-be ex-wife on the God damn phone," Irene hisses as her voice raises a few more octaves than the woman would want to. "Or are you incapable of doing that as well?"

"I am capable of plenty."

"No, you're not," she laughs, and my stomach twirls. I am going to be sick. "You weren't capable of fucking her properly. That's why she came to me, wasn't it?"

My hand grasps the device, taking it away from Dorian's long fingers and lifting the phone close to my mouth. "What?"

The single word is enough for the woman on the other side of the line to let go of a long breath. I don't get it. I have been nothing but unpleasant. Pushing her away to a point others wouldn't even look back at me. But Irene appears to get off while torturing me with her presence.

Maybe she enjoys this situation. I know power is a turn-on for the woman.

"You barely looked my way today, and we have a meeting tomorrow morning," Irene says. "I thought maybe we could talk."

"We have nothing to talk about, Irene."

"If it's because of your husband tell me. I can take care of that. I can wait Ari-"

"Don't call me that. In fact, don't call me at all. This is my personal number. For anything work-related, you have my office number. It's either that or email."

She doesn't even get the chance to reply as I end the call. I take a deep breath before turning and lifting my eyes to meet two furious ones staring back at me.

I don't blame him. How could I?

Dorian and I are in a situation far more complicated than most people could understand. Our lives changed in the blink of an eye. Darkness spread between us, and we both pushed each other away. I won't take the whole blame for my failed marriage. But I will for cheating on my husband. We have been grieving for over a year, and the pain we have felt is one I don't wish upon anyone. I was wrong, I knew I was, and yet I acted on it anyway. I owe my husband an apology for it and I will apologize for the rest of my life if I have to.

I am not perfect. Perfect is a fantasy to those who wish to make people to think their lives are either black or white, a lie told to people that can't see the grass is not always greener on the other side. Sometimes it's rotten, others it isn't even grass at all, but it's how the seller advertises it that matters, isn't it?

Dorian doesn't speak. Instead, he turns away from me, heading to his desk and grabbing everything to leave. Something tells me he needs to calm down before getting into his car and driving us both home. It's probably the trauma from last year that's worrying me. Even though I was driving at an average speed, I still managed to end up in an accident.

I try to reach for him, but he looks over my head, pretending he isn't seeing me. "Dorian," I plead. My voice shakes as I try to hold myself together. "I finished it. I did. She-"

"Is a bitch who isn't used to the word no. Ari, I get it. I am not angry at you right now. I am angry at the situation. I asked you before. Let it go."

"It's not that simple," I breathe out. "There's work. I'm forced to see her, and the plan-"

"What plan, Ari?" Dorian asks, and I shut my eyes. "I get you have to work with her, but your revenge can drive us apart. Your plan can end this relationship once and for all. Your plan won't bring Raphael-"

The words hang in the air as our eyes meet, and Dorian nods, composing himself and trying to remain calm, forcing his voice to stay even. He doesn't get it; he never will.

And again, I don't blame him.

"Ari-"

"I have the papers ready and waiting for the judge to approve a trial," I confess, raising my chin and staring straight at him. "I'm not changing my mind, Dorian. You may not understand it, or you may disagree with it, but I need to do this. I have to do this."

22
Ariella

The woman next to me whispers something to the man sitting across from her. It's obvious from her glances I am the topic of their conversation. It is normal, I suppose. I have been sitting here for over half an hour. What she doesn't know is I told her husband I would rather kiss a goat than spend a minute with him, when he hit on me before she walked through the door.

My phone rings and I glance at it, noticing Dorian's name at the top.

Dorian: Meeting the boys tonight

I let the tears slide down my face and stare at his empty seat across the restaurant booth. He forgot we were meeting for dinner. We had made plans, and he forgot. Last week was hard. The entire year has been hard. But watching my husband write the number one on that paper lantern may have broken me all over again. I yelled, and I cried when I was all by myself. I held my scream for so long, that when I finally let it all out, my ears were in pain.

One year without my son. One year of crying myself to sleep almost every night. One year of trying to find answers, but with no luck. I can't help but grow desperate. People think we managed. They see my husband and I are still together and they think we are okay. But we are not. The other day Dorian mentioned the word divorce during therapy and I died a little more. I have been fading away for twelve months.

Thinking about Dorian is not helping to lift my mood, so instead, I shift my attention and stare at the list on my phone, biting down on my nail. Red & Blue Associates has to have someone willing to speak. Mrs. Garcia said if I could get a hint, a name behind it all, our case will become much simpler.

"Is this seat taken?"

My eyes lift to find two dark ones looking down at me. She is familiar, but I can't pinpoint from where. "No."

The woman slides into the seat next to me instead of across the table. Her short red ponytail sways as she sits and she motions for a server passing by. "Bring us two martinis, please." At my raised brow, she smiles. "I saw you alone and thought what a waste of a woman to be stood up."

She glances at my wedding ring and smirks. I however tilt my head, thinking where do I know this woman from? "What's your name?"

A small smirk spreads across her lips knowing she caught my attention. I am not interested in her, at least not in the way she thinks. I am married, although not happily anymore. The last thing I want is to hurt my husband.

"Irene Rogers," she says and my stomach sinks, realizing why *she looks so familiar. "What's yours?"*

"Ariella Vaillant," I let out only above a whisper.

I dare a glance at my phone still displaying the list of people from Red & Blue Associates, and my gaze lands on one of the top names.

The Vice President. The woman who I haven't approached yet because she wasn't important at the company at the time of the accident. She worked in human resources. I had never even heard of her until a few months ago. They place our drinks in front of us and Irene takes hers to her lips. Her eyes, however, never leave me.

It is clear what her intentions are, and how little she knows about me. They nominated this woman as Vice President after the accident. In the meantime, Dorian and I had kept our names out of the papers. Even Dorian's father agreed it would be for the best if we stayed under the radar for this. Privacy is expensive, but necessary in this case. It's not like Red & Blue are worried about making things public either. Even the lawsuit my lawyer is helping me with is being kept as private as possible.

"Why are you here alone? Bad day?"

I shake my head, but my mind is racing, thinking about the chance in my hands. Irene isn't here for small talk. She is one of the people who can give me the answers I have been seeking for so long. No one even replies to my emails at the police station. I was there a few weeks ago, but the Chief refused to re-open the case. Dorian doesn't even speak about Raphael, and our therapy sessions have been less than fruitful. One year of this, and I wonder how much more I can take. I can handle the silence. The indifference. What I can't handle is the guilt I still feel and the questions I keep having. Who is the person that paid the police? They archived the case within days. By the time Irene took her place at the company's main table, no one was investigating anything anymore because the driver took all the blame.

"Bad year," I reply.

"We can't have that, can we?" Irene shakes her head. "Let me pay you dinner."

"I don't know if that is a good idea."

"Why not?"

My hand lifts and I let the light shine against my wedding ring as if to prove a point. "I am married and you clearly have second intentions."

Irene shrugs. "I don't want a relationship. I don't do relationships," she deadpans. "Even if you are married, it cannot be a good marriage when he doesn't show up."

With everything happening in my life, the last thing I need right now is to feel guilty. I want to amend my marriage, and being around this woman won't do that. All I want is distance from Irene and the people she works for.

She snaps her fingers before I can stop her. Irene orders an expensive bottle of wine, which I am sure is a way of trying to impress me. It fails, and I am about to say something when her phone rings.

"Yes," she says, taking the call as soon as she sees the caller's ID. "I am out of the office for the night. Can't it

wait? Fine, but speak fast. I don't have time. What do you mean, we are getting sued?"

My entire body grows cold as I watch Irene glancing at me before shifting and whispering into the line. "It's been a year… do we have a name? Well, why can't we have one? How can we silence this?"

I lift my drink and sip from it trying to put on my best nonchalant face. Irene steals glances in my direction, and I smirk every time. It seems to have the effect I was looking for because when Irene hangs up, she apologizes.

"I am sorry. It was work."

"Bad day at the office?"

Irene bites down on her lip, studying me. "You can say as much."

How do I approach this woman? How do I make her talk about what I need? As soon as I gave her my attention, her demeanor changed… a lot. My finger twirls a string of my hair and Irene drags her attention to it.

Fuck, this is the last thing I want to do. But… what if this makes me win in court? I ignore my emotions in my chest and try to keep my head clear.

"Are you letting me buy you dinner?"

I bite my tongue not to tell her where she can shove her proposal. Irene has already finished her entire martini, so instead of replying to her question, I gesture with the empty glass to a server who nods at me. She is getting drunk tonight. Maybe this way I can get a proper answer.

"What if we drink a smidge more?" I say. "I still know nothing about you."

"You know my name," she cocks her brow. "Is that not

enough?"

I shrug. It doesn't go unnoticed she is too eager to get things rolling. Not everyone has the patience my husband had to win me over all those years ago. But then again, not everyone is the man I married. "A name is just that, a name. I know nothing about you. Would you mind telling me what do you do for a living?"

She thinks this through, staring back at me, and leaning forward. Her hand slides over my leg gripping my thigh as if for support but I know it's anything but. My entire body stiffens, and she smiles. For a brief second, I hope she will pull away, but when Irene whispers in my ear, I realize she is reading this wrong. She thinks I am nervous.

"And yours is a name I would love to have on the tip of my tongue every night."

Bile rises up in my throat, but I take a long breath. I want to slap this woman. To tell her who I am and what I have to do. Yet there are rumors of a possible merger between our companies. I have been quiet about this, trying to take advantage of the situation if such a thing is true. There is a lot one learns when behind the curtains of how businesses come together. And having Irene wrapped around my finger would not be a bad idea.

So I do my best to keep my nausea down. "Not so fast. I am not one to jump head first."

She snickers. "I love a good challenge."

"What else do you love?"

"My job," she says, brushing away a loose string of her ponytail.

"And what is that job?" I try again.

She chuckles, finding my curiosity funny. "I am the Vice President of Red & Blue Associates," she says, puffing out her chest. "We work with retail."

My opening is so obvious I can't even hide my triumphant smile. "I know. I am one of the designers of Wear a Kiss. I believe your company has been trying to get a hold of us for a while now. But something about your PR not being very good held us back."

As my brow raises, Irene drops her smile. "Rumors," she shrugs, recomposing herself. "People will believe anything they read about. Big companies love to spread rumors about their rivals."

"Then I suppose if the rumors are false, so is the reputation you all have for being ruthless?"

Irene chuckles. "Oh, I am ruthless sweetie," she leans in. "It's part of my job. Someone has to deal with all the shit thrown at my company."

It becomes clear as I get some answers about Irene's promotion. They knew they could have people picking on their actions. So they chose someone from the inside. It also becomes clear how I will get my answers.

Irene will not speak unless I spend time with her. Unless I give in to something. Cheating is not an option for me. But this is my son, the truth about who killed him. Irene slips her company card to me when she realizes I am not giving up so easily. She leans again and before I can say anything or run from the woman, her hand slides between my legs and grips my inner thigh. It's possessive, and as she kisses me, I smell alcohol coming from her.

These were not Irene's first drinks. She doesn't even realize I am too stunned to kiss her back.

"Call me," she mumbles. "We have a lot to talk about."

I watch as she slips away into the street, too stunned to even move. Only when it hurts do I dare to breathe and look around to see if anyone saw us. No one is even paying me attention, and my shoulders slump with relief. I decide it's safe to make a run for the bathroom. A woman comes out of a stall and I step in, closing the door behind me. All I had in my stomach comes rushing up and I fall to my knees in front of the toilet. The tears threaten to fall before breaking free and stream down my cheeks as I cry and empty my stomach over and over again until it hurts. Until there is nothing else left.

I don't cheat. I never did. But I need answers. Dorian's name flashes on my screen and I groan, hitting my head against the bathroom stall.

Dorian: Josh will drive me home. Don't wait up.

He doesn't deserve the mess I made in our lives. He doesn't deserve to grieve like this. And I don't want to stay in a loveless relationship. Nodding at myself, I walk out of the stall to wash my mouth and face. If I am doing this, I need to let Dorian go.

The last thing I do before walking to my car is email my lawyer, asking if she can draft me a divorce settlement.

"So this thing with her," Thea says, sitting across from me in my office as I finish explaining how I met

Irene. "It started slowly."

I dip my chin. "I never meant for it to happen and it was never more than a few kisses and me groping her once to distract her," I sigh. "But now, even with Dorian knowing the truth, I can feel myself slipping through his fingers, Thea," I confess as my eyes stay on the scenery outside the window. "He asked me to let go of everything, to forget what I want to know."

"Is there more?"

"There is," I nod and explain to her the little I can about wanting to know the culprit.

"He is trying to survive," my friend replies.

I won't tell her everything. I am not crazy like that. Thea wants me to open up, and I will, with time. Right now, I have to explain to her my fear of losing my husband, of ruining our marriage.

"I know he is," I breathe out peeking at her, taking notes. "But so am I."

"Ariella," Thea calls. "Sooner or later, you will have to choose."

"Why?" I scoff. "Why do I have to choose when I want both? Why can't I have him and make Red & Blue Associates pay?"

"Because Dorian wants to let go of his anger. I don't think he wants to slip back into that state of mind and relive all you two have been through."

"I don't want it either," But I reply to her. "I want them to pay Thea. I need them to pay. Dorian hates them as much as I do. I don't-"

"As your friend," she compels me to calm down, and I take a deep breath. "All I can tell you is to talk to him. I know he wants answers just as much as you do, but he isn't willing to sacrifice his happiness. If that means losing you, he won't have it."

"Thea," I sigh. "We lost our son. I know Dorian thinks this won't bring back Raphael, but at least it will bring some justice-"

"You may think that. But are you willing to risk your relationship if you are not sure?"

I have been avoiding her. It's the only thing I can do as Irene keeps coming to the company for unnecessary meetings. Every time I hear whispers of her name in the hallway or they call for me to be present at one of these things, I avoid the woman as if I am a vampire and she is the sunlight.

After talking to Dorian the other night, and him confronting Irene over the phone, I know I will have to choose soon. Dorian is my choice. he will always be my choice. But letting go of the answers and the justice I still haven't found… I am not sure if I can do that.

"They're calling for us," Louis warns me. "I tried to stall them-"

"It's okay. You go ahead. I'll be there in a few

minutes. I want to send this email."

Louis dips his chin and heads to the door, leaving it ajar as I stare at the screen and the lie I just told my friend. Yes, there is an email, but I have sent it for over five minutes, and it's not even work-related. My lawyer is informing me today about the lawsuit and when the court is calling for us to be present.

My desk phone rings, and I pick it up, noticing someone walking into the office as the girl on the line gets frantic while the door closes.

"I'm sorry, Mrs. Vaillant, I couldn't-"

"Don't worry, I'm sure Ms. Rogers won't stay for long."

Irene smiles, amused at my words but mostly since I am granting her the courtesy be alone with me for the first time since I ended everything. She walks in a circle before heading to the desk where I wait, ignoring her eyes and her lean figure, desperate to call the attention I don't give her.

"You're not at the meeting," she states the obvious.

"My presence isn't necessary," I say back, still staring at the notebook and computer where the sketch I've been working on takes form. "I can't say the same about you since your company asked for yet another meeting about something we already ruled out days ago."

"I have someone in there for me. We just need to confirm everything before you start production to sell across the country," she shrugs. "We need to talk, Ariella."

"No, we don't."

Irene takes a long breath, displaying the thin patience she is grasping onto. "I have been missing you at night. The meetings with the lawyers keep dragging and-"

"So, you didn't pay the woman yet?"

My feigned innocence results as Irene shakes her head. Maybe I filled a void in her life because she doesn't have many friends, isn't open to others, and is lonely. Two months of me grasping for answers and getting hindsight on how her company works made me realize they have nothing. They have no idea how to fight back. I will be sorry for everything I have done one day, but not now. Now I need to know.

"The lawyers want to, but she isn't willing to meet out of court."

"Smart one," I chuckle. "You can't fix everything with money, Irene."

"Money is always the answer," she brushes off.

The opportunity appears right in front of me and I speak before it slips away. "Was money the reason the lawsuit is only happening now? Was money the reason you didn't get the police on your tail the first time?"

Irene raises her brow, tilting her head as her tongue grazes her teeth before she kisses them. My tone is off, but I was never gentle with the woman. Yet, I have no time left to tiptoe on the subject. This is happening soon. If they are meeting with lawyers and trying to buy their way out, I have less time than I first thought. Few weeks. As far as I know, they will send the notification letters soon.

No judge will allow me to stall for long before calling us.

She also knows that if I am making questions, it is because I will talk to her, and right now, Irene is desperate enough for attention.

"Money solves problems, and we had a situation that needed to be fixed."

My hand clasps on the sheet of the notebook, tearing the paper as I take hold of my emotions, not to throw the keyboard at Irene's head.

"I can't listen to your chitchat," I let out, focusing on anything else than her. "I have work."

"Well, you may want to put work to the side."

"Irene, do you realize I can make your life miserable? That I can end this deal you think you have with my boss?"

"Cut the crap, Ariella," she scoffs. "We both know your boss will never pull away from this. You will hear me first; then you will decide what to do."

Irene's smile is nothing but cold and twisted. She reaches for a small folder inside her purse, and turns to me. She throws it in my direction. My phone rings as I pick it up, sighing when Dorian's name appears, and as I am picking up the call, Irene speaks once more, making my entire blood freeze.

"Those have copies," she giggles." I took photographs from the security cameras images of the places we met. I am the one who can make your life hell. Still want to play games with me?"

The last thing I need is for her to make the photos public. If she leaks them, then Irene has control of the narrative of the story. And I can't have it happen. My phone rings and I take the chance to interrupt her. "Yes."

"What time are you arriving home tonight?" My husband's voice sounds on the line.

"Is that the idiot?" Irene scoffs. "Tell him you can't talk now."

I walk away from Irene. "I only have one meeting, then I will head home straight away."

There is silence on the line. One that stretches before Dorian speaks. "She's in your office?"

"Yes."

"Alone?"

"My secretary is right outside Dorian. I am trying to make her leave-"

"No, you are not," Irene chuckles loudly. "We were having a great time."

"Dorian-" I call.

"I'll see you when you get home," is all he says before hanging up on me.

23
Ariella

My eyes still burn as I sit in the car, staring at the house. A fight is brewing; I know it. But the reason my eyes burn is the tears I have shed while driving home. I sigh, opening the door from the car and heading into our house. By the time the door is closed behind me, I spot Dorian on the kitchen island. His eyes not meeting mine, his lips pressing into a thin line as his hair falls over his eyes, shielding them from me.

But what catches my attention is the notebook and sheets he is staring at.

My plan. All of it, including court documents I kept locked away. How the man I love managed to find them is unclear.

"Dorian," I let out, placing my things on the chair closest to the cabinets before grasping it with my hands. "I know what you're thinking-"

"She was there again, Ari. Alone."

Before I turn to boil some water in the teapot and take my mug, placing it on the kitchen island in front of me. I inhale a deep breath without paying proper attention to what I am doing.

My entire focus is on the silent man at the table.

There's this thing when no one speaks, and the environment becomes heavy with guilt and apprehension. The one who deals with guilt is the one who breaks the silence. “I can't control when she is there,” I reply, pouring water into the mug and watching the tea blend before turning towards him. “You know that.”

“What I know is I have asked you, pleaded more than once, and you seem to ignore that.”

“I'm not,” I breathe out, trying to reach for him as he stands up, but my husband pulls away. “I'm not ignoring us.”

“Really?” He scoffs. “Then why didn’t you pull back? Why are you still going through with this?”

“Dorian-”

“You haven't given up on your crazy plan, Ari. I had time to read this, you know… You can’t even be sure if you will win. You don't even know which wounds this whole thing will open again,” my husband accuses, taking a step towards me with a finger pointing at my chest. “You are still in that mindset.”

Mindset.

It’s what my husband calls the need in me for justice. I get it; not everyone can be so driven to the point of elaborating on something as complicated as what's happening in my life right now. Still, from everyone, I thought Dorian would understand *me*.

Though he doesn't accept it, I thought he would understand I can't let it go. I was wrong.

"My mindset keeps me going, Dorian."

Our eyes lock as a staring contest begins. Two stubborn people who always enjoy going at it and bumping heads whenever their point has to be proven. That's what I loved about him from the start.

"Can't you let it go?" He asks. "Can't you forget everything and stay with me?"

"I *have* to do this. Why can't you understand it?"

"I don't know, Ari. Maybe because you say it was for answers, and still you were with Irene every damn chance."

Ah, so it's again the cheating. I can let it go from his end, but he can't forgive me. Cheating is cheating. I don't care how many times it happened, and even if Dorian has a point, because Irene is still around. But I was not one to tell him to fire his secretary. I could have let it go, even with her still working for him.

Because I trust him.

But this isn't about trust. It's about pride and peace. I cannot control when Irene is around me, but I have been doing my best to be there for Dorian.

"I told you before nothing happened between us," I speak through my teeth. "I kissed her. I didn't have sex with her. It's not like you're innocent, either."

"Because I was with Zoe once? Sure," he scoffs. "Same thing, isn't it?"

"Just because I cheated on you doesn't make it okay for you to cheat," I say, glaring in his direction. "I told you I wanted to sign the papers, but you said no."

"You want me to sign the papers?" He asks as his voice raises. "Will that make you happy? Will that make you run into her arms-"

Dorian slides something from beneath my planner and I recognize the envelope. It's the same one I left on the kitchen table weeks ago. The one he hid from me because he didn't want to file for divorce.

My confidence shakes as I stare at him. "I have nothing with Irene," I confess, done with the fight and taking my mug into my hands. "I told you, Dorian-"

Why is it so hard to see that I am holding onto him? How can't he understand that I don't love anyone else? I don't want anyone else.

"Still, you can't let her go, so what am I supposed to believe?"

"Me! You are supposed to believe me."

Me.

The woman with your name on the ring she carries. The woman to who you promise the world. The one who tells you she loves you every single night for the last weeks.

He is supposed to have faith in me, not be jealous or afraid. He is supposed to believe me, as I believe him every time he tells me to let it go.

"Right. That always worked out fine, didn't it?"

"I have nothing to do with her, Dorian," I explain, placing the mug back on the island. Tears prick against my eyes and so I shut them and take a long breath. "I'm tired of fighting. Please Dorian believe me."

All I want is for us to make amends and for things to be okay. But the way he is staring at me makes it clear my husband and I are in two different mindsets. And that's when he pulls the rug from beneath my feet.

"I will believe you Ari… if you choose."

"What should I choose?" I blink, uncertain of what he is about to say.

Dorian picks up the envelope and takes a deep breath. "Either you stay with me and we work on our marriage, or we talk this through and figure out what it is you want. I cannot deal with all of this, Ariella. I cannot go through it again."

My eyes burn, but I don't cry. I refuse to break. He watches me, his resolution wavering but still holding on to his words. "You are making me choose? Dorian, I wanted to divorce you to spare-"

Dorian scoffs. "Fine. You want a divorce? Then let's divorce," he says and slams the envelope on top of the island.

The envelope falls with a heavy thud, but as it

does, it clashes against the only thing close to it. My favorite mug slides off and falls to the floor, shattering into dozens of pieces. Silence spreads when we both notice the words broken on the floor. The same three ones I won't ever hear from my son's lips again, making the word 'mom' stick out against the floor. Dorian stares back at me, all anger vanishing from his eyes.

"*Merde*. Ari… It wasn't on purpose."

I nod but take a step back, the tears I held as best as I could break free. I watch one of the last remains of my former life shattering. Wiping my cheeks, I turn around to head outside, slamming the kitchen door behind me.

24
Ariella

The house is silent; my feet touch the warm wooden floor as I make my way to our bedroom and notice the closet doors are open. After our fight, I jumped into my car and drove without knowing where I was going. I drove until I reached the shore. The sea helped calm me down, so I could cry as no one was around to see. To scream while no one could hear me.

I didn't want them to.

Why would I allow anyone to see my pain again?

There's one person who knows how it feels, and yet, he decided to leave. My fingers scan the empty spots where his favorite clothing used to hang. He didn't take everything, but enough for a week. I sit on the bed and pick up the yellow post-it he left behind.

I am going to stay away for a few days. It's for the best if we spend some time apart to understand this.
I am sorry Ari. I didn't want to break the mug. I promise we will talk whenever you are ready.

Je t'aime mon amour, et je suis désolé.

Staring at the room around me but not focusing on anything as the pain invades me once again.

The same from that night, the absence of something

He left. Dorian had enough and left as I wanted all those months ago.

25
Dorian

The doorbell rings into the apartment, and I hear my friend mumbling something about it. I should have let him know I was coming here. But in the haste of leaving, I didn't even think. Footsteps approach and before I lift my gaze to meet Eli's, I let go of an exhausted breath. He stares back at me, but I can't make for what he is thinking. Probably wondering why I have a bag in my hand and a defeated look about me.

"I am sorry," are the first words leaving my lips. "I am sorry for Zoe."

"Me too," he scratches the back of his neck. "I may or may not have overreacted."

Eli steps aside and I walk into his apartment. The place is vast enough for a single man to live in comfort in New York City. All in browns and grays with the best gaming system. I could have gone to Josh's, but with Thea around… not the best idea. I stop in front of him and my friend sighs, wrapping his arms around me and pulling me into a tight hug. It is weird how much I needed it. How much I needed someone I care about to comfort me. I am not a touchy guy by any means unless it is my wife. But right now, I needed a hug. I rest my forehead against his shoulder and try to calm down the emotions running freely inside of me. Ari is blind by grief, and although I understand her, I don't know what to do.

"What happened?" Eli asks and I walk towards his sofa.

I plop myself on top of it and watch him grab two beers before joining me. How do I explain this to him? Eli hands me one and I open it, taking a long gulp. "Ari and I had a fight."

"About Zoe?"

"No," I say, shaking my head. "She knows about Zoe, and I know about whatever she had going on." I pick at the corners of the label from the bottle, intending to give it my full attention and not dwell with whatever I am feeling. My wife said they never had sex, and I can live with that. I can live with knowing Irene never touched her, although it hurts like a bitch. But I cannot live with doubt. "She is suing Red & Blue Associates."

Eli frowns. "She is?" I nod. "And you're mad about it?"

"I am not mad because she is suing," I explain, rubbing a hand on my face. "I am mad because the person with whom she was involved is Irene. The Vice President…" Eli's brows disappear behind his hairline. "Exactly."

"But- wait. Let's go back. So Ariella cheated with this Irene woman?"

"Yes."

He takes a sip of his beer and I do the same. Both my friends know my wife isn't straight. It came up in conversations before about how many women Ari had dated. "But she ended it?" I nod. "And then you found out she was suing them and got mad?" I nod again. "Okay. Why?"

"She can't let go."

Eli blinks, staring back at me and I feel myself shrinking under his attention. "Dorian, I realize you are dealing with losing your son and you want to move on, but your wife is still struggling with guilt. Can you blame her for wanting to do this?"

"No," I say, letting go of an unhumorous chuckle. "That's the problem. I am proud of her for this and I understand she can't let it go. But I don't think I can be around while she does this. We… it's complicated, Eli. I don't want to see Ariella going down the path she has been walking out of. I don't want to go down that path again either… It was hard enough to walk out of it once."

"And you think the best way to do so is leaving? Listen man, I get it," he raises his hands as if to say he isn't fighting me on this. "You both went through hell. But if she feels like she has to do this… well, then you should let her. And when it is done, you can figure it out what to do." My friend stares at me as I take a long chug from the beer. "I suppose there is more to this story, isn't it?"

"The Irene woman?" He nods. "Well, she is still after Ari. Ari says she pushes her away, that nothing happens. But because she has business with the bitch, she is around all the time. I asked Ari to explain this to her boss. To tell him she isn't comfortable."

"And?"

"And she told me her boss had a brief explanation about Ariella moving on from old grudges."

"She really needs to leave that company."

"She does," I scoff. "She wants to."

Eli stares at me for a long minute. He crosses his arms over his chest and leans back in his seat. Silence spreads between us and I can feel my skin becoming clammy. The difference between talking to my friends is crystal clear. Josh explodes and listens. Eli makes me think about what I did wrong. Which I think is always a lot worse considering how guilty I feel every time he does it.

"Do you love her?" I give him a look as if to say he is an idiot for considering otherwise. "Then don't turn your back on your wife. Not fully, anyway. Let her deal with this, but don't walk away from her life."

I want to punch something. I feel like an idiot. I don't know what to do. I shouldn't have walked away. I shouldn't have left. But having to deal with the aftermath of the fight, especially since I broke the damn mug… I can't even look at Ari, knowing she will not forgive me.

To others, it may be just a mug. To us, it is a reminder of our boy. One I took away from her.

"You are welcome to stay as long as you want," my friend says, patting my shoulder. "Do you know what you are going to do?"

I raise a brow. "I will support whatever it is Ari does."

Eli shakes his head. "I was asking if you're going to be at court when she is called?"

My gaze drifts away from Eli, considering it. "I don't know Eli. It's hard enough to know bits and pieces of it, but I also don't want my wife going through this by herself. If Ariella wants me there, I will be."

26
Ariella

I feel empty, fueled by only one thing for the last few days.

Revenge.

It is the only word on my mind since Dorian left. Although it hurts, I understand what he means by saying we need to figure this out separately. He hasn't touched on the topic since that night, not that he has touched any subject at all. Dorian and I have barely spoken. He needs his space and I doing my best to let him be.

Louis has been curious. For the last few days, I have been working more, staying until later at the office. I haven't told him yet. I have told no one. Between the pain and the menace of people staring at me differently, I don't think those words will ever slip through my lips. Not until I know what will be of us.

So, I focus on the job I have to do. Irene is due to come here today representing her company once more, and this time I won't let her walk away without the freaking name. I've had enough of it.

The bad news is bound to come… we already have a day to be at court.

"Mrs. Vaillant?"

The knock on my door makes me sigh as I stop the pen over the screen, dismissing my work and focusing on my secretary, who is peeking by the door.

"Let her in," I reply before the woman has time to announce the one behind her.

Putting my glasses down, I massage the bridge of my nose as Irene's stilettos march towards me. Demanding attention as usual, for someone who says she is independent, that she doesn't want anyone in her life, that her job is her priority, this woman clings to me.

Irene is a little more complicated than the people I have dealt with. It's not like it's easy for her to open herself to others. It's why I had to distract her with something more. When she isn't thinking straight, it is easy for the truth to slip through her lips.

"You're early," I say, staring straight at her. "Any reason?"

"Word on the street is that you're going through some rocky situation," Irene speaks, smirking. "Everything okay?"

"Work," I shrug, leaning back in my chair. "The company has been busy, and I need to focus more on what happens here."

"I see. Nothing else? Not even that husband of

yours."

"I told you before, and I will tell you again, my husband is none of your concern, Irene. You should know how to listen. If you play nice, maybe we can talk about it," I state as she approaches, gliding her hand over my desk. Her eyes come alive with hope, but we both know she is here because she wants someone she can vent to. Irene is lonely. "What's wrong?"

I don't want to know what's wrong in her life; if I am right, the next words she confesses will be hard for me not to react to. So I force my expression to soften and my lips to turn up the slightest to seem as if I care.

"The company is going through some shit," she acknowledges. "That lawsuit we had against us is going through. Our lawyers say it is a matter of days before we are called."

"So it's really happening?" I ask, pressing a key on my computer and making sure the app is running before I stand up and walk to the window.

She isn't here because she wants me back. Irene wants someone to vent her frustrations. Loneliness must have crept in. I could never entirely push Irene out of my life. I could cut ties with her, but she would still come around, no matter how much I tried. My secretary and even security had instructions for not letting her in without my permission, and yet somehow here she is. This woman is stubborn. If she wants something, she will get it.

I glance at her over my shoulder. "You told me once it was something out of your control, an event you could not stop, but the company wasn't to take the blame," I tiptoe, and she sighs as I notice her walls coming down. Now is the time. This is the nicest I have spoken to her in weeks, and maybe the vulnerability will help. "If you want me in those meetings, I need you to let me in Irene. What happened?"

"You saw it in the news. The accident concerning a car from my company? The one your husband mentioned the other time. A little boy involved died. Someone needed to take the blame, and we had to move fast. It was bad enough that there was a mortal victim, but being a toddler… The public would not take this well."

My breathing comes to a halt as Irene approaches me, staring outside, and I notice the way she loses her gaze on the city beneath us, recollecting the day. I hold on to dear life not to scream, not to speak, not to say anything that will give away everything I have worked for.

I may have already lost my husband because of this. I am not going to ruin it.

"What did they do?" I ask when she stops talking.

"The chairman called the entire legal department and HR. He was furious, yelling in every direction and trying to find something or someone to put the blame on. He wanted to know how he could get out of it without closing the company. We explained to him that the board made the final decision as to which company would be in charge of the vehicle's maintenance and they somehow went with the simplest plan. When he realized the guilty ones were him and his associates, he changed the target of his anger. Saying whatever happened could not take action against the company, it wouldn't end well for us. We needed a scapegoat, someone who would take the blame and let us walk around the topic; Red & Blue Associates was already facing some serious issues by then, other lawsuits from other companies saying we had stolen business deals from them. All is fair in love and war, and this was war. So-"

Irene stops speaking and takes a deep breath. I glance at the desk, my heart pounding against my chest in anticipation of knowing all is in place, and then turn to the window once again. There are no emotions, nothing but the way my nails dig against my palms, not to make her understand who I am or what I want.

"When no one came up with any ideas, I told them we could pay the driver to take the blame. I had read his file. His family struggled with his gambling addiction. We all knew he would take the money. It's not like he was innocent either. They also promoted me from HR director to Vice President.

My only task was to help the company come out clean. They promised me I would make it to the board over the next four years, but this lawsuit is delaying everything. I won't get my promotion if someone sues us for the accident."

As the truth sinks in, I swallow the words I want to say. My voice will give away my emotions if I don't play this right.

"You told them to blame an innocent man?"

"Yes," she shrugs. "Everyone has a price, and for five years in jail, he has the sum he wants waiting when he leaves, plus his family is taken care of. The family who was in the other car also wanted privacy and I thought they had let this go…" She sighs and looks my way. "I'm not telling you this for you to hate me, Ariella. I know it is not helping much about my case. I want you to see we all make poor decisions. Mine led me to you."

His absence hurts the most when I step inside the house every evening. However, things are not as they were this morning, which means Dorian was here. I can smell his perfume. A spark of hope lights up in my chest. We haven't spoken since that night, but as I make my way towards the closet, not caring to turn the light on, my stomach drops noticing he took more than his clothes.

Dorian's items aren't on his bedside table anymore.

Instead, I find a note.

I came by to pick up some things for work. Let me know if you need anything, or when you are ready to talk.

His notebook, Raphael's photo, the agenda where he keeps his appointments. None of those are in their usual place, and I try to calm myself down. He needs them, and this is something I knew could happen. My husband needs to think.

My feet take me to the bathroom. I turn the shower on and step inside. I let the hot water run through my body and ease my nerves. Irene confessed. She finally said it. It forced every nerve of my body to let her talk and then tell her I needed to leave so I wouldn't give away my emotions. I don't want to celebrate my achievement. It only reminds me of what I gave up to be here though. I know well I would do it again.

I lean my head back before a sob escapes me, and the pain invades my senses all over again. I try to keep my crying and sadness under control, but it's too much. Everything is too much. My body drifts to the floor as I curl up and hug my knees, resting my head on my arms and letting the pain take over.

We were healing. That's what hurts the most. If he had left before, I would have been heartbroken, but it wouldn't be like this. Before, I thought there was no salvation. Before, I thought we were drifting apart, and we would never find each other again.

He made me believe we could. Dorian made me believe we could be together, no matter what.

Everyone leaves. That's the thing about me that most people don't know. Maybe one day I will explain my life. I will explain why I never speak about my family, about my past before him. The past can hurt me in ways most people can't.

It is a door I sealed shut in my life.

Dorian is the only one who knows about it, about them. He is the only one I confided in about the struggles of traveling to New York and leaving those people behind me.

I didn't need a family, I didn't need anyone, but then he appeared, and now he is gone as well. Loneliness crawls into my heart and taints my thoughts. The dread of life alone when I had pure love. I lost my son, and now I fear I have lost my husband.

And again, I will never blame him for leaving me, not after all we have been through. Some part of me is glad he is moving on with his life. The other is crumbling apart.

The phone rings, and I move from my spot, listening to it until it dies further away in the bedroom. I take a while to get out of the shower, put a towel around my body and make my way to the closet to choose something to wear. Not even my pajamas seem appropriate right now, and instead, I grab a set of sweatpants and a shirt. His shirt that I keep in my drawer because he gifted it to me years ago so I would have something to wear while at his place.

A sound reaches my ears before I realize it's my phone again and Thea's name pops on the screen, but I don't answer. She will ask questions that are too hard to answer right now. If I am doing this, I need to distance myself.

I close my eyes, and for the first time in months I pray once again to the God I do not believe in that I don’t wake up.

But my dreams do not let me rest, and the doorbell rings throughout the house. My bare feet step on the cold floor before I pull the door open. Thea smiles at me, but it does not reach her eyes. She is worried I haven't taken her calls the entire evening, which isn't natural.

Sighing, I step aside and let her enter the house to shield her body from the frosty night. Josh stands by the car. He waves at me, taking in my figure as I wave back. “Is he okay?” I ask.

Josh nods. “Stubborn as ever, but he is fine.”

“Do you want to come in?”

“I think you two need to talk alone,” Josh says, tipping his chin towards the place Thea was standing. “And I also think you should stop being as stubborn as your husband is."

I raise a brow at him but know he is at least half right. When I close the door, Thea is already waiting.

"You're not answering your phone," Thea says, peeking around the house and taking her jacket off as I make my way into the living room. "Everyone is worried, Ariella."

"I'm fine," I breathe out, staring at her while sitting on the sofa. "I haven't been in the mood to speak."

"Well, I can understand that," she says, tilting her head. "I talked to him."

Of course, she did. Why else would Thea be here to check on me if not because Dorian already told her and our friends he left?

But curiosity takes over me as usual, and I just need to know this one thing. Even if Thea tells me, it's stupid that I still need to ask.

"How is he?"

"Bad," Thea assures me, sitting in the armchair. "He was worried you had done something stupid."

I snort. "But not worried enough to come check himself."

"Ariella, we were the ones telling him not to come. At least not until you two figure it out. He told me about the plan. I-"

"I don't expect you to understand."

"That's the thing," she chuckles. "I do. I understand why you need to do it, just as I understand why Dorian doesn't want to be involved. It scared him to lose you for that, so-"

"He left anyway, Thea," I state, rolling my eyes.

"True," she says, pressing her lips together. "But there's always hope. I don't expect him to take you back, and I don't think it's a good idea for you guys to be together now. But maybe after this, after you heal. Maybe then."

Maybe.

I wish I could hold on to that word.

"What if I have lost him completely by then?"

"If you do, you will survive anyway. You're a fighter, Ariella. You have been through enough, and for that reason, I am by your side on this."

27
Ariella

She is coming today, and I doubt she will be smiling.

How do I know Irene will pay me a visit to the office? Simple, I received my letter at home before driving here. The one from the court with the hearing date, and on that letter are all of our names. Mine, Raphael's, and Dorian's. We kept my name secret until the papers came, but it was bound to happen. She knew the name her lawyers gave her. The same one my lawyer "accidentally" let slip once. I needed them out of my scent.

Irene isn't completely stupid. She will understand what has been happening, and as I make my way through the atelier, gaining a few glances from the women who work in the department, I know it's not just Irene and Red & Blue Associates who are not pleased with what's happening.

My boss probably isn't either.

Louis watches me approach my door. He shakes his head for me not to step in, and I sigh, knowing someone is already inside waiting for me. I am only glad that Dorian will get a notice about the lawsuit today. I asked my attorney to keep him involved.

He is our son's father. He should at least know what is happening, even if he doesn't want to be in the courtroom, even if he doesn't want to be with me. The decision to be present or not is up to him.

As soon as I push the door open, I almost laugh. My boss stands behind my desk. This office may be mine, but the attitude tells me the company is his, and he is still the one who pays me my salary.

"Ariella," he lets out, turning to face me. "Punctual as always."

Mr. White walks towards me as I extend my hands to the small armchairs around the coffee table. Far away from my computer, which has information and drawings, I don't want him to find out. It's his problem if he doesn't let me be original, so it's my right not to show him everything I sketch. We sit; he licks his lips in anticipation as I try not to smile, knowing the motive for his visit.

"What do I owe the pleasure of you being here, sir?"

"Something came up," Mr. White states, bouncing on his heels. "Red & Blue Associates informed us about a conflict of interest between you and them."

So, he has been waiting for me here ever since Red & Blue Associates called. Not Irene, but someone higher in the hierarchy.

"A conflict of interests?" I ask to make sure, when in fact, what I want is for him to continue speaking, as I don't want to say anything he might use against me.

"Yes, they called us this morning in the early hours, explaining you have a lawsuit against the entire company."

"That's not true," I reply, stopping him, and Mr. White sighs in relief. "Not the entire company. Just Ms. Rogers and the board."

The way my superior's face constricts as I confess the truth could be funny if the conversation wasn't so serious.

"Is there a problem, sir?"

"You could say that. They say because you are doing this, they won't make a business deal with us, and Ariella, the deal we have going on, is quite crucial. There's a lot of money involved-"

"They're calling it off?" I ask, narrowing my eyes. "Sir, it's fine. If they do, you will have other companies that can take the brand. Better ones."

"Other companies are not as cheap," my boss interrupts me, and my blood freezes in my veins.

Of course.

Leave it to men like him to put money ahead of interest, pride, and principle.

"Cheap doesn't mean better, Mr. White," I do not break eye contact. "I am suing them because they are cheap bastards. Sir, Irene confessed the company neglects things over money. I could pretend and look the other way when you did business with them. You knew they were the ones whose car crashed into mine last year, but you still went ahead with it."

"Ariella-"

"No, Mr. White, I am still speaking and you would do well to hear what I have to say this time. You knew. You knew very well that my son died that day and Red & Blue Associates was involved. Still, as someone with money at stake, you took the chance, but it was very heartless of you to put me on that project. You could have chosen anyone. Louis, for example."

"Louis isn't as capable. He is not the head of the department-"

"I am not done," I tell him, raising my finger, and the man grunts, trying to open his mouth for the third time. "He may not be by your standards, but we could figure it out. Forcing me to be around them was cruel. I even told you I wasn't comfortable and you brushed it aside. You ignored I lost my son because of them. You looked at the technicalities."

Mr. White stands all of a sudden as I do the same. He fumes and pants as I approach him, ready for what is coming. "You are stepping out of line, Ariella. I treat you all like family. If you weren't comfortable with the project, why didn't you say so?"

I roll my eyes. "Don't you remember, sir? You called my grief a grudge. You, as my superior, as the *family* you mention, should take the interests of the people that bring the money inside this building. Let's face it, sir. I have been helping you to become *very* rich."

"You do what I ask you to, just like anyone I hire around here. You do what I pay you for, or you'll suffer the consequences."

Well, I don't want to do this right now, but this man isn't giving me any more time. Silly of me to try to make him understand. I love my job, I love what I do. But I do not have the time nor the patience to deal with this. If the accident taught me something is that I only have one life and I need to make the moments count. Spending my hours somewhere I am not appreciated, and dealing with people who drain my happiness is not worth it. In a little over a year, I already lost so much that I know losing this job will not be the end of me.

"Then do it," I shrug, and he blinks. "You came here to intimidate me to stop the lawsuit, which won't happen. I do not expect you to know what it is like to lose a child. Thankfully, you have all of yours with you. But I was hoping you would put your employees ahead of money. Since that isn't happening and we can say clear as day I am not giving up, then hire someone to do my job."

He doesn't show it on his face, but his Adam's apple wobbles. I smirk, taking one last step and placing both my hands on my desk while leaning forward. I can see him fuming, wanting to say more but scared of the consequences. But I don't care about the consequences at this point. I have lost so much already. There is little more to lose. My son is dead. My husband and I may as well never get back together if Dorians' silence is any proof of it. The job I love doesn't appreciate all the time I put into it.

"I am going to make it simple for you, Sir. In my top drawer, there is a letter of resignation from my lawyer. I ask for a nice sum of money to keep a secret of what I know about this company, plus interests from all my time here. Either you pay me the amount I ask for, or you fire me and pay a much larger sum."

28
Ariella

I wish someone had told me how I would feel comfortable seeing my scars. Both physical and mental.

I have gained a lot of scars throughout my life. Now I have nasty ones branded against me. Sometimes my scars remind me why I am who I am, and why I came all this way. When I stepped inside the building this morning, I was aware I could be without a job by the end of the day. It is exactly what happened.

After a talk with my boss, he wasn't pleased. Now I pack my things and put all of my belongings inside a card box. Still, I smile as I do so. They will promote Louis, which will be amazing for his career, and if they try not to give him the proper recognition, I'm sure someone else will. As for me, I have my plans.

Maybe now I can take a long break and start my own business. The dream never faded away, lingering in the back of my mind all this time. It came a few years before I wanted it to, but I have the funds and contacts for it.

Everything is in the box. Funny how my life here inside this room can fit into something so small as this. The entire floor is silent since they heard the news I was leaving. My secretary is pouting with the uncertainty of who she will work with from now on. No one else seems to be pleased with my boss either, since word got out about why I was leaving.

I got news from the security that someone arrived at the building minutes ago. I'll allow her to make a scene in the building and let my former boss deal with the temper Irene has shown me throughout the last year. The same Irene who shoves the door open, hand in the air with a document I know so well. She stomps towards my desk before slashing it against the wood. She ignores Louis, who frowns in my direction.

"What the fuck is this?"

She only got the news now? Interesting. Her bosses have known for hours. It shows Irene's promotion is not because she was the best for the job, but because they wanted to silence her after getting rid of the other idiot. She is qualified for the job, but I doubt they would even consider her for it if it weren't for her idea. Everything she does with the intention of being the best will bite her in the ass one day.

"It's a letter," I explain, tilting my head. "Someone writes them, then puts them in the mail, for you to receive. Do you want me to read it for you?"

"Don't act like a stupid bitch, Ariella. Why are you suing us? Why didn't I know Ariella wasn't even your real name? Have you been using me the entire time?"

"Yes."

There, it's out in the open. I can be a bitch sometimes. I am aware of it. But Irene has to walk a mile in my shoes, as does anyone else, before I allow them to say any hurtful things about me. The fact that I have made mistakes in my life doesn't allow anyone to judge my actions. Sometimes the first one's pointing fingers have the most terrible secrets.

Like her.

She can complain about me using her all she wants, but she is the reason I cry myself to sleep so many nights.

"I knew you were cold, but this-"

"This is an act of vengeance," I state, taking a deep breath, circling the table, and standing in front of her with my chin held high. "You are getting nothing more than the consequences of your actions."

"It was your kid," Irene scoffs. "That's why that stupid moron of your husband was so infuriated at the fashion show. The kid was yours."

My tongue glides inside my mouth against my cheek as I take a cautious step towards her.

"Wash your mouth before talking about my family."

"Does your dead son know what his mom was doing all these months? Does he know she is a cheating whore-"

The slap that lands across her face shuts her up. She lifts her palm to her stained cheek as I control my breathing, enjoying the cherry red spreading across her skin. I almost threw a punch, but it would leave a scar and I want to avoid giving her anything she can throw back at me. I never lifted a hand to anyone in my life. I am not violent. But when it comes to my family, I am willing to kill someone if I have to.

"I warn you. Do not speak about my family. What I am taking from you now is not half of what I lost."

"You won't get away with this," she threatens, leaning towards me and trying to make her warning clear while pushing a finger against my chest. I don't move. Louis steps by my side so fast I barely notice him coming from the door. "I am going to ruin you. You will beg in court to keep your job. I'll make you wish you'd die that day."

Her hand wraps around my arm pulling me closer. But I don't move and put my fingers over hers. Irene whimpers as I tug them from me. If I break one of her bones, so be it. She came searching for blood, but it doesn't have to be mine. I am done bleeding.

"I already do," I reply. "It is the difference between us, Irene. I know how to love someone. You do not.

People will never love you for who you are, just as you cannot love people back. You are too selfish. Too self-centered. And as for your threats, they fall short. You should focus on how you are going to handle the judge."

"This is not a threat," Irene hisses, her fingertip poking my chest once more and stepping so close her breath hits against my skin. "You will end up with nothing once we are done."

"Try me."

My chin lifts as I stare her in the eye, and Irene almost burns a hole in my skull with the power of her stare. There's something unusual about intimidation: when you think they can take something away from you, it's frightful, but I couldn't care less about it now.

They won't take anything I haven't lost already.

"You bitch," she grunts, heading for the door. "You'll regret this."

A snicker appears on my lips. "I doubt it."

29
Dorian

"Let's walk through another painful memory," Anna, my new therapist, tells me.

Thea recommended her, and although Ari and I were doing our sessions together, I have been avoiding those telling Anna I have a busy schedule.

All days are fine for me to work on my marriage, but I'm not keen on the idea of facing Ari before the trial. It's an uneasy feeling because although I love her, I fear she will bring back the one thing I don't want to talk about. Divorce. So instead I let my gaze stay on the dark-haired woman staring back at me. Her blue eyes plead with me to collaborate, and I do.

Might as well help us both out and do what she wants. I know the hearing is happening soon. I got the letter the other day. Ari did not waste time, and I am both proud and angry at her for it. She could have told me from the start. The question is, would I have listened?

"A painful memory?" Anna dips her chin at my question. "That would be the day of the accident."

The man pulls the blue sheet and my entire body runs cold. There is no pain able to describe the way my entire soul breaks as I watch my little boy on the morgue table. His angelic face as if he is sleeping. I glance at the man, taking a cautious step forward and he nods. My hands hover over my son. I want to hold him. I want to tell him he will be okay. My eyes burn, a sob erupts from the ends of my heart, and I kneel next to the table when my legs fail me.

"How?" I ask. My voice fails to project the word loud enough.

The man exhales deeply, staring at Raphael. "We will perform an autopsy. I cannot give you an accurate cause of death yet, sir. But it was most likely the impact of the truck against the car," he says, but I don't look at him. "The boy died at the scene."

The man shifts on his feet while I pour my heart out and shed tears for the boy I loved more than life itself. "You have to cut him?" I realize what he means and taking my child's small hand between mine.

He is cold. So cold.

I have known pain and grief. Yet nothing compares to this. It is as if a part of me is gone. A piece of myself slipped away into the dark and I will never see it again. I will never hear my son's laughter, hear his voice, or see him waking up. I will never hug and kiss him, drop him at school, or put him to bed. I will never be his father again.

"I do, sir."

A hand rests on my shoulder and I look back to find a

doctor staring down at me. I did not hear him entering the room. His eyes plead for forgiveness, but he still speaks. "Mr. Vaillant, I am Doctor Williams. I called you to come to the hospital?" He asks, but when I don't reply, he continues. "Your wife has come out of surgery. She should wake up soon."

I dip my chin and slide the sleeve of my shirt over my face to wipe away the stream of tears still falling. I press a kiss on Raphael's hand and mumble I am sorry to my son before standing. I am sorry. So fucking sorry for this. For not being there for him when he needed me the most.

Ari is out of surgery. The doctors told me she had to be rushed to remove a piece of glass from her back. It was life-threatening, and no one knows how my wife survived with it stuck in her back. Or how she stayed awake for so long when the truck hit her side of the car. They said she crawled to the back seat. They said the paramedics found her holding our son's body, and then she passed out. Doctor Williams called it her will to live. It did not surprise me.

My wife sleeps in the bed while I sit by the chair at her side. I almost whimper watching her bruised body. She is fine, she is safe.

But anger curls around my stomach at the same time as grief. A part of me is numb enough to realize the anger I feel is not towards Ariella but at myself. At the low piece of shit I have become. The man who had to work and passed on a chance to be with his family. As she moves on the bed, I keep my gaze on the city outside the window. Tears stream down my face as I watch the woman I love lift her hand to the tube on her nose. The hospital called while I was packing to leave work and I knew. I knew something was wrong with my wife. But I still can't process what I am feeling. It should have been me in that car. If it were me, maybe Raphael wouldn't be dead. If it was me, maybe I could have done something to save them both from this.

"Dorian?"

Her voice sounds hoarse and distant. They said they had to force a breathing tube down Ari's throat while they were bringing her in. Ariella's body looks so frail, so small on the bed. So broken. She wraps her hands around the bed sheet and tugs it up, covering her chest. There are bruises on her hands. The same hands that put our son to sleep last night. The same hands I kissed this morning before leaving the house.

"I'm here," I whisper and turn to face her. I bite down on my lip, staring at the woman I love but whom I cannot tell how I feel. It is not fair to her. As it is not fair to Raphael. "Are you okay?" She dips her chin. So many questions run through my mind, but I need to know. Before anything else, I need to know. "Do you want something else for the pain? Do you want me to run get a nurse to check on you?"

"No," she breathes out. Her eyes glisten against the dimmed lights of the room.

She knows. I know she knows. I can see it in her face. My parents prepared me for a lot of things in my life, but they never prepared me for the loss of the people I would love. Or how to support someone when they are going through it. I watch Ariella on the bed and breathe out a sigh of relief. "I know you may not want to talk about it, but I need to know what happened, Ari."

The question slips before I realize it. She looks at her hands as she speaks and I take the chance to wipe away the tears. They do not seem to stop.

"There was a truck," she mumbles. "I tried to reach him-"

I turn to face the window once more. Ariella shifts on her bed and tries to sit. I am about to tell her to stop, but then her hand tries to reach for me, and somehow, without me realizing why, I lean out of her reach. I don't want her to touch me. Not because I am mad at her, but because I am mad. I am just mad. At the world, at God and at myself. I don't want her to see what a failure I am as a father and a husband that I couldn't even protect the ones I love.

I failed. I failed both of them.

30
Ariella

The place feels crowded, and I am used to being in rooms with a lot more people. Still, I can't shake the feeling that there are too many people inside the courthouse. Thea suggested earlier for me to enter the building through the side door, not wanting to grab the media's attention outside. They are all gathered at the front, cameras pointing at whoever passes, hoping to get the best shot or even a remark from me or Red & Blue Associates. Thea doesn't say it, but I know there's more to this.

I know Dorian is coming today.

A sigh of relief left me before I grew nervous. These days haven't been easy, and the fact this entire thing is taking place on the 17th feels like irony.

"Did you talk to him?" Thea asks by my side as we head towards the coffee machine. "Josh said he would be here around 9 a.m."

"No," I reply. "I haven't talked to him for a few days."

"Ariella..."

"I can't Thea." I say as she presses a button. The

machine buzzes in reply and the paper cup makes the distinct noise of falling in its place. "I don't know what to say or how to say what I feel. He texted the other day to let me know he had to pick something from our office while I was at work and all I could reply was 'okay'. Okay. As if he said the store didn't have the bread I wanted. He texted yesterday saying he would be here today, and I didn't know what to reply."

The two hours staring at my phone while trying to figure out what to type were a torment. After I don't know how long, I reacted to his message with a heart and saw the ellipses while Dorian was typing. Whatever he was planning to say, he regretted it because he never sent the second text.

"You two need to talk. Even if you don't end up together, you need to talk."

"Even if we do," I say as the small beep from the machine gets my attention, and I take my hot beverage from it. "What do I tell him? How do I start that conversation? Hi, I know I hurt you deep enough with all my vendetta plans, but do you want to have a drink?"

Thea presses her lips together, pretending to choose what to drink when I know she is stalling for an answer. I know what is stopping me from talking to Dorian. Since we haven't spoken after the night he left, I am fearing he is still upset.

I'm scared if we talk, he will tell me he is ready to

file for our divorce. He took the papers with him. The other night I couldn't sleep, so I decided to pick them up and throw them out, but they were not there. I don't know what to make of it... did he take them to sign the papers? Or because he doesn't want me getting ideas?

He can ask for a divorce; he has the right to do so. I am scared, but I know I will survive. I have survived it all so far.

I have to heal, and I will only do it by closing this chapter of my life. I will take down those who drew my son away from my husband and me. Bringing down Irene and the company she works for. They do not care about people's lives if they put money over emotional well-being.

The cruel world we all live in.

So, if I can delay the conversation bound to happen with my husband, I sure as hell will avoid it for as long as I can. Dorian will too, and maybe it's for the best. If it ends, if our marriage is over, I want to deal with it with a clean mind.

"Oh, there he is," Thea lets out, tapping me on the shoulder as I turn to watch Josh walking in our direction. "God, that man. Look at those thighs-"

I block the sound of my friend's voice as she drools over her boyfriend, and instead, my eyes spot Dorian right behind Josh. I designed the suit my husband wears. A dark-gray slim fit, with almost unperceivable green lines. He paired it with a black button-down shirt and no tie. Our eyes meet, and my lips part. The suit used to cling to his body, but now it doesn’t. Dorian stops in his tracks and it is as if we have a silent conversation. He dips his chin, looks at something behind me, and then taps Josh on his arm. Josh points inside the courtroom when Dorian glances at his watch and walks away.

It's fair. I get it. Whatever happened between us was too much for him to endure. Still, I can't shake the feeling he’s a coward right now, and I’m angry about it.

A hello wouldn't hurt.

Irene’s voice reaches me and I glance over my shoulder to watch her having a heated argument with her lawyer. A frown makes its way between my eyebrows as I consider if seeing her is what made Dorian walk away.

Josh laces his arms around me, pulling me into an embrace and almost knocks all the air out of my lungs before whispering the words that have my wobbly legs getting under control.

“You can do this.”

I can, and I will.

This trial took something from my life, and I gave enough to those people already. My son’s death was their fault; my marriage falling apart was mine.

I almost don't ask, but the question is out of my mouth before I can rethink my decision. “Did he say anything?”

Josh licks his lips as I watch Eli walk to us and

smile in his direction. They all came, which is more than I was expecting. I thought I was going through this alone; I thought my husband wouldn't come.

"If you are worrying if Dorian is upset with you, all I have to say is that he is a stubborn ass sometimes," Josh replies. "He can't understand it entirely, or rather why you kept it a secret for so long. Eli has talked him through it most nights, and it's sinking in. But he hasn't stopped loving you. He needs time, Ariella. You are stirring something he was ready to let go."

"I know Josh," I reply, stopping him. "I know that all too well."

"He came. It must mean something," my friend smiles at me. "He also told me to let you know you are beautiful today."

I give my friend a small smile, not knowing what else to say. But I don't have to think about it, as we are called to go to our places. Voices surround me in a whisper from every end of the courtroom when I walk into it. I sit right by my lawyer's side, and my eyes move to the man behind us as I notice Dorian fidgeting with his hands. He doesn't stay still as Josh taps his shoulder, and they share a knowing glance. Josh murmurs something, squeezing his fingers in reassurance before looking at me, and the corner of his mouth lifts.

The murmur stops when the door at the right corner opens, and a woman walks inside the room wearing a long black cloak. If I prayed, this would be one of those things I would pray for. No matter how much I don't believe in God, I prayed hard for whoever watches over us to send me someone who would have a warm heart and not be blind with greed. Let's just hope my last act of faith doesn't come to bite me in the ass.

"Ariella," Josh calls as I turn to look at him, trying not to land my gaze on Dorian and failing. This time, he doesn't look away from me. His eyes study mine for a little before drifting to my left hand, and I dare to glimpse at his fingers as well, noticing his wedding ring still there. "You can do this," Josh says, giving me a double thumbs up.

"I know," I reply with a smile, tugging at my lips.

From the corner of my eye, I notice the Red & Blue Associates representative, and their lawyer, everyone growing impatient as Irene appears unbothered. This facade is one I am fully aware of, but it is one that has led her to where she is today. There aren't many people that can think with a clear head under stressful situations, not letting their emotions cloud their judgment.

Like my husband and I do.

Dorian and I always react based on our emotions. It is why our fights were always passionate. It is why he cannot stand to be by my side now, because he hurts. I have to endure this, hiding my feelings the best I can with the sole purpose of revenge. Still, if I think about it, my heart betrayed me didn't it? It's why I am here. I want them to suffer.

When I turn to stare at my friends, Dorian is watching me and I don't look away from him either. His gaze doesn't appear to carry the anger of the last time we spoke. This time, it is soft, as if he wants to talk but doesn't dare to say what's holding him back.

As usual.

It's Dorian's biggest flaw. He says nothing of what he feels, especially when he knows he already hurt someone. I can understand it, I do, but right now, I can't allow myself to care about it.

I have come too far, and *we* will have to wait. With a sharp inhale, I focus on what brought me here. The pain lingering in my chest that doesn't let me sleep at night. The times I wake up screaming, clutching my chest with my bare hands before deciding to walk away from my bed. Without my husband by my side, our bed feels empty. Will I tell him this? Maybe one day. Anna and Thea have both worked with me, reassuring my fragile mindset that I can relay my emotions to him. I should, as I did when we were happy and together. It will only happen if he wants me back.

Twelve people enter the room, their heads down. No one meets my eye, but I know my lawyer, Mrs. Garcia, chose them based on their family ties. When they are all in front of their seats, the rest of the room stands. I stare straight at the woman who carries my faith without even knowing it before glimpsing at the lawyers and Irene. Still unbothered, but trying to smile at the judge. If I am covering my emotions behind a mask, so is she. The difference is I don't want my feelings bare in the open for everyone to see my broken heart.

"Good morning, everyone," the judge greets. "I'm judge Carel. Who is Mrs. Vaillant?"

I raise my hand and nod at the woman, who then drifts her eyes to the other side of the room.

"And I suppose you are Red & Blue Associates representatives and Ms. Rogers? Alright, then let's get started."

It's time.

"Thank you, Your Honor," Mrs. Garcia says, sitting in her spot by my side. "The issue that brings us here is rather sensitive. It involved my client and a car accident last year..."

My attention remains focused on the judge as my lawyer explains the circumstances of the accident, what happened in the car and how the witnesses described it. But not everything. There are still some things I won't admit. Not even to Thea. Not until I am ready to face the demons that lurk in me at night.

Minutes pass, hours, and time seems irrelevant as both parts of the room present the case to the woman who will dictate our future. From the corner of my eye, I notice part of the jury glancing at me. Curiosity wins every time. One woman, in particular, looks like she wants to come around the room and give me a hug.

It gives me hope.

Someone moves behind me as the lawyer speaks. Dorian, I suppose, since I can see his shoes from the corner of my eye. This part is as uncomfortable for him to listen to as it is for me. Right now, I wish I could hold his hand or he could hold mine.

I wish he were by my side. Not that I need it, but it would be easier.

The lawyer for Red & Blue Associates stands. He does their opening statement and is not as subtle, bringing back my past and how I ran from home. However he found out about it.

The hours drag. Mr. Byrne, the defense lawyer, focuses on how I came into the city without a plan. How reckless I was as a teen. He goes further, hinting about my marriage, and I glare at him.

"I think I have heard enough for now," Judge Carel states once the defense lawyer is done. "We shall continue this tomorrow at 9 a.m."

We all nod, knowing today is going to be about explaining why we are here. Knowing this will take a while until it's finished. Thea and Josh look at me when I stand. I glance at the man I love who doesn't walk away this time.

"I'll see you tomorrow?" At the end of the sentence, my eyes land on Dorian, despite me asking all four of them. It's a loaded question, but the dip of his chin tugs at my heart strings.

"We will be here," he says, watching me. His answer does not give any hint if he is meeting me tonight or not.

Maybe his lips part to speak again. Maybe he takes a step in my direction, but right now, I can't stand to be in this room any longer, especially today. I need fresh air; I need to gather my emotions. It's like a fire pit. If I stand too close, I can burn myself, but without him, I feel cold. Thea gives me a small peck on the cheek before whispering what I already know.

"Baby steps. I'm proud of you both, but let's do one thing at a time."

The frosty night greets me like an old friend as I make my way to the tree behind the house. It's the 17th, reminding me once more of how long I have been absent from seeing the most beautiful smile on Earth. Of the eyes that had nothing but innocence, love, and adoration in them. The resemblance of Raphael's gaze to Dorian's never failed to amaze me. It makes me miss whenever my husband would look at me like I was the only person in the world. Rare occasions over the last year, but I keep them all close to my heart. A lantern has to be raised to the sky tonight. Although Dorian is not staying in the house, I intend to do it by myself if I have to. I will wait for him, as I did all the other months since we started this ritual. I will wait because I always do.

But the minutes pass, turning into half an hour, and there is no sign of Dorian anywhere. Thus far, I have tried to be optimistic, but I am considering if today was too much for him. Hearing the technical part of how the accident happened when he only knew bits of it may have left a deeper scar in my husband. Reopening the wound he was recovering from.

I sigh, staring at the stars trapped in the darkness in a distant space I somehow think is where my little love is. Up there, watching the mess, we became. The mess I am. Someone fueled by anger and revenge. Someone who once loved so much is now incapable of understanding her emotions. Someone who is sure this is the only path.

"I'm sorry," I mumble to the cloudless sky before resting my forehead on my knees and folding my arms around them, letting the sadness and memories take over me.

There are times in my life when I need to cry. To let it all out before I face the world again. Dorian was the only one who used to see my tears. He was the only one I let close enough. My hands clutch my elbows, pulling me closer as if I were about to break.

I'm alone.

This time is not like when I ran away. This time it hurts so much my breathing becomes heavy and a heavy fist grasps my heart, squeezing it until it bleeds. I know I will survive this. You can't die from the pain of a broken heart. I should know. Dorian may love me, like Josh said earlier. But even being in love with someone is not enough. Sometimes love struggles and falls apart no matter how much we want it to hold itself together.

Something snaps by my side, and I lift my head to spot Dorian walking toward me. My stomach flips, sinks, and butterflies go crazy inside of me as I try not to make a big deal out of this. I shift on my seat. Dorian pushes his lips together, coming to a halt and watching me. He carries the lantern in his hand, lifting it in my direction as I shift my gaze to the one waiting for mine.

"Sorry I am late," he says, scratching his brow, and it takes me a couple of seconds to achieve the thought he spoke to me. "I forgot how bad it gets when you have to leave the city. I texted you."

"I left my phone in my purse," I say and eye the bag in his hand.

Dorian takes a blanket from inside with a soft smile, hands it to me so I wrap it over my shoulders. The fist around my heart squeezes it again, but this time not in a way that makes it hurt.

He stares down at me. "Can I sit with you?"

I nod, sliding further on top of the blanket I brought, grabbing my lantern, and holding it close to my chest. Dorian stays by my side, staring at the space as I was a few minutes ago.

We don't speak for a while. I don't want to say anything that will make him step away. As for Dorian, I assume he doesn't know what to say.

"You don't have to sit back there," I say, not meeting his eyes as he glances at me. "In the courtroom, I mean. You can come and sit by my side if you want."

Dorian bites down on his lip, letting the words sink in. I know I may ask too much of him. The truth is, I can do this by myself. I have planned my journey for months, but it would be easier if he were with me.

"I'm not ready for that yet," he acknowledges, and I nod, taking a long breath.

Too soon.

"I understand."

"But," he says, and my heart skips a beat. "I would like to pick you up tomorrow for us to arrive at court together."

The slow dip of my head makes the corners of his lips tug up. I don't even want to think about the logistics of him coming back here so we can head back to town. He could sleep in our bed… I would sleep in the spare room. But Dorian doesn't suggest that, so I don't push it.

My hand clasps around my lantern and the lighter, and I try not to smile when my husband leans closer as I light up our lanterns. His peppermint scent takes over me for the briefest second. I miss him like crazy. But everything at its time. My husband has always given me space and been patient with me. This time, it's my turn to do the same.

If he means for us to be back together. If not, I can survive that. We both do what we need in the night's silence before watching the lanterns reach the sky, hoping to make our little angel smile.

I stay sitting in the same space we used to watch our son, now in silence, enjoying Dorian's presence and trying not to make a big deal out of it when our fingers brush against each other. I try not to make a big deal out of it and fail, feeling myself falling further when his hand closes on mine and my heart skips a beat.

31
Dorian

It is day three of this trial. But I sit right behind my wife the entire time. Ari does not spare Irene a glance.

We talk a little. Ari isn't acting as if she is mad at me and maybe knowing she isn't is what makes me more fearful of it all. The last two days I have driven to pick her up and taken her back home. We make the drive in silence, or with me telling her how the jury is reacting to the trial. It seems in favor of Ari.

I'm the one who stays on common ground and doesn't let the conversation shift. But I need a little more time, and for this trial to be done before I can tell Ari my decision. For all I care I would be at our house again, but with everything happening, I think she needs to keep a clear head.

This trial is bringing back emotions I would like to shut down.

Sometimes I wonder how she still loves me. How is she still able to love after all she has been through? Hearing the lawyer explain the accident was the hardest part so far. Mrs. Garcia called two witnesses yesterday, a couple who watched everything. Both of them said the same thing. They could hear Ari calling for our son inside the car. They could also hear the despair from the driver, who both insisted was not drunk.

The sound I let out after they confessed it made the judge glance in my direction. I get it better now. I have been so inside my head and grief I ignored the truth. It was easier. Believing in part of what happened was much easier than listening to the last moments of my son's life or how Ari reacted to it. Ignoring it was easier than facing everything.

All of it was easier than having to deal with the ache of knowing the pain we both faced after. It was stupid of me, and I acknowledge as much. At some point last night, I was waiting for Eli to kick me out of his sofa and rush me to meet Ari. But I cannot just show up at our door. She deserves more than a simple apology.

We both did wrong, but her wrong… her wrong has made me realize my wife is the bravest, strongest woman I have ever known. And I love her all the more for it.

I watch as Josh whispers something, leaning towards Ariella. She smiles at him, but it doesn't reach her eyes. Inside the courtroom, she doesn't look as tired or fragile. Which I know she is. I see it every time we are in my car, and she lets her guard down. Here she carries her head high and looks down at everyone who dares to mention her name in the wrong tone.

"You are doing great," Josh whispers at her, and I feel a grin tugging at my lips.

Thea wraps her hand around Josh's and pulls him close. When he doesn't look at her, she tilts her head to the hallway. My brow raises as I watch the two of them interact, and the younger is oblivious to what his girlfriend is trying to tell him.

There are these moments between couples when your eyes speak more than words. Still, it doesn't seem obvious to Josh the way Thea's eyes scream at him.

"Josh," Thea breathes out. "Can you come with me? I want to buy something to eat."

"Now?" Josh asks, raising his voice. "But they are going to start in-"

"Yes now," Thea says in a more clear tone. "I'm hungry."

As if it isn't apparent by the tilt of her head and the way she opens her eyes more. Josh finally gets the subtle hint behind his girlfriend's request. He nods, turning around and walking further away, leaving Ari and me alone.

I watch them walking, Thea slapping his shoulder and mumbling curses under her breath as Josh chuckles. Those two are perfect together, and although my relationship fell apart, I am glad my friend found love. My eyes meet the two brown ones I love the most and I know at this moment I will do anything in my power to win my wife back. Even if I have to crawl and beg her to take me once more.

"Josh is right. You are doing great."

"Thank you," she replies and I catch the smallest crinkle in the corner of her eyes. "Dorian I-" the words fail her. Ari sighs. "I have been meaning to ask… Do you need anything?"

"Don't worry about me, Ari. I am good. Well, good as I can be, considering the size of Eli's sofa."

"You can always come back home," she says before catching herself. Ari bites down on her lip, readjusting her thoughts. "I will sleep in the guest room, and you can-"

"It's fine," I tell her, shaking my head. "I think this was the best decision. Me going away for this long and give you space. I needed to clear my head and understand everything, and you are not one to stop once you have something in your mind. We were on track to destroy ourselves if we didn't take a step back."

Something painful crosses over my wife's gaze. I want to hug her and promise we will be okay, but I know she wants to have a proper talk first. Ari is not one to move on without making everything behind clear.

Eli comes to the door. When spotting us, he stops in his tracks and smiles before motioning to the watch on his wrist, signaling we have only a few minutes.

"I know you said you have been sleeping at Eli's. I'm happy you two talked"

"When I appeared at his front door, the fight didn't matter anymore," I admit.

I wish it could be that simple for us.

As I am about to tell her that when this is all over, I would like to have an honest conversation. The commotion behind me makes me turn around. People gather, cameras go off, and I roll my eyes, watching as Irene walks towards us.

32
Ariella

Her heels click on the floor as her skirt and blazer sway, while Irene furrows a brow at Dorian for not walking away. She takes her sunglasses and places them inside her small purse, tilting her head.

"Ariella," Irene sings. "Or should I call you Adriana?"

"I'm not even sure you should talk to me at all."

"Oh, I know I shouldn't. My lawyer advised me not to," she says, lifting her gaze to Dorian as she speaks. A smirk taunts her lips. "But because of all the fun you and I used to have, and considering our past, I figured I might at least come here and tell you this in person."

Dorian takes a long breath, his body heat growing against mine as my husband steps closer and towers over me from behind. At this point, I don't know if he wants to protect me or drag Irene out of the way. Maybe both.

"If you have something to say, then say it. My minutes are precious, and I don't want to ruin the little time I have outside of the courtroom by spending them with you."

The corner of her mouth lifts as Irene smirks at me. She places her bag on her hip, opens it, and takes a small USB from inside while shoving it right in front of my eyes.

"This," she says, trying to increase our curiosity. "It's all I have on you. The conversations we had, the things you said about your boss."

"My *former* boss," I correct and feel Dorian's eyes on me, so I glance back to explain. "I quit."

His hand rests on the small of my back, catching me off guard, but it's an encouragement. He knew how much I wanted to do it. I hope this is confirmation enough to him I had everything planned all along and I know what I am doing. For a few seconds before Irene speaks I could swear I feel Dorian's thumb brushing against my back.

"Wait…" I say, a mocking grin appearing on my face. "No one told you I am not working there? You are out of the deal with Mr. White and Wear A Kiss?"

"Anyway," Irene continues, avoiding my question. "The press would love it. You won't work for anyone in the entire country again. I can show it on the court-"

"You didn't submit it before," Dorian snorts. "I've seen the file your lawyer didn't mark as evidence to present to the judge because it is not relevant. Not for what we are here for, anyway. I would think twice about doing it now. It must not mean much if even your lawyers are not willing to use it."

He saw the files?

I look at Dorian as I ponder when did it happen, but he only lifts the corner of his mouth in realization of what he said. I take a step back, needing the warmth of his body closer to me, and he doesn't pull away. Instead, his arm tugs me closer, wrapping around my waist.

"Even so," Irene shrugs, glaring at Dorian behind me, not enjoying how he cut her off. "Sometimes, they accept additional pieces of evidence. I'm sure the judge will enjoy knowing you and I were involved in so many ways."

Figures it's what she would do. Her company may even be the one behind this idea. It's desperation. I scared them enough they're thinking they can lose. Irene is reluctant. All her hard work has been in vain. My eyes linger on the USB a little longer before I shift in my spot, staring right ahead at Irene. If they present the evidence, will it be a reason to dismiss the lawsuit?

"I thought you were smart. We are talking about the company and how your team planned this entire thing, Irene. Ariella's actions outside of court have nothing to do with it. You know..." Dorian says with a chuckle cold enough to drop the temperature. "After all you've done, it's funny how you still think you can get away with this."

"Ariella," she starts.

He clicks his tongue. “Her name shouldn't even be on your lips, so I suggest you shut up.”

Irene rolls her shoulders back at my husband’s words, but I see her confidence wavering. “Is that a threat?”

Dorian pulls me around him. His body shields me from Irene as he whispers. “I don't make threats, Irene. I'm not a coward.”

I think my heart just burst out of my chest. My hand wraps around his as I draw him closer to me. Dorian does as I ask without words, his fingers tightening on mine, and I thank whoever is looking down at us for this. This moment made up for all the nights I haven't been sleeping.

“I didn't come this far for you to take me down,” I enunciate my words clearly. “Bring your worst Irene. We will do the same.”

She scoffs, turning around and walking away from us. Almost stumbling on Eli as he leaves the room once again to check on us. He frowns at Irene, dismissing the attitude, and motions to us that it's about to start. From behind Eli, Louis’ head pops. I told him about the trial, but his coming may put him in a tight spot with Mr. White. I don't want my friend to get caught in all of this.

“I called him,” Dorian says, noticing the confusion on my face. “He gave your boss an excuse. Your former boss, I mean,” he corrects himself.

Can I love this man more than I did yesterday?

Dorian tightens his hold on my hand as I think about going inside, but Dorian's hand still holds mine. As I am about to take a step further, he speaks.

"Ari-" he breathes out, looking at our hands. He lifts mine and his fingertip slides across the wedding ring. Dorian's gaze knocks all the air out of my lungs when our eyes meet. "They took everything from us. We lost so much already. Make all of our sacrifices... *your* sacrifices count."

33
Ariella

"The defense would like to call Mrs. Vaillant to speak," Red & Blue Associates' attorney says. I stand. I knew this was coming, and I was prepared for it. They won't fight fair. I am sure Irene told them as much as she could. When it's her reputation and job at stake, she will fight tooth and nail.

My heels make a little noise over the silence in the room as I approach the chair where the security guard gestures with his hand for me to sit. The Judge watches, and so does the jury. They read my every move. Some people seem to have a hard time hiding their thoughts while listening to the trial. Others don't even stare at Mr. Bryne while he speaks. Irene taps her nails on the table. She kisses her teeth, looking away from me as her lawyer whispers something to her, and she nods.

Dorian watches from my lawyer's side. After Irene spoke to us, or whatever one can call what happened this morning, he didn't want to go back and be a mere witness in the trial. He stayed by my side. It is a tremendous step. But he cannot seem to be still either, fidgeting with his fingers when our eyes meet.

"Mrs. Vaillant," the man asks, approaching. "Can you tell us, briefly, about the accident?"

"Briefly?" I ask, raising my brow. "Sure. I was making my way to Central Park when a man driving a truck from Red & Blue Associates t-boned my car and killed my son."

My brief description has the chubby man blinking in reply. I'm sure Irene didn't tell him about my temper. I take a deep breath while the man clears his throat.

"With a little more detail this time, ma'am," he tries narrowing his eyes at me.

"On the 17th of July 2021, I was driving after taking my son Raphael-"

"Your son the victim-"

"My son *Raphael*," I continue. "It was his name. I will address him by it, if you don't mind."

The lawyer sneers, knowing he hit a nerve. "Not at all, Mrs. Vaillant. Please continue." My gaze shifts to Dorian, who clasps his hands together and gives me a single nod of encouragement.

"Raphael wanted to go to the park. He asked me the night before, so I picked him up earlier than usual. He was excited, and as I was making my way to-"

"Where was your husband?" The man asks, pointing at Dorian as if asking me if it is, in fact, him, the man I am married to. "Where was he during all of this?"

"At work," I reply, tilting my head, not understanding the root of the question. Mrs. Garcia makes eye contact with me and puts a strand of her black hair behind her ear. Our signal. It is for me not to evade questions, but not to go into detail either. We both know this conversation can take a sudden turn. She was told not to object unless it was something out of context.

"I took Raphael by myself-"

"Mrs. Vaillant, what is the state of your relationship with your husband at the moment?"

"Objection," Mrs. Garcia calls, standing up.

"Mr. Byrne," the Judge speaks over both voices. "Relevance of the question?"

"We will get to that, Your Honor, I promise," Mr. Byrne states. "Care to reply to me, Mrs. Vaillant?"

"We went through a rough patch as expected after what happened."

Mr. Byrne strolls around the room. I follow him with my gaze, knowing Dorian is doing the same. This hearing is about to take a nasty turn. They want to show the dirt in my relationship. It will make me less of a victim against Red & Blue Associates. I never said I was one.

"Do you have a happy marriage?"

"We used to. Until our son died."

"What happened after?" Mr. Byrne asks. The

frown on his face not matching with his tone.

"I'm not sure what you mean, Mr. Byrne. Nor do I see the relevance of this story to why we are here today."

"Please elaborate on your question, Mr. Byrne," the Judge warns him. "And get to the point."

"Will do, Your Honor. It all has an explanation," Mr. Byrne feigns innocence. "Mrs. Vaillant, aren't you cheating on your husband with my client?"

"Objection-" Mrs. Garcia calls, but the Judge lifts her hand.

I take a deep breath, regaining control over the topic. My gaze shifts to Irene as I speak before it travels to the man I hurt for so long. Dorian and I stare at each other, and my eyes stay locked on his as I reply.

"I did."

"So," Mr. Byrne tiptoes around the question. "If you are capable of such a thing if you lie to your husband, to whom you promised fidelity, who's to say you are not lying about this? Maybe you are lying about not speeding on that day?"

Is he serious right now?

The police were there. They took measurements of the accident, and I was under the speed limit. His accusation is nothing but a roux to make me lose my mind and yell in court, to disbelieve my credibility. Last year maybe, but not anymore. They don't know the love I hold for my son is bigger than any anger I can feel towards them. The love I have for Raphael is the only thing keeping me going when the nights are long and dark. When all I wish for is for us to be together again.

Irene doesn't know the lengths I will go to for my little boy.

"Not that I need to explain my marriage to you, Mr. Byrne, but my husband knows I was unfaithful, and he knows the few kisses your client and I shared meant nothing. I wasn't speeding on the day of the accident either," I say as calmly as possible and look at the jury. One man makes eye contact with me and it's obvious he doesn't like what I have to say. "I was making my journey with my son in his backseat, and we were singing his favorite songs. All of a sudden, the truck appears at my left, speeding and not being able to stop-"

"How do you know such a thing?" Mr. Byrne asks.

"I saw the driver. I remember his face and the way he was panicking before hitting my car."

Mr. Byrne strolls in front of me, placing his hands behind his back and studying the emotions in the room. I fight the urge to glance at the jury.

"You think you do. But you weren't in the vehicle that went against your car."

"You are right. I was in my car, but I saw him and it was obvious. I saw the truck, and I noticed it wasn't stopping. So I turned to grab my son and tried to wrap my arms around him before the truck collided against us."

The man with eager eyes blinks at me as I speak and wait for his remark. He has something else to say. They always do. Men like Byrne enjoy diminishing women like me. It gives them a sense of power, that little other things do. It makes them feel meaningful and happy even when their life is miserable in every other aspect. Men like the one in charge of questioning me have a petty heart and pretend to be something they are not.

But I do not let him think as such. I do not allow him to pretend I am less than who I am. I won't allow Byrne or anyone to stomp on me.

"You were…" he lets the words hang in the air.

"Reaching for my son.".

"So, you let go of the wheel?"

Of course, he thought I had reacted and stayed in my place. It would be normal for so many people. To freeze in the face of danger. "Mr. Byrne, are you a parent?"

He clears his throat at my question, sliding his hands inside the front pockets of his trousers and bouncing on his heels. The gentleman always asks the questions being inquired by the person he should be interrogating. He does, however, realize the same thing I do. Whatever his intentions are, most people watching him are not enjoying the way he is conducting the interrogation.

"No, I am not. I don't think my personal life is the one thing we should focus on," he chuckles as if my question is not important.

"Then I don't suppose you would understand why I had to leave everything and try to save my son's life, would you?"

We both catch at least half the jury nodding along and Mr. Byrne clears his throat again. "Mrs. Vaillant, please calm down."

"No. You are talking to me as if I am the one to blame for the accident. You, sir, are putting in cause my morals, when all I did was drive around the corner and the truck from the company you are protecting drove toward my much smaller car. Replying to you, I left the wheel. My priority was my son, not my life. I tried to jump over the seats to put my entire body over his car seat or tried to since I didn't make it on time. I rushed to the back of the car, and my hands brushed Raphael's seat, but the moment the truck hit the car we flipped and-"

My eyes close as the inevitable memories crawl into my mind. The screams from everyone in the street mixed with Raphael's cry invade my thoughts. The smell of blood and oil burning against my nose… I take a long breath, my lips pressed together.

"Take your time," the judge tells me.

My nails dig against the fabric of my trousers. I need to do this, to explain it, so maybe the stupid man in front of me grasps the idea.

When my eyes open, I lock them on Dorian's.

I never told him, not like this. He never knew the pain of what happened that day. I didn't want him to carry the burden of it. Thinking about the little one we love in this way wouldn't do the man I love any good.

Maybe it wasn't the best decision I made, but it was my decision, and I made it out of love.

"I let go of the wheel to protect my son. I let go of the wheel because even if there was just a slight chance it was me who got hurt and not my son, I would take it. But I would do anything, *anything* I could, for my baby boy to be alive, even if it meant I would die in his place. Because I don't think you understand the despair of that moment, Mr. Byrne. How I jumped to him, how I tried to put my body over his car seat. How everything around us exploded, and it turned the world upside down. And then after the car stopped spinning after I could not feel my back bleeding, I opened my eyes, but my son wasn't moving. My son wasn't breathing."

Tears gather at my sight, and I take a long breath. No one speaks in the courtroom.

I glance at Dorian and my heart aches to hold him close to me. Tears fall on his cheeks, his body shivering but not from the cold, and holding his hands in fists in front of his mouth. His gaze stays on me, hurting like I knew he would. Hurt I still think I caused. Josh, behind him, stares at the floor as Thea rubs his back. Both Louis and Eli stare at the window as if that will hide their own pain.

"I struggled with opening his car seat. I got him free and then lifted my hands to touch my baby. He didn't move. Not even when I called his name. Not even when I screamed for help. I did this all the while, listening to the muffled sounds around me. People were yelling. I heard the driver as well. I heard the man you left to take the accusation of murder shouting now he knew the truck wasn't capable. But do you know what I was doing? I was holding my little boy against me. I was closing his eyes and kissing his hair, singing his favorite lullaby. The same one his father and I always sang at his bedtime. In the meantime, praying to a God, I don't believe in bringing Raphael back. To take me instead. And if God couldn't do it, to at least spare me of the pain and take me as well. I held my baby against my chest for as long as I could before my body gave up on me, and I enjoyed the pain because I knew I was dying. I *wanted* to die."

Byrne doesn't dare to look at me anymore. He dips his chin, mumbling "no further questions" under his breath and heading to his side of the courtroom where Irene is. She shifts her gaze, letting it go to the man sitting next to her. It's the first time I see the slightest crack in her revealing her emotions, but it's too late.

Dorian wipes away his tears while my lawyer stands up. She buttons up her jacket, revealing her slim waist, and heads towards me as her black hair sways to the rhythm of her heels. She nods at me and lets me take a few seconds to compose myself before speaking.

"Mrs. Vaillant, you said you got involved with the Vice President of Red & Blue Associates?"

"I did."

"Why did it happen?"

A smile tugs at the corner of my lips. From the start of this journey, I wasn't supposed to keep it a secret. When I tried to give Dorian the divorce papers, I had all of this in mind.

It would be easier, and yet I don't regret us making the effort to be together. At least I got a few more months with him.

"Because I knew she would confess her darkest thoughts about what happens in the company."

Irene and Byrne share a nervous glance.

"Do you have any evidence of this?"

"I do. I have recordings of it on my phone."

Whispers cover the room, lingering between the people and breaking the silence from before my lawyer turns to grab the device and show the evidence. Mr. Byrne blinks, looking at the sheets of paper and trying to figure out what he missed.

"Objection," he yells, startling half the room. "We never saw the evidence, Your Honor."

Mrs. Garcia walks to our table and picks up the evidence, handing it to the clerk, who then takes it to the judge. "Mrs. Vaillant's recordings are crucial to the case, as they contain conversations about the accident with the Vice President of Red & Blue Associates."

"Objection," Byrne says again, and the judge stares at him, waiting for him to elaborate. "The defense needs to process this evidence. You cannot allow this-"

"Considering you were the one asking in the first place about Mrs. Vaillant's activities outside of her marriage, and the importance of the situation, I think it's only fair to do this," my lawyer says, using her most charming smile.

"Your Honor," Byrne chuckles, waving his hand in our general direction. "You can't-"

"This is my courtroom, Mr. Byrne. It will serve you well if you remember it. I'll allow it," the Judge speaks over the petty man's voice. "Let's listen to it."

With a proud grin, Mrs. Garcia turns, her eyes set on Irene and Byrne as she walks to the table where Dorian is watching.

The Judge hands the USB back to the clerk, who then hands it to Mrs. Garcia. She slides it on her laptop, and Irene's voice fills the room. I fight back a smile, knowing the very first sentence is enough to win the case. *"You saw it in the news. The accident involving a car from my company? The little boy involved died. Someone needed to take the blame, and we had to move fast."*

34
Ariella

"In all my years as a Judge I have never seen such disrespect towards a case, or the people involved in it," Judge Carel says staring down at Mr. Byrne, Irene, and another man who is representing the board for Red & Blue Associates. "With that being said, I ask for you to listen to the jury's verdict in silence."

We didn't even have time to go home. After this morning, Mrs. Garcia and I were ready to go back to her office, but we were called not even two hours after leaving the courtroom.

From the jury, a woman stands. "We have, Your Honor. The Jury finds the defense guilty of all charges."

I forget how to breathe. It appears the air around me fades, and everything moves in slow motion while I take everyone in. Judge Carel talks. Her hammer sounds across the room, but I can't focus on what she is saying. My ears seem to malfunction as I watch most of the jury smiling at me. A woman nods, and I swear her teary eyes and the sad smile she gives me will stay in my memory forever.

Irene stands up. The representative from the company does as well. He walks around the table and approaches the Judge without warning, leaving Mr. Byrne calling after him. Maybe they'll have to spend the night in jail if they keep disrespecting Judge Carel like this. I couldn't care less if they do.

But Irene does not move from her spot. Her hands shake, and she takes a long gulf of breath. Her eyes meet mine for the briefest second, and she closes them. The representative from Red & Blue points towards her, and Irene walks around the table to join him and the lawyer.

Thea yelps as Josh stands, claiming victory louder than the rest. But I stay still. Dorian does too. His hand searches mine and takes it as if to check if the moment is real. When someone touches my shoulder, I look up at my lawyer, smiling at me.

We won.

"You did it." Mrs. Garcia says with a wide smile on her lips. "I'm pretty sure they will have to close the business after this comes out in the press. They're going to investigate the company. You'll get a big fat check coming your way soon."

I nod at her as the woman turns to my husband and excuses herself from the courtroom. Time isn't what matters at this moment. I stand up and my eyes meet Dorian's waiting ones. His lips part, but a voice cuts him off.

"You won't get away with this, you opportunist,"

the Red & Blue Associates man hisses behind me. The same one who directed the press conference after the accident and hinted I was speeding. Irene, however, seems to have whipped the emotions haunting her away from her face.

I can almost see the crack in Irene's intentions. But she puts walls around her and concentrates on all the wrong things. They lost, and here she is with the representative from Red & Blue, making their case valid as if they weren't called out on it.

"First," I take a deep breath. "It's Mrs. Vaillant to you, sir since I do not know who the hell you even are."

"Ariella-" Irene speaks.

"Second, I am going to get away with it because I did nothing wrong," I tell him and then turn to her. "You should be more worried about your job not surviving this crisis, Irene. They want to blame someone, and they will blame you."

"Sir?" Byrne calls. "We should go-"

"We are not going anywhere," the representative says. "Irene, do something. You have things against them. Your job is at risk here. We all are."

Irene extends a hand to silence him, taking a cautious but determined step, as if attempting to intimidate me. But I beat her to it, closing the small space between us. Someone towers over me from behind, and by the way, peppermint lingers around. I know it's Dorian.

"I wouldn't try to blackmail me about anything stupid like ruining my life. The recording will go public. Whatever you can do to me, I will do much worse to you," I say, glaring at the man behind her. "You too Sir. The company may never recover after this. I already lost everything, so don't test me."

Irene leans forward, her eyes inspect mine as she whispers the words the entire room can hear. Around us, everyone seems ready to stop this if things get out of hand.

"This isn't over, Ariella."

"Yes, it is," I reply, turning around and heading towards the door.

"I'm going to-"

"Would you shut your mouth?" Dorian says at the woman. "You've done enough. Stop trying to cross our path."

Irene scoffs. "Are you threatening me right now? In court?"

"*Une menace?*" Dorian snorts. "I am not threatening. I told you I don't make threats." his smile widens, but it's not the warm one I love. Here is the man who will have my back, no matter what. "If you even try to look at my wife, I will make sure you get your ass dragged into jail. Paying the driver cannot be the only wrong thing you ever did."

Irene stares at him before averting her gaze to her lawyer, who gulps and tilts his head while turning to leave. She follows suit, close by, not daring to glance in our direction- I can still hear the curses falling from her lips until her voice fades in the busy hallway where people linger by the door.

"There are reporters outside," Louis warns me. "We are leaving first, so you can exit through the side door without being seen."

I nod, watching my friends leave and knowing Dorian is staring at me all the while. His body is close enough and my fingers brush against his. I inhale, letting his perfume invade my lungs, telling my damn brain this is not the last time I will see him.

But I need to know anyway.

There is no way I will sleep tonight if I don't ask if I don't at least know the basics of this relationship. What we are for each other. Because even if he isn't pushing me away today, we are still not together. And I know it takes time, but I need to know.

I have hurt enough already. So has he. I need him to tell me if this is over.

Fighting the urge to bite my nails or plug the skin from my lips, I blurt out. "Dorian? Do you want to go grab a coffee?"

A smirk tugs at the corner of his mouth and my husband places his hand on my back as we leave.

"Mrs. Vaillant," Mrs. Garcia calls, turning her attention to me. "I heard from Red & Blue lawyer that they will pay this week."

"The total?" She nods.

It is a lot of money. But it's money I don't want. "I

can donate it to charity, right?" Mrs. Garcia smiles and nods again.

At my side, Dorian's hand rubs against my back in soothing circles. I didn't want to tell him what we would do with the money. It's not like we need it. Since I have no use, or desire for it, a few charities both Dorian and I donate to regularly will receive it instead.

"I think it's safe," Josh says, stepping behind us. "Louis is talking to the press. They want Ariella to talk, but… he is talking to them. The last thing I heard, he was chatting about his new designs."

I hug Thea, Josh, and Eli before walking with Dorian to the side of the court. As soon as we step outside, it pours. Dorian takes his jacket and places it over my head, shielding me from the rain. We don't walk for long, but we walk in silence.

We arrive at a small café and drift unnoticed from the press. A little shop displaying pastries of all colors. Yet the promise of food doesn't even seem to entice me. My stomach churns with nausea at how the conversation my husband and I are about to have can end.

I have a good feeling, yet something in the back of my mind keeps telling me I am hoping for too much.

My husband orders both of our drinks before turning to me. I stay quiet while Dorian chooses the last table. The window shows the grayish day outside. From here, we can see the reporters leaving as the rain grows heavier. A couple sits side by side while their friend talks on the phone. The woman, with dark red hair and a face worthy of being on a magazine cover, grins at the man by her side. The look of love mixed with lust he gives her has me shifting my attention back to my table.

Dorian and I had those moments, and not long ago. I wonder if he will ever look at me like that again.

"Thank you," I say as the server hands me my drink and I place the mug in front of me. Smoke emanating from the hot beverage as the server tries to catch Dorian's attention.

"Do you need something else?" Lust laces her voice while she asks him.

I lift my brow at her, knowing full well she is being inconvenient. Very inconvenient.

She leans forward, cleaning the already immaculate table, and still I watch this girl, who can't be over 20 years old, hitting on the man on the table as if her life depends on it. The same man who doesn't spare her two seconds of his attention, nor her cleavage which is on full display. Dorian glances at her at some point when she tries to reach further into the table to take the napkins out of the way, almost bumping into him. He presses his lips together before his attention shifts back to me.

"We're fine," he says. "We would like some privacy."

My brows rise as the girl places a strand of her hair behind her ear, peeking at me. I tilt my head and watch her leave against her will. Moving my wedding ring around my finger makes me realize that although I never took it out, I don't know if Dorian did or not. He has his hands beneath the table, so I have no way of telling if he is still wearing it today. It's not like I can ask. Well, I can, but I won't. We are not there yet. I am not even sure if we will ever be. He stares at his drink now as I shift my gaze between the people in the café and him. His hands are out of my sight, and I let my gaze drink in his figure, the places where his clothing is looser. With a frown, I shift my attention once more. I don't want to think about him not eating.

Silence is a dreadful thing when we don't know what to say or how to phrase it. For instance, I notice how Dorian peeks at me when he thinks I am staring out the window. Or when he bites his bottom lip to stop himself from talking every time my wedding ring glimpses against the light from the lamp above us.

But none of us says a word. I want to, so badly. I want to voice how my days without him are dull, but I don't want to scare him off.

Instead, I clear my throat, ready to break the quietness settling between us. Back then, we always had these moments when we didn't need to speak and enjoyed each other's presence. They were some of my favorites. How his hands would glide against my scalp or caress my stomach even without him realizing it. He used to do it often when I was pregnant, forcing Raphael to move inside my belly. How he would lean against me and nap whenever I was working on the phone or tablet while we were on the sofa. How I would enjoy his presence on sunny days, even if we barely talked for over an hour or two.

But the silence between us now is not because we spoke about everything we needed. It's because there are things I need to get off my chest.

"Thank you for this," I let out with a deep breath, holding the mug between my hands as if it's a life vest.

He places his hands on top of the table, but his right hand covers his left, and I scold myself, thinking how stupid I am being. It is not as if the ring determines everything between us. Many people don't even wear wedding rings. Not that it was natural for him to be without it, but after all we have been through, if he took the ring off, I could understand.

"Why wouldn't I?" he asks, furrowing his brows.

"I wasn't sure if you wanted to talk to me just yet."

Dorian presses his lips together while shifting in his seat. His gaze meets mine before neither of us is strong enough to hold eye contact. My heart breaks every time he does it.

"We have to talk eventually," he says without a hint of harshness. "And now is a time as good as any other."

"I agree."

"How have you been?" He asks, disarming me again. I wanted to ask first, to show him I care.

"Better," I breathe out. "I like our new therapist. She scheduled sessions to talk to her twice a week at least."

"She told me you were in a better place," Dorian acknowledges, and the confession that he spoke about me makes a certain body organ beat erratically.

Butterflies go crazy in my stomach at his words. I try to control my breathing. "I have," I admit. "Knowing this was all going to end soon helped me a lot."

"I can only imagine."

"Dorian," I call, staring out the window. "I never meant for it to turn out this way."

My husband says nothing for a few seconds and I grow anxious. "It's done, Ari."

Every time he says my nickname, my heart skips a beat. Daring a glimpse at him, I notice him looking out of the window as well. The streets are full of people welcoming the chilly weather bound to come. The lights in the buildings and trees invite the celebration so typical around this time of the year.

A thought comes at me. If this fails, I will spend the holidays alone.

Not that there is a lot to celebrate. Christmas was Raphael's season. Watching him getting excited with the gifts, having our friends over to eat on Christmas day. My family, it's who these people are. Before Dorian, I didn't allow anyone into my life. With him, I gained family, and friends. Something to care about and fill the quietness.

Back when I was a kid, family meant little. Family was a word for the people who hurt me to throw whenever they needed me to behave or do their bidding. But not him.

"I'm sorry it happened like this," I confess. "From the papers to the cheating. I'm sorry about Raphael-"

He blinks at me as my voice breaks. His hand reaches for me, and the ring on his finger touches mine. It is then that I fear my heart will break. It keeps beating faster and faster and I am pretty sure if I don't force oxygen into my lungs, I may pass out.

"It wasn't your fault," he whispers, with tears shining and threatening to fall, but Dorian takes a long breath.

We have cried enough today.

"But I shouldn't have pushed you."

"I pushed you too, Ari. I cheated as well. What happened to us was difficult. I do not wish it on anyone. But we survived. We are here. Maybe not together, but we are. And you were brave to do what you did. Even if I did not understand it back then, I can see how it was important. Why you had to do it."

"I-"

"I'm sorry for all my wrongs," he whispers, and I watch him with a new set of dread, fearing his next words. "But you have to stop blaming yourself for how our lives turned out."

Tears form in my eyes as I swallow down the pain. He is right. We cried enough.

Maybe that's why I throw caution to the wind. Maybe it's why when he slides his fingers between mine, I lock my eyes on his.

"Ari, we have been through enough. I think-" he says, but I am already speaking.

My lips part, fearing he would confess my nightmares. "I'm not ready to give up on you just yet."

My husband leans back in his seat, resting against the dark Bordeaux fabric of the booth, and I bite my lower lip, watching as his body language changes. What was once uncertainty now seems to transform into curiosity.

As he surveys the streets outside, winter makes its way into the gray canvas, and people don't realize how lucky they are. A couple runs with their grocery bags, shielding themselves from the rain that threatens to fall at any second now. An old lady walks hand in hand with whom I assume is her granddaughter.

I will always be jealous others do not understand the value of these moments. How a child can giggle and demand attention from a parent who doesn't take their eyes off their phone. How they may pout and throw tantrums, but it is sometimes the only way they know how to deal with their pain and frustration.

Yet, not even me, an adult, knows how to handle her emotions.

"I have dealt with my pain alone," I breathe out, filling the silence when he doesn't speak, and I can't take it anymore. "It took me a while, and I'm still not there, but I am healing. I'm figuring everything out again."

The ends of his lips turn up while my husband closes his eyes and takes a moment to drink in my current state. He isn't speaking because he has all of his emotions flowing. It's what Thea warned us to do. When everything feels like is too much, the first thing we have to do is stay quiet and figure out what we should take care of first.

Dorian opens his eyes again and stares at me. For the first time in months, I cannot read them. I cannot comprehend how deep his emotions are, and it scares me.

"What do you mean, you're not ready to give up?"

"I will admit I dealt with this the wrong way when we were working things through," I tell him. "Especially that I should have told you about the plan. But I feared this. That you would distance yourself once more. And I wasn't ready for it. Not when I had you again. I wasn't ready to feel empty like I did after the accident. To only feel sadness and anger."

Dorian tries to hide his smile as I speak. He shakes his head to gather his thoughts and places both hands on the table. Rolling his shoulders, my husband straightens his back.

"Thank you," he murmurs. "I needed to hear that. But you still haven't answered my question. What do you mean, not ready to give up on me?"

"Unless you have given up on the idea of us," I reply, forcing my voice to be even. "I am not saying this marriage is over yet."

Dorian blinks, puckering his lower lip while nodding in agreement. He then leans forward; a glint of emotion too fast for me to read crosses his gaze, and I tilt my head in wonder.

"So, you are done with your plan?" He asks, and I nod.

"I needed this, Dorian," I confess. "I needed to avenge what happened."

"I get it, I do, Ari but-"

A long tiring breath for a conversation we avoided for months makes its way between us as I gather the courage. He needs to listen for reassurance, and I will say it as many times as he wants me to. "It's done," I let out. "I'm not going there ever again. I can promise you."

"Ari, you're doing it again," he chuckles. "You're

not letting me speak. You say you are sorry about not including me in this revenge conquest. You say you are not ready for this to end, but Ari-" my heart stops. It breaks and shatters into a tiny million pieces I know will be hard to gather again. Maybe never. It is the thing about a broken heart. I know I will survive the pain, but something in me will die. My eyes wait for Dorian to finish, to speak the words I fear. "Who is to say I am? Who is to say I was ever going to give up on you?"

"I-"

"I never signed those papers, did I?" He asks. "Matter of fact, I threw them out when I went back home so you wouldn't have any ideas. I know I didn't deal with this in the best way, and I know I hurt you. I am sorry for all of that, Ari. I can't even explain to you how much."

As he speaks, the tiny pieces in me slide together again. I gulf in a breath, and giving air to my breathless lungs.

"I'm sorry for not being there the second time around. You needed me. I know we were working everything out, and I get your fears. I have those too. The night I saw the things you wanted to do, I understood I was losing you again, and I did not know how to manage. How to handle you when you were so determined. I was so scared about it that I took the easy way out. Eli scolded me hard about it, you know?" He asks, and I watch his eyes become amused. "There was this one night I went back home. I stayed two hours outside, staring at the door. Wondering how I could talk to you again. How I can apologize for it all?"

"Dorian-" I whisper.

"I felt powerless. So many fucking times ever since last year. Hurting about Raphael, not knowing how to deal with it. Watching you cry and be in pain was hard enough. But then I realized you were doing this. Fearing where this could go, I panicked. And I didn't see it at first. This was how you were dealing with the loss. This is what you needed. I panicked and feared that my love for you wasn't enough to keep you grounded. That it wasn't enough for you to stay with me. That *I* wasn't enough."

My love for you. How can I breathe after hearing those words? There is something about seeing the light at the end of a dark tunnel that fills my chest with hope. "I forgive you," I say.

"And I forgive you too."

This time, I embrace his words. I embrace the silence settling between us again. I embrace how he leans on the table, and his hand touches mine every few seconds. I embrace how much I love my husband, and I will fight for it. Even if I don't know if he still feels the same way about me.

"So, not giving up on me," he says. "I like the sound of it. How does it work?"

"I'm not sure," I reply, narrowing my eyes and watching the amusement on his face when he smiles and lifts his coffee to his lips to hide it.

"You know I am hard to get, don't you?"

"So am I," I shrug. "Or have you forgotten about when we first met?

"How could I?" He snorts. "It took me days to know your name."

"You may play hard to get, but you're not that hard to understand."

He cocks a brow, figuring out my plan, and I stare at him. There is a lot more we need to say, talk about, but not now.

"We will still fight," I assure him. "We will still make each other mad and avoid speaking about our emotions. But neither of us will give up and-" my voice threatens to fail as I compose myself. "I love you. I've loved you for years, and the way I feel for you is not something I can ignore. If after we try this one time you don't want me, if you don't want this marriage anymore, tell me, and I will walk away from it, granting you your wish. But if there's so much as the flicker of love inside you, that tells you we can still work this out Dorian, if you still want to try-"

His hand rests on mine. His thumb brushes against the back of my hand, caressing the wedding ring, and Dorian stares at me.

"We need to stop hurting," he says. "We can try,"

he mumbles under a shaky breath. "We need to go back to therapy together and take things slow. You have to stop thinking we will not end up together. I have no intention of letting you go. Not even in our afterlife."

My eyes drink on the image of my husband, who looks back at me. His smile is one of the most beautiful things I have ever seen. When he takes both my hands in his, I know whatever I was fearing is behind me. "In our afterlife as well?" Dorian nods. "Then you should know I don't want to be alone in our house anymore."

"I don't want you to be alone there either," he stares at me and lifts himself from his seat, coming to my side. His breathing fans against my lips and Dorian pulls a string away from my eyes before kissing my forehead.

"I love you, Ari. I didn't stop loving you, even in my darkest moments. We are both broken, and it is fine." His forehead rests against mine for a second before he kisses me sweetly. "I love all of you. Even your pain. And when we fight, when we get angry at each other, we will try. I am not ready to give up on you just yet, either."

Epilogue
Dorian

People do not tell you how painful or fucked up life is. In all the years I have known my wife, I have seen the smile I love falter more times than I would like it to happen. Right now, I watch the same smile spread across her beautiful face as she draws hunched over her desk. She tilts her head, studying her work, and I dare a peek over my wife's shoulder.

"What are you working on?" I ask, placing a coffee mug in front of her and picking up my book from the armchair close to the window.

Whenever she wants to spend her free time drawing, I find myself needing to be near her. So even if we are not talking, this is what I consider quality time with my wife. To be around her is enough. We have spent enough time apart as it is. I think after the trial, Ari and I needed each other's presence to feel normal again. I took a leave from work, letting Josh be in charge, and Ari rested for a few weeks before figuring out how to start her own company.

Ari takes a long sip and glances at me, giving me a grin behind the mug. She then turns her notebook so I can see the drawing clearly. "A new collection."

I lift the paper to observe the details of the dress. This is not her usual drawing. Ever since she started her company, my wife has been focusing on wedding dresses. Her first atelier opened a few months after we got back together and brides have been crowding the store ever since its first week. She also began a line for bridesmaids and grooms last year, when we opened her second store. The first one in Europe. It is a success, not that I doubted anything else coming from the woman I love.

"It's a little shorter than the last ones," I smirk and she rolls her eyes.

"That's because it's not a wedding dress. I am designing something for Nicole, since she has an important interview coming up."

"Your sex therapist friend?" Ari dips her chin. "Got it." I walk around the desk and place a kiss on top of her head. "If you want to start a casual wear collection, I am all in for it. As long as you try one of your designs for me."

"I thought you liked me better with no clothes on," Ari says, raising a brow and I lean forward.

My lips brush against hers and I notice how her body leans towards mine. "I like you. Just *you*. I don't care if you have clothes or not. You could wear a Yoda bath towel wrapped around your head. I wouldn't mind."

"I didn't know you were a Star Wars fan," she smiles and I swear all air gets knocked out of my lungs.

My wife and I have been in a happy place for three years. Not the happiest of our lives. I sometimes fear that part is behind us. We are together and we are well. We still fight, and we still snap at each other, but it is easier to talk it out now. We work on understanding what the other means. Couples' therapy also helps, and we still see Anna for our sessions.

Knowing I won't be able to read anytime soon, I put my book down. "I am not. I am a fan of yours, Mrs. Vaillant," I say, crouching in front of her. Ariella's hand slides around my shoulder, pulling me toward her.

Her gaze lands on my mouth and my wife looks at me as if the words are stuck in her throat. "What is it?" I ask, breaking the silence.

"We should talk about this morning... about the pregnancy test."

My entire body becomes stiff beneath her fingertips, but Ariella doesn't let go. Instead, she leans forward and rests her forehead on mine. She closes her eyes and takes a deep breath as I do the same. A field of flowers invades my lungs and takes me home as I open my eyes to meet the hazel ones I love. She brushes my cheek with her fingertip, drawing all of my attention to her.

"It came out negative," I mumble. "What is there

to talk about?"

I have been trying to bring the topic up all day, but to no avail. It's complicated to even approach it. It takes us back into a painful part of our past as a couple and as parents.

"I saw the disappointment all over your face, Dorian. It was the same as mine. I am late, and it's not like we were trying for me to get pregnant. However, even the slightest idea of it being real… I saw you wanted it and the thing is, I want it too."

A strand of her hair slides free and I tuck it behind her ear. We have talked about how the house sometimes feels too silent. How we are not comfortable moving anywhere else, at least not for the foreseeable future. So we tried to fill the silence around here. First, Ari wanted a dog. We went to the city pound and got three. Tony, Cap, and Nat. I always laugh when Ari admits she was the one choosing their names. They run free at least three times a day. We pay for someone to take them out while my wife and I both work.

Then Ari suggested a cat because they don't take up much space and are good company as well. Bubbles proved us wrong and has taken over most of our office and living room. She is the high lady of the house and rules over all three dogs. It is not a silent house by any standards, yet the void still lingers for both of us. The need for more.

I want more kids. Of course, I do. But I wouldn't

impose it on my wife. It is her decision. She will be the one carrying them. And after Raphael… I wasn't even sure if Ari would want to try, so I never brought it up. Then this morning happened. Ari approached me, saying her period was late. I bought her a pregnancy test, and we waited for the results. I could see her struggling not to cry when the single line appeared. Neither of us made it to work, preferring to stay with each other. It was emotional, it was messy, but we were together. It is the beauty of our life now.

The conversation had to happen, but I was waiting for her to be ready to talk about it. About how upset she was. I couldn't understand if it was because she wanted the test to come out negative or because she was reliving our past.

"Ari," I sigh. "We don't have to try if you don't want to. I would never force you to have another baby just because it is something I want."

She rolls her eyes. "Stop being stubborn. I am not taking the pill tonight," as my gaze widens, she clarifies. "I want to try Dorian."

"Are you sure?"

"I'm sure. I even talked about it with Anna a few weeks ago. Another baby will not make me forget Raphael and it will not replace him. That is not why I want to have a child. I want one because I love you. I want this house to be full again, Dorian. I want us to have a little one running around. To see our love born into a baby."

"I love you," I whisper, and she giggles.

Another thing I never thought I could hear. Her giggles. She looks at me with a spark of mischievousness and as I am about to ask what she is thinking, she speaks.

"You remember how fun it was to try for a baby, right?" She asks, biting down on her lip and her gaze travels to my mouth.

I lean forward, my lips resting on hers before Ari closes her mouth on mine. My tongue slips in and she moans against me as I lift my wife and carry her to our bedroom.

We pass by Raphael's room, now open, and turned into a place for Ari to keep samples of material for her business. Anna suggested keeping some of our son's things, but eventually disposing of the bedroom since it wasn't adding or helping us move on. We were reluctant, but eventually gave in.

I kick our bedroom door open and close it behind me to stop the dogs from following us. Ari smiles into the kiss. It does so many things to my body. She lets her hands travel down my chest and helps me slide my clothes off. I watch as my wife stares up at me.

Her eyes are happier. Her gaze now tells so many more stories I want to dive into. I don't waste minutes talking and kiss her until I feel she needs to breathe. All the while undressing Ari and laying her on our bed. My mouth worships every part of her body, and I make her come at least twice before thrusting into her. Her lips part mine as my wife whimpers for more and I give her everything I have. I make love to her for the entire night if she wants me to. I will stay in this house for a week until she is tired of me.

We lay in bed, my arms wrapped around her naked body, my kisses covering her shoulders, and my hands caressing her hair. Ariella falls asleep in my arms and gratitude washes over me.

People do not tell you how painful or fucked up life is. But they also do not tell you that even in the most fucked up situations, with the right person by your side, you can survive the heartache.

ACKNOWLEDGEMENTS

If you are reading this, I can only hope you did not throw the book out your window. I bet you wanted to at some point, so thank you for sticking around.

Something I don't tell most people is I used to write online for four years before venturing into this. Remember Bubbles the cat Dorian mentions in the epilogue? Well, that was the name I went by. Dreadful was one of my most read books, but it had such mixed reactions it scared me to publish it. Before I took it down it had almost 650 thousand reads. Also you may not know this, but I love to give hints about my next book. Did you pay close attention to the last chapters?

Writing a book is never easy. Writing a book about… well, about losing a child proved to be one of the hardest things I ever worked on. The other one I have saved for a rainy day, so expect news on it somewhere around the end of the year.

But now let's go to the thank you's. Whenever I see other authors thanking people, it always looks so polished. And then there's me. The one who is chaotic and made her editor go through hell. Sorry Kelly. You were very fast despite it all.

Amanda, you were wonderful and your cover is the most beautiful thing I ever had in a book. Thank you so much. The LGBTQIA+ community who I love and received me with open arms. I almost didn't make

Irene so cruel, but her character was more complicated than I would like to admit.

Now let me see if I don't forget people whom I want to thank. The TikTok and Instagram community. I do not know how I am so lucky to be friends with some of you, but thank you for sticking up with my weirdness. The Romance Riot server, I cannot praise you enough for the patience you have shown me as I go through the self-publishing process. You are amazing, and the love and support you all gave me is more than I ever thought I would get.

Meg and the girls in my book club server, the best hype people I could ask for. Each and every single one of you brings a smile to my face, and you all make the hard days easier. You are all so kind, and I could say names and things I love in each of you individually, but then this thank you would be 3 pages long. Please take my love as proof of what you mean to me.

I also want to thank my Betas, who I annoyed every day with questions about the characters while I was editing. Sorry. I love you. April and Megha, the book is finally published so now please don't throw it at my head.

To Moy and Asya: this book would not be here if it weren't for you. If there is anyone I need to thank, it's you two. I know I sometimes struggle with expressing my emotions, but just know this book is not the only thing you helped make better. If I am publishing it, if I didn't give up is because of you two. I love you, and I love you even more for believing in me when I didn't want to believe in myself. The world is a better place since I have you two in it with me.

Mom and dad, well, I didn't tell you about this book either. Love you. I'm sorry.

I would like to thank my sister not only for her support but for taking L with her whenever I had to work on my writing or editing. Think about this as the hugs you don't like. It's better, right? At least there's no body contact. I love you kiddo; you are the best sister one could ever have.

Lastly, I want to thank the readers without whom I would have stopped writing a long time ago. I can only call myself an author because I have you all willing to read what I put out there. Some of you have been following me from the time I uploaded this online. I love you. So much I don't think the English language has enough words able to describe it. Thank you so much for understanding my decision to take this path, and especially for sticking around.

ABOUT THE AUTHOR

The dream of writing came during my teens. I would write stories in class instead of studying or paying attention to the teachers. I started writing and uploading my books online during my late twenties before taking the step into publishing. I am a single mom; I love animals and lazy Sundays. I am either writing or reading most of my time, or this is what I like people to think since I procrastinate a lot and spend more time than needed on social media.

ALSO BY NYSSA WINTERS

280 DAYS OF BLOSSOM

"I want to be a mom, and I don't want to wait for a guy I have met online to fill all the spaces in the survey of my life before it happens."

A fun romance about modern women: we first meet Olivia Torres, a successful Latina in the publishing business who is tired of waiting for Mr. Right. She reads stories for a living, and yet her own feels stagnant. She chooses to go through IVF and fulfill yet another life dream and goal—to become a mom. Haneul, her best friend and confidant ever since college, is always supportive. He is Olivia's favorite person in the world and the one she can count on at any time. But what he and Olivia fail to realize until later on is that the semen used in Olivia's IVF was a donation Haneul had made earlier.

As the pregnancy develops, their relationship changes. Feelings Olivia thought long forgotten begin to arise, and their friendship is put to the test.

Ingram Content Group UK Ltd.
Milton Keynes UK
UKHW011952240423
420698UK00011B/1138